Fancy Stepped Out of the Cold Stream, Keeping the Blanket Tucked Tightly Around Her . . .

Jeff looked at her longingly and said, "Damn it, woman, you resurrected me. I didn't want you to, but you insisted." He caught her hand in his and pulled her beside him. "Marry me," he said gruffly.

That again. Anguish swept over Fancy. She knew he only needed someone to replace the woman he lost, the woman he loved. "Damn you," she choked out, "why can't you just find yourself a whore and leave me alone?!"

His hand was strong on her chin, forcing her to face him. "I don't want a whore, Fancy. I want you . . ."

Dear Reader,

We, the editors of Tapestry Romances, are committed to bringing you two outstanding original romantic historical novels each and every month.

From Kentucky in the 1850s to the court of Louis XIII, from the deck of a pirate ship within sight of Gibraltar to a mining camp high in the Sierra Nevadas, our heroines experience life and love, romance and adventure.

Our aim is to give you the kind of historical romances that you want to read. We would enjoy hearing your thoughts about this book and all future Tapestry Romances. Please write to us at the address below.

The Editors
Tapestry Romances
POCKET BOOKS
1230 Avenue of the Americas
Box TAP
New York, N.Y. 10020

A TAPESTRY BOOK
PUBLISHED BY POCKET BOOKS NEW YORK

Books by Linda Lael Miller

Banner O'Brien
Corbin's Fancy
Desire and Destiny
Fletcher's Woman
Willow

Published by TAPESTRY BOOKS

This novel is a work of historical fiction. Names, characters, places and incidents relating to non-historical figures are either the product of the author's imagination or are used fictitiously. Any resemblance of such non-historical incidents, places or figures to actual events or locales or persons, living or dead, is entirely coincidental.

An *Original* publication of TAPESTRY BOOKS

A Tapestry Book published by
POCKET BOOKS, a division of Simon & Schuster, Inc
1230 Avenue of the Americas, New York, N.Y. 10020

ISBN: 0-671-52358-9

First Tapestry Books printing August, 1985

10 9 8 7 6 5 4 3 2 1

Printed in the U.S.A.

For Sally Jean Lang—
the girl with snowflakes
in her hair

Prologue

Port Hastings, Washington Territory December 24, 1887

THE GREAT HOLLY WREATH JIGGLED ON ITS HOOK AS JEFF Corbin slammed the front door behind him, wedged his hands into the pockets of his heavy seaman's coat, and stomped down the steps.

Almost immediately, the door opened again. "Damn you," barked a hoarse voice, "wait a minute!"

Jeff paused in the middle of the snowy walk, his shoulders tense, his jaw set in a hard line. He did not turn to face his brother; feeling the way he did, he couldn't. Even when Adam came to stand before him, Jeff refused to meet his eyes or acknowledge his presence.

"How long are we going to keep this up?" Adam demanded, his hands rising to his hips.

Jeff said nothing, though imagined shouts of anger and hurt were reverberating through his mind. Because he rarely hid his feelings, it was especially difficult for him to remain silent.

"It's Christmas, Jeff," Adam reminded him, with uncommon patience. "You can't leave now."

"I *have* to leave now," Jeff breathed, his gaze still carefully avoiding his older brother's. His mind and heart were full to aching with pictures of Banner, his sister-in-law, and of the children she had borne Adam. They were twins—a boy and a girl. . . .

"Jeff."

Jeff forced himself to look at Adam. The wind was bitterly cold that Christmas Eve; it stung both men and blew between them, severing the chain that had once joined their two souls. "I've got to go," he said. "The *Sea Mistress* sails at dawn and the crew is already aboard."

"Damn the *Sea Mistress!*" hissed Adam, lifting one hand to the back of his dark head in frustration. "I had to keep Papa's illness a secret from you and everyone else, Jeff! Don't you understand that?"

Jeff nodded. "I understand," he said, but it was only a half-truth. For five years he'd believed his father dead; finding out that the man had been alive all the time had jarred him deeply.

"You don't understand," rasped Adam. "Jesus, Jeff, he had leprosy—"

"I know. And he had you to take care of him. The devoted son. Why in hell would Papa have needed me when he had you?"

Adam flinched slightly, but stood his ground. "It's more than that, isn't it?"

Jeff lifted his chin. "Yes, it's more than that," he replied evenly. "I love your wife, Adam. I love Banner and I wish to God that those two babies in there were mine. Does that make the problem clear enough?"

The explosion Jeff half expected didn't come; Adam only sighed and tilted his head back to search the snow-shrouded heavens. Glistening, prismlike flakes gathered on his lashes and the strong planes of his face. "You'll get over what you're feeling now, Jeff. Just give yourself some time—"

Battling his emotions, Jeff made his way around the barrier of his brother's tall frame and started toward the gate. "Time heals all wounds, doesn't it, doctor?" he called back, glad that Adam could not see his face. "I'll be gone about six months, so don't wait up."

Suddenly, Jeff felt himself whirled around. He was thrust backward against the heavy stone fence. Fury stung him, but its pulsing venom left him oddly weak and quite immobile.

"You are going to listen to me," Adam drawled, glaring into Jeff's face like a blue-eyed demon.

Jeff managed to thrust his brother's powerful hands away from the lapels of his coat, but he could do no more, and his breath was coming hard, as though he'd just run a great distance. "Go to hell," he said.

"I love you, too, Jeff," Adam replied. Then he sighed again and spoke without the sarcasm that was so much a part of his nature. "Please, don't go. Not like this—"

It happened. The sobs Jeff had been holding back broke free, tearing themselves from the depths of his chest, harsh and raw. "God damn you," he choked out. "*Damn* you, Adam—*I can't stay*—"

Adam drew his brother close, held him for a moment, then stepped back. His voice was hoarse. "You know, don't you, that I wouldn't have seen you hurt like this for anything in the world?"

Jeff nodded. "I know."

Briefly, Adam touched Jeff's shoulder. Then, without another word, he turned and walked back toward the house, where Banner waited. Banner, with her lush, cinnamon hair, her green, green eyes—

Jeff, so anxious to leave only moments before, stood still for a time, gazing up at the great stone structure that had always been his home, for all his travels. Tonight, however, it seemed to exclude him.

After almost a minute, Jeff Corbin unlatched the gate, opened it, and walked through. Oblivious to the cold and the biting snow, he made his way down the steep hill to the town, and then to the harbor beyond.

Reaching the long wharf where the *Sea Mistress* was moored, he drew a deep breath, hoped to God none of his grief showed in his face, and marched up the shifting, snow-laced boarding ramp.

His men greeted him with coarse jocularity, as they always did; he spared them a desultory wave of one hand and strode toward his cabin, his head down. Whiskey. What he needed now was whiskey.

The first thunderous blast shook the clippership just as Jeff reached the steps leading below deck, hurling him down into the companionway. There were screams and then another explosion sounded, seeming to tear at the innermost timbers of the ship.

Dazed, Jeff half crawled back up the steps to the main deck. There was fire everywhere; crimson flames crackled through the rigging, consumed the sails, skittered along the deck itself, and danced hellishly on the railings. Men jumped overboard, their hair and clothing afire, their cries of terror and pain incongruous with the petal-soft snowfall wafting down from a hidden sky.

The heat was unbearable and, as he lunged over the port side of the ship toward the darkness and oblivion that awaited him, Jeff thought he heard the devil laugh.

Chapter One

Wenatchee, Washington Territory
May 12, 1888

THE RABBIT WOULD NOT COME OUT OF THE HAT.

Fancy could feel the creature with her right hand—it was crouched deep inside its black velvet bag, shivering and stubborn and heavy. The crowd of children in front of the gazebo pressed closer, their freckled faces intent and smudged with strawberry ice cream, their eyes fixed on the battered top hat.

"She can't make no rabbit come out of there!" one little boy complained. "That ain't even a lady's hat!"

"Maybe she ain't no lady!" observed a barefooted demon.

Perspiration trickled between Fancy's breasts and shoulder blades. She tugged harder at the rabbit, conscious of Mr. Ephraim Shibble's cold glare of warning. Beyond his bulky frame, the glorious pink and white blossoms of the apple orchard seemed to shift and shimmer in a haze. Fancy noted distractedly that colorful ribbons, dozens of bright balloons, and even presents hung from the boughs of one tree.

"Don't do this to me, Hershel," she pleaded. A breeze scented with blossoms and bruised grass and picnic food cooled her burning cheeks and loosened the damp tendrils of silvery saffron hair clinging to the back of her neck.

"I told you she couldn't do it!" howled the small heckler who had spoken first, squinting up at Fancy in hostile challenge.

Stung anew, Fancy wrenched at Hershel, hard, and he came out of his hat at last—the black bag that had hidden him hanging from his hind legs like a grim flag of defeat.

The adults who had gathered to watch shook their heads and turned away, some grumbling, some chuckling, some pitying the proud young woman who stood stiffly in her ridiculous star-speckled dress, still holding the rabbit aloft.

As the children scattered, too, Fancy bent and thrust an unrepentant Hershel into the wire cage secreted beneath her folding table. When she straightened, she was met with the condemning gaze of Mr. Ephraim Shibble, her employer.

The heavy man, suffering in his tight-fitting suit, bent to take up the worn placard that had stood in front of the table and perused it with calm disdain. "'Fancy Jordan,'" he read, in mocking tones. "'She sings. She dances. She does magic.'"

Fancy winced and clasped her hands together behind her back. "Mr. Shibble, I—"

Shibble interrupted by shaking the signboard; a shower of time-dulled glitter fell from the large, carefully formed letters. "You are a fraud," he accused, in a scathing undertone. "You are an embarrassment! *And you are out of a job!*"

This was what Fancy had most feared, but she retained some semblance of composure and met Mr. Shibble's small, watery eyes squarely. "You cannot leave me here," she said, in even tones that betrayed none of the hysteria rising within her. "I have no position, no money—"

Shibble shoved the battered signboard into her hands. "Then I suggest that you sing and dance, since you are apparently incapable of magic. You will not travel another mile, Miss Jordan, with my company!"

"But—"

"No! You have humiliated me for the last time!" With that, Mr. Shibble turned and stormed away to watch one of the other members of the small traveling show perform. For a moment, Fancy, too, watched the Great Splendini wobble upon his "high wire," which loomed all of five feet off the soft ground.

When she was sure that she would not be observed, Fancy sank down to sit on the gazebo's top step, resting her head against the white-washed railing. A long, despondent sigh escaped her.

"You weren't all that bad," remarked a gentle, masculine voice.

Fancy, on the verge of tears, looked up to see a tall man standing before her, his arms folded, his azure eyes revealing both amusement and sympathy. He wore dark trousers, a vest over a pristine white shirt, and a clerical collar.

"I was bad enough to be fired," she argued.

He bent, took the signboard from the gazebo floor where Mr. Shibble had dropped it, and read it pensively, as though it were some lofty treatise. "Can you really do magic?" he asked, after some moments.

Fancy blushed. Though one would never know it by the way her act had gone that afternoon, she was, as it happened, a fairly accomplished magician. She could draw coins from behind people's ears, for example, and she could make fire flash from her fingertips. Once, on a particularly good night, she had even sawed a woman in half and put her back together again. Volunteers for that trick were hard to come by, though, and the props had been borrowed from another magician.

"Yes," she said, with dignity, "I can do magic."

"We could use some of that around here," reflected the young minister.

Fancy looked about, really seeing her surroundings for the first time since her arrival earlier that day. Since then, she, like the rest of the troupe, had been too busy preparing for the noon performance to pay much attention.

Now she saw a massive, gracious stone house, the acres of lushly blossomed apple trees that flanked it, the green-gray river tumbling past the sloping front lawn, the gardens with their budding rosebushes and marble benches. "Do you live here?" she ventured, thinking it a marvel that a man of the cloth could be so prosperous.

"Yes," replied the reverend, with a slight bow of his head and an amused twist of his fine lips. "My family owns the land, actually, and I manage it."

Fancy was impressed. Once again her gaze caught on the particular apple tree with the balloons, ribbons, and presents dangling from its boughs. She was certain that she had never seen such a festive sight. "Is it someone's birthday?" she asked.

The reverend laughed softly. "No. My family has a tradition of celebrating the blossoming of the orchard. The entire community is invited and each of the children gets to take a gift from the tree." He paused and frowned thoughtfully. "Sounds a little pagan, doesn't it? Like a rite of spring or something."

Despite her circumstances, Fancy smiled. "It's a lovely idea," she answered.

"I'm hungry, Miss Jordan," the man announced suddenly. "How about you?"

Fancy was ravenous. There had been no time to eat that morning after leaving the train in nearby Wenatchee, a small but thriving settlement along the same green river that flowed past the house. "I have a rabbit we could roast," she suggested, only half in jest.

The pastor grinned and offered his hand to help Fancy up from her perch on the gazebo steps. "That would take far too long, wouldn't it?" he reasoned.

Before taking his hand, Fancy looked down at the worn skirts of her performing dress. One of the silver stars she had stitched onto it was coming loose, and she attempted, in vain, to smooth it with her slender finger. "I don't know your name," she said.

"Keith," he replied informally. "Keith Corbin."

Corbin. The name stabbed the pit of Fancy's empty stomach and spun there before whirling through the rest of her system like a stormwind. Dear God in heaven, surely the family this man spoke of could not be the *Port Hastings* Corbins!

Reverend Corbin crouched to peer into Fancy's bloodless face, her hand still warmly cushioned in his. "What is it?"

"N–Nothing," lied Fancy. In her mind, however, vivid, flashing images collided with each other—the explosion aboard the ship anchored in Port Hastings' busy harbor; Temple Royce, then her employer and avid suitor, laughing as he lifted a glass to toast the demise of the vessel's captain.

"Something to eat might help," speculated the pastor, rising to his feet and pulling Fancy with him in one fluid motion.

After filling their plates at the long refreshment table, Fancy and the minister returned to the gazebo steps, where they sat together, eating in silence. Fancy was grateful for the feast of ham, candied sweet potatoes, green beans, and hard-crusted bread—heaven only knew when she would eat again, now that she'd been dismissed from her job.

"You'll be needing a new position," remarked Reverend Corbin presently, as though reading Fancy's distraught mind.

Glumly, Fancy nodded. From what she had seen of Wenatchee, it was a small place and opportunities would be limited indeed. Probably few of the residents, if any, employed servants, and she had not seen a restaurant where she might wash dishes or wait tables until she'd earned enough for train fare. "I know," she said.

"I could give you money," ventured the minister.

Fancy shook her head in immediate refusal. Debt was a burden she carefully avoided, remembering the anguish it had caused her parents. "I must earn my own way," she insisted, her chin high now, her plate balanced on her knees.

"Then work for me, here. I'm afraid there isn't much call for magic in Wenatchee."

Coming from another man, an offer of this nature would have immediately put Fancy on her guard. After all, she'd been on her own three years already, though she was just nineteen, and she'd learned readily enough to beware the double-edged kindness of "gentlemen." But this man was different from most, she knew, and it wasn't only because of the collar he wore. "What would I do, Reverend Corbin?"

He smiled. "Please—call me Keith so that I can call you Fancy."

Again, this was not a point Fancy would normally have conceded, being wary of familiarity with the opposite sex. "All right, Keith," she answered. Then, feeling oddly hopeful, despite a lingering disturbance over his surname, she asked again, "What work could I do here? The apples aren't ready to be picked—"

Keith took her empty plate, stacked it atop his own, and set them both aside. "No, the apples won't be ready until fall. But there is a job for you here, Fancy—one that will, I'm afraid, call for no small amount of magic."

Fancy waited, oblivious to the milling crowds, the frolicking children, the preparations for departure being made by Mr. Shibble's ragtag "theatre" company.

"Last Christmas Eve, my brother's ship, the *Sea Mistress,* was at anchor in Port Hastings harbor—"

Fancy's heart seemed to plummet to her knees, then shoot up to hammer against the inside of her skull. Oh, God, she thought. God, no. This *is* the same family!

Keith stopped, fixing Fancy with haunted, sky-blue eyes. "Do you know where Port Hastings is?" he asked. "It's near Puget Sound, on the Strait of Juan de Fuca—"

Fancy nodded, unable to speak. Again, Temple Royce's ugly, triumphant laughter echoed in her ears.

"Anyway, Jeff—that's my brother—was badly burned. He still has scars on his back and along one of his arms, but the worst marks, of course, are inside him."

Fancy closed her eyes, bile scalding the back of her throat. Damn you, Temple, she thought frantically. "But he didn't die," she said, thankful for that much, at least.

"No, not quite. Like a lot of the other men, though, he was forced to jump overboard. The water was colder than usual and it was awhile before he was brought ashore. He caught pneumonia and almost didn't survive that." Keith sighed, gazing pensively at the decorated apple tree, where laughing children were jumping and scrambling for the gifts and balloons that graced it. The joy of the scene was at terrible variance with the story—the all too familiar story—that he was relating. "Jeff is here—once he recovered he didn't want to stay in Port Hastings. There is some kind of rift between him and our oldest brother, but neither of them will talk about it and it's really beside the point in any case. The fact is that Jeff is dying, Fancy, though he should be over the physical effects of what happened."

Fancy shivered. "I don't understand how you think I could help," she managed to say. "I'm not a nurse—"

"Jeff doesn't need a nurse so much as he needs a companion—someone who can spend time with him and bring him out of that inner world where he's hiding. Between the orchards and my parish, I can't work with him the way I should, but I love my brother, Fancy, and I don't want to lose him."

"I w–would spend time with him? What would that accomplish?"

"I'm hoping that you'll be able to stir some emotion

in him—anything. Make him laugh, make him cry, make him mad—I don't really care."

Fancy swallowed and looked down at her skirts. In every fiber of her being, she ached with the shame of what Temple Royce had done to Jeff Corbin and to his family, not to mention the crewmen who had not survived the blast aboard the *Sea Mistress.* She was not responsible for the attack, of course, but just knowing who was weighted her with guilt. She had not told the authorities what she knew; instead, she had just fled the town to try to forget.

Now she studied Keith Corbin's earnest face and wondered what would happen if she told him that it had been Temple Royce who had ordered the charges of dynamite to be laid on and beneath the decks of the ship. In the end, she decided that she did not dare.

But further worries waited to be dealt with. She had worked as a performer in Port Hastings aboard the *Silver Shadow,* a clippership converted into a saloon. Suppose Captain Jeff Corbin had seen her there and recognized her now? Worse still, suppose he recalled that she had, at that time, planned to marry Temple Royce—a man he no doubt regarded as his worst enemy?

Fancy's predominant instinct demanded that she flee, that she put this town and this family behind her, before one of its members remembered her as she was now remembering them. But she did not have the means to escape, having lost her job, and besides that, a small part of her longed to atone somehow for what Temple had done. "I'm not sure I can help you," she muttered, plucking at a star on her skirt with nervous fingers, "but I'll try."

"Thank you," said the pastor, and his large, calloused hand closed over both of Fancy's, encouraging and warm.

Jeff watched from an upstairs window as the guests began clamoring away in their assorted wagons, carriages, and buggies. The seedy little circus, hired for the special amusement of the children, had long since gone, but one of the performers had stayed—that disturbing, elfin creature wearing stars on her dress. Something about her made Jeff feel uneasy, though even from a distance there was no denying that she was an appealing little piece.

He sighed, not quite able to turn away from the window. She was talking earnestly with Keith, he could see that—in fact, the two had never been very far apart all day. Who was the woman, anyway, and why hadn't she left with the others?

Jeff's features formed a scowl. Come to that, why was Keith squiring a good-looking woman about, when he was engaged to marry Amelie Rogers in less than a month's time? He was still pondering this question when the imp suddenly stopped her conversation with Keith and stared up at the window where Jeff stood. She couldn't see him—that was impossible—and yet she seemed to be bidding him.

Because something inside Jeff urged him to obey her, he turned quickly away from the window. Shirtless, he went to stand before the mirror above his bureau. He turned to one side, just far enough so that the crimson, puckered scar on his back was clearly visible. It made a broad swath between his right hip and the top of his left shoulder. That scar, like the similar one on his arm, was rooted deep inside him, reaching beyond muscle and bone to his very core. He closed his eyes and tried to summon Banner O'Brien, now his brother's wife, to his mind. Instead, he saw a small, fair-haired vixen with a galaxy strewn upon her dress.

Through the open door of his room, Jeff heard footsteps on the stairs. He cursed and dived for the closest shirt, which was hanging over one of the posts of his bed. He was fastening the first button when Keith rapped at the doorjamb.

"There's someone I want you to meet," the pastor announced with that peculiar combination of tenderness and determination that only he could manage.

Jeff glared at his brother and muttered a round curse. Perhaps out of deference to the man he had been before he'd lost his father, Banner, and his ship practically in one fell swoop, he ran the fingers of his left hand through his hair.

"Hello," said the imp, stepping out of the shadows and into the doorway. "My name is Fancy."

Diplomatically, Keith turned and walked away. His boot heels made a forlorn, echoing sound on the stairs.

"What the hell kind of name is 'Fancy'?" Jeff snapped, all the while taking note of the wayward, sun-colored hair curling around a saucy face. Her eyes were a deep violet.

"It's a nickname for Frances," the sprite retorted, ignoring his rudeness.

There was a dimple in her chin—just the tiniest dimple. "Where did you get that silly dress?"

The dimpled chin lifted, the violet eyes flashed, but Fancy stood her ground. "I made it myself. I wear it when I perform."

Even though he was standing in the middle of the room, Jeff felt oddly cornered. He ignored the fact that the sensation wasn't all that unpleasant. Setting his feet wide apart and lifting his hands to his hips, he made a deliberate effort to look ominous. "Unless you're going to tap-dance or something, why don't you get the hell out of my bedroom? A man could get the wrong idea, you know."

"You're full of wrong ideas, I think," imparted the minx, completely undaunted. Her pert little nose crinkled disapprovingly. "Goodness, it's musty in here," she said, and then she had the unmitigated gall to march over to the wall and wrench open one window and then another. This done, she proceeded to fetch discarded shirts and trousers up from the floor, bunching them under one arm.

Jeff stared at her in furious amazement. "What the devil do you think you're doing?"

The violet eyes met his squarely. "I'm helping you, of course. That's what your brother hired me to do."

"Damn his hide. I don't want any help!"

"That's your major problem, I would imagine. That and the fact that you're acting more like a spoiled little boy than a grown man." Incredibly, she strode to the doorway and flung the laundry she'd gathered into the hallway. After that, she advanced to the bed, pulling off the blankets and sheets, denuding the pillows of their cases. "It's time you stopped sulking and started acting your age, Jeff Corbin."

Jeff was appalled for a moment, but then the singular humor of the situation came home to him and he began to laugh. What a ridiculous, delicious sight this Fancy was, her wild hair tumbling from its pins and silver stars coming loose from her dress. As she bent to gather up the sheets in both arms, Jeff felt a familiar stirring inside him.

She paused, looked at him uncertainly for the first time. "What's so funny?"

"That dress. Your name. Everything."

Fancy's lush little body stiffened and that perfect chin jutted out in fierce pride. "I'm glad you're amused," she said. "Perhaps that's a step forward."

Again, Jeff ran a hand through one side of his hair and, with one fleeting glance at the mirror, saw that his fingers had left ridges above his right ear. "Just what did my brother tell you? That I'm some kind of recluse? That I need to be saved from myself?"

"Something on that order, yes."

Jeff was furious. "I love a woman I can't have," he said. "In fact, she's my brother's wife."

"Life is tough," said Fancy, with a shrug.

"I lost my ship!"

"People lose things every day." She paused, looking around the spacious, well-furnished room. "From what I've seen, you have more—much more—than the average man, anyway."

"You don't understand!"

Fancy dropped the sheets and came to stand in front of him, looking up into his face. "I'm afraid I do. You've been hurt. You're angry. And now you're throwing a tantrum!"

"A tantrum?!" Rage sang through Jeff's veins; for the first time in months he felt fully alive. "How dare you say that?"

"I dare," she assured him evenly.

Jeff had absolutely no answer for that. He watched Fancy in silent fury as she turned away, retrieved the sheets, and started toward the door. What was she going to do next, pull down the curtains? Roll up the rug?

"Damnation!" he muttered.

"I'll be back with fresh linens in a few minutes," she sang out, without even bothering to look back.

Jeff was not used to people—especially women—reacting to him in quite that way. The chit was downright obnoxious, that's what she was! "Wait a minute!" he roared.

She stopped, looked back over one trim, bestarred shoulder. "Yes?"

"I don't want you to help me, do you understand? I don't want you gathering my laundry and changing my sheets—"

"Someone has to do it," came the flippant reply, before the minx disappeared entirely.

Jeff lunged to the doorway, gripping the framework in white-knuckled hands. "Not you, God damn it!" he bellowed.

Fancy spread one of the sheets on the floor of the hallway and then bundled all the other laundry into it. "Why not me?" she asked, without particular emotion.

"Because—"

"Yes?" urged the imp, swinging the enormous bundle up onto her back like a female Saint Nicholas.

Again, Jeff Corbin, always glib, was stuck for an answer. Hellfire and spit, he'd never met a more annoying woman in his life!

By the time she'd returned, this time carrying a stack of neatly folded sheets, he had had a chance to come up with some ammunition. Sprawled comfortably in a chair near the window, he watched as she began remaking the bed.

"I never would have expected this of my pious brother," he said. "But he may have hit upon just the therapy I need."

She was flipping the bottom sheet expertly; the crisp scent of starch filled the now-freshened room. "What therapy is that?" she asked, again without any great interest.

"Don't tell me that, with a name like 'Fancy,' you don't know?"

The sheet wafted slowly to the mattress and she turned to face him. "I beg your pardon?"

Triumph surged through Jeff; he bit back a grin. "I mean, you'll be sharing that bed with me, won't you? That would heal me faster than anything."

An explosion was brewing in the wide, violet eyes but, to Jeff's disappointment, it faded away, along with the pink bloom that had shone in her cheeks. "You know perfectly well that I will not share your bed, Captain Corbin," she said.

Another long-dormant emotion moved within Jeff—sweet challenge. This was one game that he'd mastered. "You underestimate my charms, Fancy," he said calmly.

"On the contrary, I find them quite unspectacular," she replied.

"Have you ever been intimate with a man?"

"That is certainly none of your business but, as it happens, no. I haven't." She turned back to making the bed and Jeff was afforded a view of a firm, softly curved derrière. His determination was renewed.

"Good," he said. "I always like to be the first."

She finished her task without another word and strode stiffly out of the room, her proud head held high. Jeff laughed to himself then, though he couldn't have said why. He rose from his chair and went to the bureau to brush his wheat-colored hair into order.

Fancy stood at the top of the stairs at last out of sight, and trembled with rage. Never, never, in all her life, had she ever encountered a more impossible man! Nor a more attractive one, she admitted to herself. Wishing that she'd passed up this questionable job, no matter what the consequences, she drew a deep breath and descended into the kitchen.

There, the housekeeper and several helpers were bustling about, heating water, and scraping dirty plates that arrived in stacks.

Keith came in as Fancy was preparing a tray for his nasty-minded brother, carrying a huge platter of ham slices. "How did it go?" he asked, with such hope that Fancy's angry mood softened a little.

"It isn't going to be easy," she said, spearing one of the ham slices for Jeff's plate. "I'm going to take him some supper and then I'll come down and help clear away."

The housekeeper, a slender woman introduced earlier as Alva Thompkins, flashed Fancy a grateful smile. The prospect of having a friend lifted Fancy's spirits.

"He won't eat, you know," Keith said worriedly, setting the ham platter down and starting back toward the door again.

"Yes, he will," said Fancy, with confidence.

Keith gave her a lopsided, sympathetic grin and left to carry in more of the litter left from the picnic. It was a job that would probably take half the night, even with all of them working.

Exasperation filled Fancy as she put cold sweet potatoes and wilted salad on the plate she meant to take up to Jeff. His help would mean a lot right now, but he probably wouldn't deign to give it, intent as he was on wallowing in self-pity!

Balancing the heavy tray, Fancy started back up the stairs. And the things he'd said to her! Her name was funny, her clothes were funny, and would she share his bed?

By the time Fancy reached Jeff's room again, fury was singing through her veins. Damn it all, even if she ended up sleeping in a field and roasting poor, plump Hershel over a campfire to keep from starving, she wasn't going to put up with this kind of treatment!

Jeff smiled pleasantly as she approached him, as though he hadn't said all those inexcusable things.

With savage delight, Fancy stood in front of Jeff's chair, returned his smile, and dumped the entire contents of the dinner tray into his lap.

Chapter Two

THE CLATTER OF CHINA AND JEFF'S BELLOWS OF OUTRAGE were audible even from the lawn. In the deepening twilight, Keith Corbin lifted a washtub-sized bowl of leftover baked beans into both arms and grinned. Thank you, he said silently to the God who lived beyond the distant skies and yet walked beside him always.

When Keith reached the kitchen, his lips still stretched into a smile, Fancy was there. Stars brighter than those stitched to her dress snapped in the depths of her purple eyes and her fine cheekbones glowed with righteous wrath.

"I'll pay for the broken dishes out of my wages," she said, furiously.

"No need," said Keith, exchanging a triumphant look with Mrs. Thompkins, the housekeeper. The two of them had been trying to reach Jeff for months, and this little snippet had managed it in a single evening!

Fancy was rolling up the sleeves of her frayed dress. "Then I'll help carry in the food," she insisted, and she proved an industrious worker, though perhaps her energy was fed by her ire.

When the leavings of the picnic had been dealt with, and night had settled, gentle and black, over the Wenatchee Valley, Keith urged Fancy to retire to her room, knowing that the next day would be a difficult one for her.

The tired amethyst eyes widened. "Mercy," breathed Fancy, putting one hand to her throat. "I forgot all about Hershel!"

The rabbit. Keith laughed. "I imagine he's hungry."

Mrs. Thompkins promptly supplied a bowl of green salad left from the picnic. "See you keep that critter out of my vegetable garden," she warned, but her attempt at sternness didn't fool anyone.

"We can put him in the barn for tonight," Keith said. "Tomorrow, I'll build a hutch for him."

Fancy smiled with a weary sort of relief, and Keith was touched. She did, for all her earlier annoyance, love that uncooperative rabbit. "Thank you," she said.

Fancy's room, situated off the kitchen like Mrs. Thompkins's quarters, was very spacious. She immediately opened the window and the sweet scent of a million apple blossoms wafted in to settle her spinning mind. The vague hum of the Columbia River met her ears and, somehow, comforted her.

She slipped thankfully out of her star-speckled dress and into the long flannel nightgown that had been laid out on the bed. It was pretty, if modest, boasting bits of lace around the sleeves and collar, with embroidered doves on the bodice. Silently, Fancy blessed Mrs. Thompkins for providing it.

Barefooted now, Fancy unpinned her hair, heavy and scented of the outdoors, and let it fall to her waist. Then she emptied her carpet bag, which contained everything she owned except for Hershel and the few props she used in her act, and thought how badly she needed a new dress. Besides the gown she wore to perform, she had one grim frock of calico and one of heavy gray wool.

Biting her lower lip, she fought down an old desire for pretty clothes of lace and lawn and silk. Such things were for wealthy women, not for the likes of herself.

There was a soft rap at the door just then, and Fancy started, jolting out of thoughts leaning dangerously toward self-pity. "Yes?" she said, alarmed even though she knew she was safe in this gracious house.

"It's Alva," chimed the housekeeper.

Fancy swallowed—some part of her had expected that obnoxious Captain Corbin—and lunged to open the door.

Alva Thompkins stood in the shadowy hallway, her arms burdened with garments of every color. Fancy spotted a pretty sprigged cambric morning dress, a soft pink wrapper, and a velvet gown of deep gold. "See if these fit you," the woman said matter-of-factly.

Fancy stepped back in amazement, one hand to her throat. "I—what—" she stammered.

Alva smiled and strode to the bed, where she dumped the lovely garments right on top of Fancy's pitiable wardrobe. "These things belonged to Miss Melissa," the woman announced. "That's the reverend's young sister, you know. Whenever she leaves after one of her visits, there's things in her room that she don't want no more. Usually, the reverend and I give them to the church, but, well, it would be my guess that you could use them, Miss Fancy."

Fancy was all but overwhelmed. It seemed incredible that one could just think of a lack and immediately have it remedied—such a thing had never happened to her before.

"Try this on," urged Alva, holding up a day dress of lavender cotton and assessing it with speculative eyes. "I'd say you could use a bit more room in the bosom, but we could fix that easy like."

Fancy fairly snatched the lovely garment from Alva's work-reddened hands, her eyes wide at the prospect of owning such a thing of splendor.

Alva chuckled on her way to the door. "You come on out into the kitchen when you've got that on," she said. "I'll see what it needs and we'll have a cup of chocolate together, you and me."

Her heart feeling warm and full, Fancy nodded quickly. The moment she was alone, she tore off her nightgown—probably it, too, had belonged to the fortunate Melissa, she reflected—and pulled on the lavender dress.

As Alva had predicted, it was a little too small in the bodice, though it fit everywhere else. The crisp cotton whispered and rustled as Fancy moved and, in her looking glass, she saw a person transformed.

Presently, she stopped admiring herself and hurried into the kitchen, where the kindly housekeeper waited. "That looks right nice," the woman said, rising from her chair at the table to take a closer look.

Fancy was filled with sudden despair. "The buttons barely meet—" she mourned, indicating the bodice with one nervous hand. Never in her life had she worn, let alone owned, such a dress. If it couldn't be made to fit, the disappointment was going to be all out of proportion to good sense.

"I can fix it," said Alva, with confidence. "Sure—I can let the darts out. You go and take that off and bring it back to me."

Hopeful again, Fancy scurried off to obey. When she returned minutes later, carrying the dress and wearing the soft pink wrapper, Alva had fetched her sewing basket and lit several more lamps.

The two tired women sat at the table, enjoying their hot chocolate and talking. Except when she paused to take a sip from her cup, Alva's strong fingers worked without ceasing, the dress a billow of lavender glory in her lap.

"How's a snip of a girl like you come to be traveling with somebody like that Shibble feller?" the housekeeper demanded with good-natured disapproval. "Ain't seemly."

Fancy shrugged. With another person she might have felt defensive, but she knew that Alva was only curious. "It was a job," she replied.

"A body'd think you'd have a husband," persisted the older woman, her silver needle catching and flinging bits of light as it went in and out of the lavender fabric. "Pretty thing such as you and all."

Fancy's sigh seemed to come from the very depths of her. "I could have married, I guess, if I'd wanted to stay in Newcastle." And be like Mama, added a voice in her mind.

"Where's Newcastle?" asked the intrepid Alva. "I don't believe I've heard of that place."

"It's north of Seattle," reflected Fancy, idly turning

her china cup round and round in its delicate saucer. "There's a coal mine there."

Alva nodded, not looking up from her work. "Right hard life, I reckon, diggin' for coal. That what your daddy does?"

It was Fancy's turn to nod. And though her body was sitting with Alva, in that cozy kitchen, her mind had wandered back to the poverty and discouragement of her earlier life in Newcastle. Lord knew, she was still poor, but she was free as her mother and others like her could never be.

"Pretty poor, your folks?" urged Alva, making a slight slurping sound as she took a draft of her cocoa.

"Yes," said Fancy directly. Though she was far away from Newcastle and had no desire to go back, she still grieved for her family. They were caught in the trap of debt and illness, forever trapped. "Papa is sick, but he still keeps working in that mine."

"Don't reckon he has much choice," observed Alva. "A body's got to eat."

"They barely manage that," mourned Fancy, her eyes distant. "The mine owner pays his workers in company scrip, which can only be spent at his store, of course. People always owe more than they can ever hope to earn."

"But you speak like a lady," Alva pointed out after biting off a thread with strong, sure teeth. "How'd that come to be? And how'd you ever learn to work magic?"

Fancy smiled. "As soon as I left, I got myself a job as a lady's maid in Seattle. I listened to her and I read books when I wasn't working, and pretty soon I came to speak the way Mrs. Evanston did. Her son studied magic as a sort of an avocation, and he taught me as much as he could."

Remembering Tim Evanston made Fancy smile, though somewhat bitterly. He'd wanted to teach her more than magic, that was a fact. In the end, he'd been the reason she'd left her job and struck out on her own, armed only with a rabbit caught in the woods behind the Evanston house, a hand-lettered sign optimistically listing her talents, and an old hat discarded by the senior Mr. Evanston.

"You been sendin' most of what you make back to your folks, ain't you?" Alva guessed, with uncanny accuracy.

"How did you know that?" asked Fancy, honestly surprised.

"Easy. A girl as pretty as you, she'll usually spend every nickel she can get on hair ribbons and geegaws. You ain't got nothin' but that fat rabbit and what you carry in your handbag."

Fancy blushed, embarrassed. It wasn't that she didn't want nice things—God knew, she ached for them sometimes—but there would have been no joy in spending money that was so desperately needed at home. "Like you said, people have to eat."

"Don't they now?" commented Alva, handing over the lovely dress she had just altered.

Fancy thanked her profusely and the two women parted, both exhausted, both filled with the joy of finding a new friend.

"Are you going to dump that all over me, or do I get to eat this time?" demanded Jeff Corbin sourly, his ink-blue eyes filled with residual rage.

Fancy stood proudly in her new dress, her chin high, her hair neat, the tray clasped firmly in both hands. "To my mind, Captain," she said, "you shouldn't be getting trays carried to you at all. You're not an invalid, you know."

"Why did you bring it up here, then?" snapped the surly man with the archangel face, not bothering to rise from his chair near the window.

"Because I knew Alva would have to do it if I didn't," replied Fancy, setting the tray down on a small side table within his reach. "She has enough to do without waiting on the likes of you."

A grin pushed aside the scowl on Jeff's face, reluctant though it was. "The likes of me, is it? Do you really think I'm that awful, Frances?"

"Do not call me 'Frances'!" ordered Fancy. "I despise it!"

The grin became a smirk and Fancy knew that she'd made a serious mistake in revealing her aversion to the name. This man would certainly latch on to any method of annoying her that was offered. "Would you rather we were formal? I could call you 'Miss Jordan.' But, then, that isn't really your name, either, is it?"

Fancy colored, full of fury and some other disquieting emotion that she couldn't quite set a name to. "No," she admitted, without knowing why. "My last name is Gordon."

He laughed, the wretch, as he uncovered the dishes on his tray and began to consume fried eggs, bacon, and riced potatoes, with alarming appetite. "Frances Gordon. I love it!" He paused, chewing what amounted to a shovelful of food, his indigo eyes snapping with life and mirth and challenge. "It's dull," he finally went on, "but at least it doesn't make you sound like a kept woman."

"A kept woman?!" Fancy half shrieked, ready to pounce on her "patient" and tear his ears off.

"Have patience with me," he urged, speaking around a bite of honeyed toast. "After all, I'm an invalid."

"You're healthier than I am!" cried Fancy, falling neatly into his trap.

The impossibly blue eyes danced. "I'm healthy, all right. One of these days—or nights—I'll prove it to your satisfaction. But let's not tell my brother, all right? He might make you go away and if that happens, I guarantee you, I'll be unsalvageable."

Fancy kept her distance, but she couldn't quite bring herself to leave the room. Or, more specifically, the man. Drat it all, what was it about him that drew her to him, even as it repelled her? "You're already unsalvageable," she retorted. "How a man as nice as Keith could have a brother like you is beyond me!"

Unwittingly, she had nettled him. He flashed her a quick, attentive look, then pushed away the plate he had raided so voraciously only moments before. "'Keith,' is it? You're on very informal terms with my brother, it would seem."

"We're friends," said Fancy, understanding but wishing that she didn't. Keith Corbin was practically the first man she'd encountered, since her father, who liked her for herself, and she valued that.

"He'd be quite a catch," reflected Jeff. "Lots of money, all this land. And he's a solid citizen in the bargain. Too bad he's taken."

Fancy was so outraged that she couldn't speak.

"I, on the other hand, am quite free. And I'm no pauper," Jeff went on.

"And no 'solid citizen,' either, I'll wager," sputtered Fancy, again possessed of a need to slap this man silly.

Jeff laughed, rubbing his strong, recently shaven chin with one hand. "Unfortunately, you're right about that. But you're not exactly respectable yourself, are you?"

Fancy was stung, and worse, she was suddenly certain that he remembered her from Port Hastings. "W–What makes you say that?" she countered.

"It's just a guess," he said, his eyes averted.

"No, it isn't. You know me, don't you?"

"Should I?"

Fancy bit her lip, unable to answer.

Jeff sat back in his chair, crossing his long legs at the ankles, his magnificent face reflective and far away. "'Fancy Jordan,'" he mused, again rubbing his chin. "'She sings. She dances. She does magic.'"

Fancy was now not only unable to speak but unable to move. She waited, in horror, her hands gripping each other in white-knuckled dread.

"Let's hear you sing," said Jeff, stunning her anew. "Better yet, why don't you sing *and* dance?"

"H–Here?"

"Why not?"

"I couldn't. I–I won't."

"Why not?" he asked again.

"I wasn't hired to do that."

"What exactly were you hired to do?"

"Why, to t–take care of you!"

"Take care of me, then. Right now, a song, a dance, or a bit of magic seems crucial to my recovery."

Fancy trembled, certain that he had recognized her

and yet unable to believe that he could have. She couldn't have sung then if her life had depended upon it, and dancing, under the circumstances, would be ludicrous. Still shaking a little, she approached Jeff, reached out, and drew a half-dollar from behind his right ear.

"A parlor trick," he said derisively, his blue gaze boring into Fancy now, hurting.

Tears burned in Fancy's eyes, threatening to spill over. "What is it that you want from me?" she whispered.

"I want you to get out," he breathed, with incredible cruelty. "Leave me alone. Now."

Wildly confused and injured in the bargain, Fancy turned with dignity and marched out of the room, closing the door behind her. In the hallway, however, she sank against the wall and wept into both hands, overcome by his rancor and by the awful possibility that he knew her, that he remembered.

Temple Royce's woman. Hellfire and spit, it was just his luck! With a flailing motion of one arm, Jeff sent the tray and all its contents hurtling off the side table to clatter on the floor.

The door of his bedroom opened again, almost immediately, and he lifted his head, expecting Fancy, ready with a fresh spate of scathing invective. But instead of his "nurse," he was met with the furious azure gaze of his younger brother.

"What the devil did you say to Fancy?" Keith demanded in an undertone reminiscent of the days before his ordination as a Methodist minister.

Jeff ached for a fight, but, given his brother's inclination toward turning the other cheek, there didn't seem to be much chance of that. If only Adam were around! Jeff's fists clenched and unclenched. "Fancy," he bit out contemptuously.

"Yes, Fancy!" snapped Keith, his jawline tight. "I just found her sobbing her heart out!"

"A physical impossibility. The slut has no heart."

Keith's effort at control was visible. Perhaps there was hope of a good brawl after all. "Don't call her that again, Jeff," he ordered through clenched teeth. "Fancy is a nice young woman trying to get by, like the rest of us. According to Mrs. Thompkins, she sends practically every cent she earns to her family—"

"How noble!" rasped Jeff. And he thought of Fancy lying, prone and lush, in Temple Royce's bed. The image made him ill. "I want that bitch out of this house, Keith—now."

Keith folded his arms across his chest and cocked his head to one side. "This house is mine," he reminded his brother in even, yet dangerous, tones. "Fancy stays. However, big brother, if you think you can override my decision, you do it."

Jeff rose slowly to his feet. "Is that a challenge—little brother?"

"It's whatever you want to make it. Fancy needs this job and she stays."

"Let's discuss this outside," suggested Jeff, a peculiar euphoria sweeping through his system at the prospect of battle.

"Let's do. Since Mama isn't here to break it up with her buggy whip, maybe we'll get it settled," replied Keith, gesturing suavely toward the open doorway. "After you."

The two brothers walked down the steep stairway

single file, both grim with anger. In the kitchen, Mrs. Thompkins smiled, looking pleased and surprised. "Why—" she began, only to fall silent when Keith pushed open the back door with a sharp crack of his right palm and strode out onto the screened porch.

Jeff followed, ready for what was to come. Relishing it. The sun and the fresh air felt good after his long exile, and the song of the river was pleasant in his ears. None of these things, however, lessened his need for an all-out, no-holds-barred fight.

In the side yard, Keith suddenly stopped and pointed upward with one imperious hand. For a moment, Jeff thought he was going to call down a thunderbolt or something. "See that?" he said.

Jeff looked up, puzzled. "It's the sky," he answered.

"I'm glad you remember. You've been hiding in your room for so long, I thought you might have forgotten!"

Shame brushed against Jeff's spirit, but just briefly. He was scarred for life. He'd lost his ship and the only woman he'd ever wanted to marry. If anybody had a right to retreat from life, he did! "What if I did?" he roared. "Who the hell needs the goddamned sky?"

Keith stood straight and tall, though not quite as tall as Jeff himself, and shook his head. "You do, Jeff. We all do—we need the sky and the wind and the trees and the land. We need God and we need other people."

"How the hell do you manage to turn every conversation into a sermon?"

Keith shrugged. "Second nature, I guess."

"I want to fight!"

"I know," replied the pastor, looking pleased and damnably unruffled at the prospect. Didn't that Bible-jockey know when to be scared?

Jeff advanced on his brother; he was going to hit him—even though his conscience stung like hell, he was going to hit him.

Except that Fancy Jordan suddenly flung herself against Jeff's chest. The impact of her gave him a swift, sweet, piercing jolt.

"Stop!" she screamed.

Jeff caught her shoulders in his hands and even this contact, born of anger as it was, caused him a strange mingling of joy and alarm. "What the—"

"Step out of his way, Fancy," Keith interceded quietly, evenly.

Fancy's small, straight back stiffened and she glared up into Jeff's face with those wide violet eyes, daring him to do God-knew-what. "No," she said in a clear voice.

Mostly to make a rather unadmirable point, Jeff lifted Fancy off her feet and set her aside as though she were a doll.

She immediately returned, but this time there were tears standing along her thick eyelashes. "Please," she said. "I'll do anything—I'll go away or whatever you want. But, please, don't do this!"

Jeff stared down at her in amazement, moved by her tears and infuriated that he could be deluded by one of the oldest of feminine wiles. The desire to fight was gone, replaced by another kind of need. . . .

"You'll be late for church," she said pointedly, looking back over one shoulder at Keith.

Keith grinned and shrugged. "Sorry, Jeff, but the lady is right. Anybody want to come along?"

Jeff made a rude snorting sound, but his eyes kept going back to Fancy's upturned face, no matter how he resisted. What magic was she working?

They stood like that, in a mutually stricken silence, for some minutes, the spell breaking only when Keith and Alva drove away from the house in a buggy, on their way to services.

"Why did you do that?" Jeff managed to ask.

One golden eyebrow arched, and the tears that had stung him so were evaporating in the bright sunlight. A breeze made a tendril of her hair dance. "Do what?" she retorted.

Jeff was maddened. "Why did you break up the fight before it could get started?"

She shrugged and turned to walk away. "Keith was late for church," she said.

Jeff grabbed her by the shoulders and whirled her around to face him again. "Damn it, Frances, don't you dare walk away from me!"

"I don't answer to that name," she said loftily, and then she had the gall to turn away again.

Jeff swore loudly, wrenched her back toward him, and, to his total and absolute surprise, kissed her. Her soft, full lips had all the resiliency of a brick for the first moment or so, but then they softened and parted for him. He took full and savage advantage of this, all the while thinking that Temple had trained her well.

Seeming to know what was going through his mind, she backed away, glaring up at him with furious eyes, her cheeks flushed. "Don't ever do that again," she choked out.

"I intend to do far more than that," Jeff replied flatly.

"Try it and I'll rip your lips off," she shot back, whirling and storming off toward the barn in strides far too long for her short, slender legs.

Jeff stood still for a moment in the middle of the

lawn, stricken by her, infuriated with her, wanting her more than he'd ever wanted a woman. Then, having no choice, he strode after her. Damn it, no woman but Banner O'Brien had ever spurned him and he just wasn't going to tolerate that again!

He reached the wide open doorway of the barn and halted, breathing as though he'd just run all the way from town. Letting his eyes adjust to the shadowy interior, the sweet scent of hay came to greet him, drawing him in. "Frances!"

Silence.

Jeff sighed, ran one hand through his hair in exasperation. "Fancy?"

He heard her then. She was crying softly, hopelessly. The sound broke over Jeff like a tidal wave.

"Fancy?" he repeated, entering the barn.

"Go away!" she sobbed indignantly. "Just go away and leave me alone!"

Jeff approached her. She was crouched on a bale of last year's hay, leaning against the barn wall as though she wished it would absorb her. "Why are you crying?" he asked reasonably.

"I just feel like it!" she wailed.

He perched on the bale beside her and then pulled her onto his lap, cradling her head against his shoulder, stroking her wayward golden hair under one hand. There in the cool shadows of the barn, she allowed him to hold her, gradually relaxing. When he lifted her chin to kiss her again, she didn't resist.

The passion she stirred in Jeff Corbin was almost more than he could bear. He allowed one skilled hand to slide upward, from the curve of her small waist to the plump rounding of a generous breast. She stiffened, then whimpered when Jeff began to stroke a hidden nipple with the side of his thumb.

He felt the enticing nubbin harden in response, and the need of this woman ground within him, painful and all-consuming. "God in heaven," he muttered.

It was an unfortunate choice of words. Fancy sat bolt upright, and her blush was visible even in the relative darkness. "Stop it!"

Jeff thought it interesting that she did not try to leave his lap. Brazenly, acting on well-honed instincts, he lowered his face to her generous bosom and gently bit the very tip of her right breast. She trembled and cried out, and he deftly opened the first button of her dress, then the second, the third. He had not taken this particular sort of nourishment in months, and he craved it now.

"No," she whispered, even as she tugged her camisole down to reveal one delectable, rose-pointed breast for his pleasure.

Jeff plucked at the morsel with his fingers and then with his lips, delighting in her soft gasps, in the way she cupped the breast in one hand and uplifted it in offering. "Delicious—" he muttered.

She made some strangled, nonsensical reply, and Jeff chuckled as he feasted. He knew she'd shared Temple Royce's bed, knew she'd given suckle to his worst enemy in just this way, but he didn't give a damn.

Chapter Three

FANCY FELT DAZED, FULL OF WONDER AND CONFUSION. The warm mastery of Jeff's mouth plundering her breast was a strange mingling of both heaven and hell—the pleasure shot through every part of her, causing her body to demand things it had never asked for, or even known about, before. Involuntarily, she arched her back, allowing him even greater access.

He was greedy, and yet he was gentle, and when he suddenly stood Fancy on her feet before him, she was startled and off balance. She swayed a little and he caught her, steadied her, his hands strong on the curves of her hips.

Knowing full well that she was at this man's mercy, Fancy stood perfectly still, waiting. She knew that she should run away, or at least resist, but she couldn't bring herself to do either of those things. Her complete conviction that Jeff Corbin would not force himself upon her if she protested did her no good at all.

In silence, Jeff looked up at her and she saw an amazement in his face to match her own. His hands began easing the skirts of her new lavender dress slowly upward, ever upward, and Fancy felt an odd, heated chill. A protest climbed into her throat and then lodged there, unutterable.

He had brought her skirts to her waist and she stood before him in only her drawers, having no petticoats to provide further interference. He bent forward, very slowly, and nipped at the now-heated center of her womanhood.

A groan escaped Fancy, along with a strangled, senseless, "What are you—oh, God—"

His deft fingers undid the ties of her drawers, slid them downward. She was completely revealed to him now and she trembled with a certain delighted helplessness; never before had she permitted a man any liberty such as this. On the other hand, even though she despised him, Jeff Corbin was not just any man. There seemed to be a separate set of rules governing him.

With two fingers, Jeff unveiled her. What would he do now? Did he mean to hurt her? Fancy's mind swirled with unanswered questions and unspeakable desires—the foremost of which he immediately fulfilled.

Jeff's tongue touched her in that most vulnerable place and some primitive part of Fancy's nature came to the fore, completely taking her over. Her head fell back, with no order from her, and a soft cry of surrender escaped her.

He began to kiss her, to nibble at her as though she

were the most delicious delicacy, and she groaned his name, her fingers tangled, frantic, in his butternut hair. She still did not know what magic he offered, but she was already prepared to beg for it. Unconsciously, she widened her stance to permit him greater enjoyment and he chuckled brazenly as he tasted her and lapped at her with his tongue. Finally, he took full suckle, and when he did that Fancy gave a choked shout of triumph.

Heat surged through her, all of it coming from the delicate bud where his mouth at once caressed and punished her. She shuddered as the joy built toward some unbearable conclusion, and his strong hands gripped her bare bottom, holding her close, making the anguished pleasure inescapable.

"Ooooh!" she shouted, and there was a great, brutal trembling inside her as this unknown need was fully, finally met. When the last tender explosion had ebbed away, Jeff stood, then calmly removed Fancy's new dress, her displaced drawers, her camisole.

"What are you—" she managed to choke out. "I've never—"

"Oh, certainly not," agreed Jeff, with tender sarcasm, as he lowered her to the clean straw covering the barn floor. Then he removed his own clothes and Fancy thought distractedly how magnificent he was. The hard, muscular length of him was something of a shock, though, when stretched out upon her.

"Jeff—you must listen—I—"

His head slid to one bare and generous breast, causing it to welcome his attentions. Fancy was lost, because that same mystical, blinding need that had consumed her before was back again, dictating the actions of her body, silencing the protests of her reason. With one knee, Jeff gently forced her legs apart.

He entered her swiftly—too swiftly, for there was a tearing pain as her seal was broken. Fancy stiffened and gasped aloud.

Jeff lifted his magnificent head to stare at her, his face draped in soft shadows. "Fancy?" he questioned, in a hoarse, stricken voice.

The pain had faded and Fancy was aware again of the wild urgings that came from within her and yet could not possibly be contained by one small body, so infinite was their scope. She clasped at the muscle-rippled small of his back, desperate for the completion she knew she had not yet achieved.

"A virgin!" he muttered distractedly, but he was again moving upon her, slowly, smoothly. It was as though he wanted to stop but couldn't.

Fancy began to rise and fall beneath him, instinctively allowing him to lead her. And yet he moaned a soft plea, as though it were she who commanded.

As his thrusts increased in power, so did Fancy's passion. She was delirious with it now, clutching at the muscled curves of his buttocks, driving him deeper and deeper. Their separate bodies became fully one, heaving with the exertion demanded of them, glistening with a sheen of perspiration.

Fancy seemed to burst through the barn roof, spinning. She clutched at Jeff in a beautiful sort of terror, but his cries and the ceaseless thrusts of his fierce manhood only drove her higher. She was certain that if she could only turn her head, she would find herself looking down on the house and the river and the apple orchard.

Suddenly, his great body stiffened and he rasped her

name as his seed rippled into the depths of her, again and again. She spoke softly and soothed his broad back with her hands as he shuddered upon her.

Finally, Jeff sank to her, his breath harsh, his frame still quivering with the brutal force of his release. "God—Fancy—oh, my God—"

Reality came crashing down on Fancy in that moment. She realized what she had done, what they had done together, and struggled beneath his inert frame, a choked sob coming from her throat. "Let me up!"

Jeff eased away from her, still breathing hard, his eyes glazed and distracted. He watched without apparent emotion as Fancy frantically grabbed for her clothes, stood up, and struggled into them.

"You were a virgin," he observed in a flat voice, while Fancy grappled with her underthings.

"I tried to tell you that!" she burst out, tears streaking down her face.

One powerful, burn-scarred shoulder moved in a shrug. "I didn't believe you," he replied matter-of-factly, as though that made everything all right. "You used to work on the *Silver Shadow* in Port Hastings. I remember you."

"Does that make me a whore?" hissed Fancy, tangling one foot in the hem of her cherished lavender dress and nearly toppling back onto the straw again.

Idly, Jeff reached for his trousers and shirt. He was almost fully dressed before he answered, "It certainly doesn't make you respectable. The place is a brothel, after all."

Fancy wanted to strike him, but she knew that he would restrain her easily, perhaps even laugh at her. And right then she couldn't have borne that. "My father works in a coal mine!" she shouted senselessly, as she struggled with the buttons Jeff had found so easy to manage. "He's dying of lung fever! My mother washes other people's clothes and they're still in debt to the company no matter what they do! Therefore, Captain Rich-and-Spoiled Corbin, I'll work anywhere, as long as I'm paid a fair wage!"

He stopped buttoning his straw-flecked shirt to watch her. "To send to them?" he prompted.

"Yes!"

Jeff chuckled, low in his throat. "You're certainly worth your wages, Nurse Jordan."

That did it. Fancy lunged at him, still only half-dressed, a furious animal sound rattling deep in her throat. She flung both fists at an impervious, rock-hard chest, frantic to hurt Jeff Corbin, to make him bleed.

He caught her wrists in a firm hold and, to her eternal surprise, pulled her close. His arms were around her instantly, the palms of his massive hands cupping her small bottom, kneading the still-tingling flesh there into a submission that soon spread throughout Fancy's being. "I'm sorry," he said gruffly. "I was only teasing you."

Fancy was determined not to be caught in his trap again. "I came out here to build a rabbit hutch!" she yelled.

Jeff threw back his head and laughed uproariously. When he finally sobered, he looked down into her flushed, furious face and said, "Lord, woman, the way you build rabbit hutches could send a man to an early grave."

"Wretch!"

He bent and kissed the tip of her pert little nose.

"You'd better go inside, Miss Jordan, and repair your appearance. At the moment, you look as though you'd just been deflowered on the barn floor."

Fancy broke free of him and strode toward the house. It wasn't until she reached her room and forced herself to look into the mirror, that she realized how right Jeff had been. Her hair was full of straw and falling around her shoulders in untidy loops, her dress was mussed and not properly buttoned. A telling apricot blush pulsed in her cheeks and her eyes were as bright as the sunny heights where she'd soared.

Trembling, Fancy took the pitcher from her wash stand, stomped to the kitchen sink, and pumped cold water into the vessel so vigorously that her arm ached. Then she swept back to her room, poured the water into the waiting basin, and splashed her face until some of the heat faded away and her heart slowed to its normal pace.

After that, she took her hair down and brushed it, causing it to crackle and flare around her face. She exchanged the lavender dress for her own gray woolen, unsuited as it was to the warm weather, and then pinned her thick tresses into a severe coronet at the back of her head. Maybe she wasn't innocent anymore, but she certainly looked the part, and that was what mattered now. If Keith and Mrs. Thompkins had seen her in her earlier, scandalous state, she would have been mortified.

Jeff was in the kitchen when Fancy dared to return to that room. He'd stripped off his shirt and he was washing industriously, noisily at the sink, the sparkling water flying in every direction.

Of course, Fancy took in the long scar stretching

across his broad back and her anger softened, just momentarily, into tenderness. She longed to walk across that room and touch the mark with her fingers, tracing its path from his shoulder to his hip.

He turned to see her frozen there in the doorway, his face and hair dripping water from his impromptu bath. Mirth danced, deep blue, in his eyes. "How very prim and proper you look, Miss Jordan. I liked you better with hay in your hair."

Fancy blushed but she did not avert her eyes, though she longed to. This was a contest of wills and even if she could not win, she had no intention of being cowed, either. "I'll thank you not to refer to that—that indiscretion again!"

One toasted-gold eyebrow arched in eloquent amusement. The muscles in Jeff's furred chest rippled as he reached for a towel and began to dry himself. "Is that what it was, Frances? An indiscretion?"

Fancy's cheeks ached and burned. "Yes!"

"That's a pity—that you feel that way, I mean. Because I intend to have you again, first chance I get." He paused and his maddening, handsome face was speculative, mischievous. "It'll be in the carriage next time, I think—"

Fancy swayed and groped her way to a chair at the table, falling gratefully into it. "The carriage!" she gasped, stunned at his audacity.

He nodded. "You're a tasty little morsel," he reflected, ignoring the new surge of color in Fancy's face, the trembling of her clasped hands. "I'd like to set you on the carriage seat and—"

"Stop!" wailed Fancy, mortified.

"It would be delicious," he continued, "for you as well as for me."

"Nothing will be 'delicious,' Captain Corbin," Fancy spouted. "I intend to leave this place immediately!"

He came to stand disconcertingly near, the towel stretched taut between his hands. Fancy's heart fluttered wildly for a moment, for she thought that he meant to choke her.

As if to add credence to this idea, he caught the moist towel behind her neck and pulled until she was forced to stand, facing him, within inches of his conquering body.

But Jeff did not strangle Fancy; he merely kissed her. His lips were soft upon hers, cool from his washing, tasting of spring water and a lingering trace of her own soaring joy.

"Don't leave me," he muttered.

Fancy broke away from him, but with difficulty. And she was still imprisoned by the towel he held. "I was not hired to serve your base instincts, Jeff Corbin," she managed to say.

He bent, caught her lower lip between gentle teeth, then tugged at it. A jolt of renewed need rocked Fancy. "Don't go," he repeated in a throaty voice. "Promise you won't, or I swear I'll carry you upstairs and demonstrate every single reason why you belong in my bed, Fancy Jordan."

"I d–don't belong in your bed!"

He let the towel go and bent as if to lift her. While Fancy knew that she could not permit such a thing, a part of her wished that Jeff would make good on his threat. "Oh, no?"

"I'll stay!" she burst out.

His hands came up to brazenly cup her breasts. "Promise?"

"I pr–promise!"

"Good." He plucked pert, woolen-covered nipples into prompt obedience. "Now, let's try to look as though we've been good while the pastor was away, shall we?"

"H–How?"

In complete contrast to his own words, Jeff was unbuttoning Fancy's prim gray dress at the bodice. "We'll build a rabbit hutch," he said. "But first, I want another taste of you. Nourish me, Fancy."

Fancy willed her hands to rise up and stop the steady baring of her breasts, but they would not. "You can't mean—"

"I want a breast," he said, bending his head, closing his mouth over one camisole-sheltered nipple, leaving a moistness there to taunt the puckering treasure beneath. "Nothing more, but nothing less, either."

His voice was sleepy and compelling and Fancy ached to grant him what he asked. "N–Not here—" she argued, in a choked little voice.

Jeff smiled and caught her hand in his; the towel was still draped over her shoulders and she arranged it to cover her gaping bodice. He led her into a small parlor off the kitchen, sat her down at the end of a long sofa, and then draped himself, on his side, across her lap.

And Fancy bared one plump breast to nurse him, loving every thrilling moment, every gentle nip of his teeth, every greedy suckling, every flick of his tongue. At the same time, she hated Jeff Corbin for being able to make her do such an outrageous thing so willingly.

Finally, when he'd had his fill, he calmly replaced her moistened camisole and buttoned her dress.

Fancy was both relieved and disappointed. While it would certainly have been imprudent to let him take her again, her entire being ached for just that.

Maddeningly, he knew exactly what she was thinking and feeling. He patted her cheek in a rather patronizing fashion and muttered, "You'll be tender for a while."

Fancy colored richly but said nothing. The gauzy fabric of her camisole clung to her well-worked nipples, giving rise to a frantic and very unladylike urge to scratch.

Jeff stood up, looking down at her, frowning slightly. "Why didn't Temple make love to you?"

It was too much. Fancy was already mortified by what she had done with this man, what she had allowed him to do to her. She shot to her feet and glared into his rugged, aristocratic face. "Temple Royce is a gentleman, unlike you!" she shouted, and the fact that she was lying through her teeth mattered not at all.

To Fancy's surprise, Jeff flung back his head and laughed a great, roaring, lion laugh. "Royce, a gentleman!"

"What's so funny about that? He wanted me to save myself for marriage."

Jeff continued to laugh.

Fancy stomped one foot. "Well, he did!"

Finally, Jeff's amusement began to subside. Replacing it was something far more alarming—a glitter of dislike lurked in the dark blue eyes. "It's far more likely that he was saving you for one of the backrooms on the *Silver Shadow*, Fancy, and we both know it."

Speechless with humiliation and impotent rage, Fancy tried to press past Jeff Corbin. She would pack her things, collect Hershel, and leave this wretched, wonderful place before anyone could change her mind.

Except that Jeff caught her arm and pulled her back. "I'm sorry," he said gruffly.

Somewhere over the Columbia River, she grappled
She gazed up at him, unable to speak for the torrent of conflicting emotions washing over her. She despised this man and yet she needed him, too. Perhaps she even loved him.

Fancy shuddered at the thought.

He drew her close; she felt again the hard strength of his chest and thighs, the warmth of his bare flesh. "Cold?" he breathed.

She pulled back. "Put on your shirt!" she scowled.

He chuckled and, incredibly, did as he was told. By the time Keith and Alva returned from church, a lovely dark-haired woman perched on the buggyseat between them, Fancy and Jeff were kneeling in the side yard—industriously building a rabbit hutch.

Keith was both pleased and unsettled by the change in his brother. It was nothing short of a miracle that Jeff was out of his room, actually doing something constructive, and yet there was an elusive element in his bearing, and Fancy's, too, that boded ill.

With the softness of Amelie pressed so close to him, it was natural that Keith would consider the most unnerving possibility—that Jeff, with his legendary way with women, had seduced Fancy.

He drew the buggy to a halt at the barn door, jumped down, and helped Amelie to alight. The turn his thoughts had just taken made him wonder how the devil he was going to last a full month until the wedding.

The steady *thwack-thwack* of Jeff's hammer ceased. Both he and Fancy had been kneeling on the grass, one on each side of whatever they were building, but they rose together, their faces watchful, wary.

Oh, no, thought Keith with real despair.

Jeff's eyes met his brother's squarely and held, though his words were directed to Amelie. "We have a guest," he said, unnecessarily.

Keith was diverted by the mention of the woman he loved, probably because he wanted to be. He felt a familiar thrill as her small, gloved hand slid through the crook of his arm and squeezed. She was a vision with her bright green eyes, her dark, glistening hair, her slight but womanly figure.

"It's so good to see you out and about, Captain," she said sweetly, her gaze touching Fancy and then dismissing her. "I do hope you're feeling better."

Jeff flung one look at Fancy—a look Keith knew as well as he knew the twenty-third Psalm—and then answered, "Much better."

Fancy's furious blush told Keith all he needed to know. "I'd like to talk to you inside," he told his brother, in a tightly controlled voice.

Jeff agreed with a nod and dropped the hammer to the ground. "Anything you say," he replied, with biting good humor.

Fancy stood nervously, taking in the compact beauty of the woman Keith had abandoned on the lawn. She was a wonder—her dark ringlets gleamed in the sun, her skin was flawness, her teeth were small and white and even.

"That Keith!" the vision trilled, as Alva flung her one unseen and inscrutable look on the way into the house. "He was rude not to introduce us!" She extended one immaculately gloved hand and stepped toward Fancy. "My name is Amelie Rogers."

"Frances Gordon," replied Fancy, accepting the offered hand and squeezing it firmly.

Amelie's frown was pensive. "I thought Keith said your name was—Fancy."

Fancy blushed. "That's my nickname."

"It's really so—colorful."

Fancy did not know whether to thank the woman or be offended. Because of that quandary, she said nothing at all.

Amelie caught her arm and ushered her along toward the house. Though her smile never waned, there was a certain challenge in its bright sparkle. "I hope that you and I can be friends, Fancy, but—"

"But, what?" demanded Fancy, stopping cold in her tracks.

Amelie had the good grace to look embarrassed. "Well, you are living here, with two unmarried men, and there is—well, there is some talk. Your being an actress—"

Considering what had gone on in the barn and then on the parlor couch, Fancy had a degree of difficulty maintaining her righteous indignation. "I am not an actress. Furthermore, Mrs. Thompkins shares this house also!"

Amelie bit her lower lip, regarding Fancy's flushed face squarely. "I've made a miserable mess of this," she murmured, after several moments of silence. A becoming blush moved up over her high, finely shaped cheekbones. "Oh, there's nothing for it—I'll just have to say what's on my mind! I love Keith Corbin very much and we're to be married next month and it's obvious that he likes you—"

Fancy was both annoyed and relieved. "I've no

designs on your intended, Miss Rogers." Your future brother-in-law, she added in rueful silence, is, unfortunately, another matter entirely.

Amelie heaved a delicate sigh of relief and, not for the first time, Fancy wondered why women always saw her as a threat to their romantic interests. Not until that very morning had she ever behaved in any way that could have been called wanton. "We shall be friends, then—very good friends. Tell me—have you ever met the Corbin family?"

Fancy shuddered. Jeff had not pursued her relationship with Temple Royce, but that was no guarantee that his family wouldn't. Come to that, they probably wouldn't approve of her in any case, given her brief career in show business. "No, I haven't." She didn't add that she hoped she never would.

"They're all coming here for the wedding, you know," Amelie reflected innocently, as they entered the house through the screened porch at the back. "I declare, I'm so nervous I could just perish! Mrs. Corbin is an important woman."

"Undoubtedly," said Fancy, feeling just as nervous. How stupid she'd been not to anticipate this, not to realize that the rest of the Corbins would attend Keith's wedding! How in heaven's name would she face them?

But then, she thought, as she and Amelie trekked past a silent Alva on their way to the main parlor, she was little more than a servant in this house. She would not have to suffer formal introductions or take any real part in the celebration.

Amelie sat down in a chair near a massive, white-rock fireplace and distractedly removed her gloves and then her fetching Sunday bonnet. "I'll die if they don't like me," she said.

Fancy was suddenly filled with sympathy for the bride-to-be; she could well imagine how Amelie felt. After all, the Corbins were an imposing group. "I don't see why they wouldn't," she said honestly, sitting opposite Miss Rogers and folding her hands in her lap.

The distant echo of angry masculine voices reached the parlor and disrupted Fancy's train of thought. Amelie looked concerned.

"What do you suppose they're arguing about?"

Fancy was afraid she knew—there had been an angry, knowing look in Keith's eyes when he'd arrived. A new thought occurred to her: that the reverend, in righteous outrage, would send her away. She was amazed at how badly she wanted to stay.

She lifted her chin and tried to look placid. "I think they just naturally argue a great deal," she said.

Amelie arched perfect, raven-black eyebrows. "You may be right."

In that moment, Fancy craved solitude more than she ever had in her life. Her thoughts were spinning and she needed to be alone to grapple with them. She did not know whether to stay or to go and worst of all, she had a nagging suspicion that she might be falling in love with Jeff Corbin. That, despite what had happened between them, would be disastrous.

Furthermore, how was she going to face Keith from day to day? How was she going to live under the same roof with Jeff and escape having the events of that morning repeat themselves over and over again?

She sighed. Keith and Amelie would soon be married, and she would be very much in the way when that happened. So, for that matter, would Jeff.

"What are you thinking?" Amelie asked, with gentle directness. "You look so sad."

Fancy was sad. Sad because she could no longer pull rabbits out of hats. Sad because her virginity was gone forever. Sad because there was such a vast difference between Amelie's future and her own.

"I'm only tired," she lied.

The future Mrs. Keith Corbin clearly didn't believe her, but she didn't press. When Keith strode abruptly into the room, Amelie's face lit up and they might have been the only two people in the whole world.

Fancy slipped out, unnoticed, and left the house by the front door. She walked around to the side yard, approaching the gazebo where she had been so roundly humiliated only the day before. She plopped despondently down on its top step.

The grounds bore no trace of yesterday's celebration, except for one: Ribbons, now forlorn-looking, trembled in the gentle spring breeze, hanging forgotten from the boughs of the apple tree that had looked so glorious during the lawn party.

Suddenly, Fancy felt as denuded as that tree, and she lowered her forehead to her upraised knees in total despair.

Chapter Four

FANCY KNELT BEFORE HERSHEL'S CAGE AND PUSHED A dish of fresh water through the little door, along with a handful of lettuce leaves. She tried not to think about what had happened in this very barn only hours before, but the effort was useless. Never, no matter where she went, what she did, or how old she got, would she forget the magic that had been revealed to her here.

One tear slid down her cheek and she wiped it away angrily, forcing herself to square her shoulders and lift her chin. She'd made a mistake, a terrible mistake, but sitting about crying over it would change nothing. No, the only thing she could do now was leave before matters got any worse.

With a sigh, she latched Hershel's cage door and rose to her feet, dusting straw from the skirts of her gray dress as she straightened. When she turned to leave the barn again, though, she found herself face to face with Jeff Corbin himself.

Though she was distraught, Fancy's heart leaped within her and then fell into place again, spinning. She glared at Jeff in despairing anger. Why hadn't he left her alone? If he had, she would have been able to stay.

But she was wrong to blame him completely, and she knew it. She had been every bit as selfish and irresponsible as he had.

"What do you think of Amelie?" he asked, crossing his arms across his broad chest and leaning indolently against the gate of a nearby stall.

Fancy's shoulders lifted in a deceptively nonchalant shrug. "Is my opinion important?" she countered.

Jeff grinned. "I guess not. Still, I'd like to know what it is."

"I like Amelie," Fancy said truthfully, trying to avoid those discerning indigo eyes.

"So do I."

"But?" urged Fancy, though the answer really wouldn't matter much to her, one way or the other. At the moment, she was feeling frazzled and just a bit sorry for herself.

"I don't think she has enough spirit for Keith," Jeff observed. He'd brushed his hair and changed his clothes for dinner—the first meal he'd taken outside his room in months, according to Alva—and he looked so handsome that Fancy ached to touch him.

Of course, she refrained. "How much 'spirit' does a minister's wife need?" she replied, a little annoyed.

"I have no idea," Jeff responded, "but I know how much spirit a Corbin's wife needs."

"Keith is different than you."

Jeff chuckled appreciatively. "You innocent. He's a man, not a saint."

"He's also a minister!"

"That will be small comfort in his marriage bed. He should wait for some infuriating snippet to come crashing into his life—the way Banner came into Adam's." He paused, but when he went on, his voice was very soft. "The way you came into mine."

Color climbed up Fancy's cheekbones. She stood still, her heart lodged in her throat and pounding there like a huge drum.

Jeff came closer, tangled an index finger in a curled tendril at her temple.

Fancy leaped backward as though burned by his touch. "Don't—please—I can't bear it—"

He sighed and his hands came to rest gently on the sides of her waist. "Fancy, I'm sorry. Not for making love to you—I can't say I regret that. But I do apologize for the way you're feeling right now."

Fancy's chin shot upward; pride was the only defense she had left. "And how is that?" she snapped.

"Used, I think. Maybe slightly taken-advantage-of."

"Slightly?" Every muscle in Fancy's small, trim body seemed to contract. *"Slightly?* Tell me, when and if I should marry, what am I to say to my husband? That losing my virtue was part of my job?"

"Fancy—"

"Damn you, don't you dare try to reassure me! You're a rich man, used to getting what you want, and nothing else matters to you—including the effect this could have on the rest of my life!"

His hands left her waist for her shoulders, gripping them gently. "Will you listen to me?" he pleaded, in such earnest tones that Fancy was almost fooled, almost lulled into believing that he really had her best interests in mind. "I'm trying to tell you that—"

"Don't tell me anything! I'm not interested in being placated!"

"Do you think I'm that pompous, that arrogant?"

"Yes!"

A muscle flexed in his jaw, then stilled. "Fancy, we can't stay here," he went on persistently. "Not after what's happened."

Fancy had already come to that conclusion herself, but it was surprising to hear it from Jeff. "I completely agree," she said, in stiff tones, wishing that she had the nerve and the strength to break free of his grasp and walk away.

"Good. Then perhaps you'll also agree that there is a magic between us that has nothing to do with your pulling rabbits out of hats."

Fancy stared up at him, wide-eyed. "Magic?"

"I've never before felt the way I did with you, Fancy. Not ever." He sighed and his grip on her shoulders eased a little. "Will you go away with me?"

The idea had more appeal than Fancy would ever admit. "And do what?"

"And be my mistress."

Any dreams that might have been stirring to life were instantly dashed. Of course he would suggest that, after the way she'd encouraged him. That was no surprise. And yet, after only one day, she'd dared to hope that Jeff was beginning to love her.

She lifted her hand and slapped him with all the force of her grief, her confusion, and her shame. He was stunned enough to slacken his hold and Fancy whirled away to run, her skirts bunched in her fingers.

Certain that she could not bear to face Amelie or Keith or the understanding Alva, Fancy avoided the house and plunged into the orchard. Her breathing was ragged and raw, dry little sobs tore themselves from her throat as she fled.

"Frances!" bellowed Jeff, and she heard him behind her, gaining fast.

She tried to accelerate her own pace, caught one foot in the hem of her dress, and went tumbling to the soft, blossom-cushioned ground. Jeff was upon her instantly, wrenching her onto her back and then pinning her beneath his delightful, reprehensible, inescapable weight.

"What the hell is the matter with you?" he demanded, looking fierce in the gathering twilight.

Fancy could not form sensible words; she wailed with grief and writhed, trying to free herself. The frantic sobs continued to well up from within her.

Jeff caught her face between both his hands and stayed the motion of her head, though her body still rebelled beneath his. "Stop it!" he hissed.

Something in the tone of his voice reached Fancy's reason and she was still, though tears were streaming down her face and her chest was still heaving. "Get—off of—me!" she choked out.

"Not until you listen to me, damn you! I wasn't trying to insult you when I asked you to be my mistress!"

"Well, it's an honor I can do without!" croaked Fancy.

"What the devil do you want from me?" he retorted furiously. "Marriage?"

"I wouldn't marry you!"

One of his imperious eyebrows arched in contemptuous disbelief. "Oh, no?"

"No!"

He looked oddly pensive. Even reflective. "It *would* solve a few problems," he mused.

"Not for me it wouldn't!"

Jeff held Fancy firmly beneath him, quelling any possibility of struggle. "Wouldn't it? Think, Fancy—you wouldn't have to haul that rodent from one town to another. And, of course, things would be very different for your family—"

Fancy's eyes widened and though Jeff stretched her arms out above her head and pressed them to the soft ground, she did not resist. "What do you mean?"

"You know very well what I mean."

Fancy dared to imagine her mother and father freed from the ceaseless drudgery of their lives and her throat constricted. "Y–You would take care of them?"

"Yes. And you." He chuckled. "And even your fat, stupid rabbit."

Fancy's wrists were caught together, in just one of Jeff's hands, and still she didn't struggle. "What about you? How would you benefit?"

Jeff laughed and Fancy felt his fingers at the buttons of her bodice. A delicious tremor of terror and need went through her. "How indeed?" he taunted, reaching beneath her dress and camisole to cup one straining breast in his palm.

Fancy groaned as he stroked the nipple, causing it to stand erect. "You don't have to marry anyone to get that!" she protested.

"I do if I want it all to myself," he replied. "Marry me, Fancy. Do all your magic in my bed."

"But you're not—we're not in love!"

"True enough. But I can't have the woman I love, ever. You've already worked miracles—maybe you could even make me forget Banner."

Fancy had never been more wounded. She closed her eyes and wished that she could die. "You let me up, Jeff Corbin. Right now!"

His hand, sweetly tormenting her right breast only a moment before, was now dragging her skirts upward, now sliding intimately along her inner thigh, now undoing the ties that held her drawers in place. He still gripped Fancy's wrists firmly, though there was no pain, and his mouth was at the breast he had so skillfully prepared for conquering. He circled the taut nipple with the tip of his tongue and simultaneously slid his hand inside her pantaloons to her abdomen.

Fancy arched her back in unwilling response as his fingers found the nest of curls at the junction of her thighs and passed beyond to caress the tiny, swelling treasure hidden there. "You said—ooooh—you said I would b–be too tender—"

He chuckled at her breast, flogged the pulsing nipple with a gifted tongue. "Not for this," he rasped, and then his fingers were plucking at the moist morsel that guarded her womanhood, causing Fancy to anguish and yet to thrust her legs wide apart so that he could have fuller access. Her reward was a steady, circling caress that made her breath come fast and sent her hips into a frantic dance all their own.

"Jeff—oh, God—Jeff, Jeff!"

Fancy's soft whimpering drew a groan from him; he bared her other breast and roused its nipple to saucy impertinence with his teeth. But instead of suckling, he talked to her, in low, gruff tones, promising her the most outrageous of erotic pleasures, describing them in detail.

Fancy was overwhelmed by needs he seemed determined to spawn but not grant. Somehow, she got her hands free and they came unerringly to the front of his trousers, making short work of the belt buckle and buttons there. Feverish, she clasped the bared, heated length of his shaft in her hands.

Jeff gasped and then trembled, now her prisoner as she was his. A low moan grated past his lips as she plied his magnificence to an even grander state.

Aware of a new and undreamed-of power, Fancy shifted to her knees, facing him, stroking him in a hand-over-hand motion that made him shudder in a splendid sort of surrender. He bore the pleasure as long as he dared, then thrust Fancy backward, onto the soft orchard grass, hiking up her skirts and disposing of her drawers with a desperate swiftness. Cupping her firm bottom in both hands, he lifted her up and entered her in one searing thrust.

Fancy uttered a gasping whimper, for he had built her to such a pitch of need that her body immediately convulsed in brutal release. This early triumph permitted her yet another new joy—watching the wild passion in Jeff's face, feeling it play in his body like a symphony.

She slid her hands underneath his shirt, glorying in the warm power of the muscles in his back. Softly, wickedly, she urged him on and on until he cried out in desolation and victory, lunging deep within her and shuddering as she received the fruit of his passion and cradled it within her.

It was late and the road was dark. The moon, riding high in the sky, was waning, part of it smudged away as if by some celestial finger. At the sound of an approaching wagon, Fancy leaped off to the side of the road, her valise in one hand and Hershel's cage in the other, to cower in the ditch.

A trail of thin golden light spilled ahead of the team and wagon and a man's voice rose in a raucous baritone. Fancy closed her eyes and prayed she wouldn't be seen, but the snorts of the horses and the squeak of a brake lever forewarned her that God was not hearing the pleas of wantons who coupled in barns and orchards with men who weren't their husbands.

"Say!" boomed a friendly and totally unfamiliar voice. "What are you doing there?"

Fancy straightened and stepped up out of the ditch, nearly losing her balance, Hershel, and the valise in the process. "Just walking," she lied.

The outrageous prevarication made the man in the wagon seat laugh. The dim light of the headlamp affixed to the side of his wildly decorated vehicle revealed him to be a harmless looking sort with thatches of thin red hair sticking out from beneath his bowler hat. His suit was an obnoxious plaid and he was a small man, smaller even than Fancy herself. "Just walking, is it? And would you like to ride awhile?"

Fancy paused, studying the man, listening to instincts well-developed by three years of traveling largely on her own. "I don't know your name," she said.

"I don't know yours, either, as it happens."

Fancy smiled, despite her weariness and the churning pain that ground within her. "Fancy Jordan."

He doffed his hat in a comical motion. "I am Phineas T. Pryor," he replied.

Fancy squinted at the side of his decorated wagon and saw that he advertised himself as a man who could both fly and cure a startling array of ills. She supposed that was no more outrageous than her own claim to sing, dance, and do magic. "Are you a gentleman, Mr. Pryor?"

"Oh, indeed. Are you a lady, Miss Jordan?"

Fancy thought of the episode in the orchard earlier that evening, and decided that it was to her advantage to lie. "Yes," she said.

Phineas T. Pryor climbed down from the wagon box and, after tipping it once more, replaced his hat. He took Fancy's valise and Hershel's cage and placed them carefully in the back of the wagon, along with the battered signboard proclaiming his companion's talents. That done, he proceeded, as if determined to prove that he was indeed a gentleman, to help his passenger up into the wagon seat.

They were well down the dark road before he spoke seriously. "You'll be safe, you know."

Fancy had known that much intuitively. "Yes, I know," she said, all the same.

"Can you really sing, dance, and do magic?" he asked, his gentle eyes on the road ahead. Obviously, he'd read the signboard.

"Can you really fly and cure diseases?" countered Fancy. The loss of Jeff Corbin was a throbbing ache in her heart, but she couldn't let herself think about him or his proposal or his lovemaking. After all, she wasn't suited to him, the way Amelie was to Keith.

"I can fly," conceded Phineas, with a wry grin. "With a little help from my balloon, that is."

Fancy squinted at him. "Balloon?"

"Yes, ma'am. She's a veteran of the War Between the States, my balloon."

Fancy was much relieved that Mr. Pryor didn't believe himself capable of flying under his own power. "I'd certainly like to see it sometime," she said, with genuine interest.

"It's a sight you won't soon forget, Miss Jordan," Phineas allowed proudly. "A sight you'll never forget."

An unbidden tear slid down Fancy's cheek and she turned abruptly away to hide it. There were other things she would not soon forget, and a balloon was the least of them.

Fancy yawned and stretched, fully expecting to awaken in the clean, homey bedroom off Keith Corbin's kitchen. Instead, she found herself in the middle of a carnival. A tent was being raised, concession stands were being assembled. And an incredible orange and white balloon loomed against an ice-blue summer sky.

"Good morning!" sang Phineas, extending slender, fatherly arms to help her down from the seat of his garish wagon.

For just a moment, Fancy stared at her new friend in bewilderment. And then everything came back to her—Jeff, her hasty departure from his brother's house, her soiled virtue. She would have cried if Phineas hadn't forestalled the action by chiming, "Come now, and have some breakfast. Fresh trout—caught it myself, in the river."

The scent of trout wafted toward Fancy from a nearby campfire and buoyed her spirits as well as her appetite. Broken heart or none, there was nothing wrong with her stomach.

Sitting rumpled and groggy on the stump of a pine tree, she ate the pan-fried fish that Phineas offered and drank strong coffee from an enamel mug. Once the edges had been taken off her hunger, she assessed her surroundings.

Though Mr. Shibble's troupe was not there, as far as Fancy could tell, there was quite an assortment of entertainments, including a fat lady, a fortuneteller, and two elephants. Best of all, though, was the gigantic orange and white hot-air balloon that shifted against the bright sky, straining at the ropes and cable that held it to the ground.

Fancy drew in a swift breath, her coffee mug poised between her mouth and her lap. "Is that yours?" she asked of Phineas, though her eyes would not leave the balloon.

There was a beaming quality in his voice. "Surely is, Miss Jordan."

Fancy was spellbound. "What makes it fly?"

"The inside of the balloon is heated with gas. Since hydrogen is much lighter than air, it naturally rises."

"How do you steer it?" fretted Fancy, still squinting at the wondrous vessel that could brave the skies.

Phineas laughed. "You don't steer her, little one. She rides the air currents, going where the wind takes her."

"Currents?"

"Yes. You see, Fancy, the air around us is much like an ocean—it flows and swirls just the way water does."

At last, Fancy looked away from the magnificent balloon. "How much do you charge? For a ride in your sky vessel, I mean?"

Phineas chuckled. "One thin dime, my dear. One thin dime. But for you—a smile."

Fancy knew a delicious terror. Fascinating as the prospect was, she didn't believe she had the courage to leave the ground that way. What if the balloon deflated, as balloons will? What if it strayed far, far away?

Again, Fancy felt dismal. It didn't much matter where she ended up, did it? No one was waiting for her anywhere.

"What is it, child?" Phineas asked directly, in gentle tones, pouring more coffee into Fancy's cup. "What makes that terrible ache in your eyes?"

Fancy trembled and took a steadying sip of the bitter coffee. How she wished that she could confide in Phineas—obviously he was a kind man—but there was nothing to be gained by letting him know what a wanton she was. "I–I'm just a little down on my luck," she allowed.

"He'll come, you know."

"Who?" puzzled Fancy.

"The man you left," replied Phineas confidently. And then he strolled away to consult with a man who carried a monkey on his shoulder.

After a moment of self-recovery, Fancy finished her breakfast and went off to explore. She found a clear stream near the carnival site and carried her plate and cup there, along with Phineas's, to wash them. That done, she cleansed her face and hands, too, and then went back to the camp, gathering dandelion greens as she went. These she gave to Hershel, along with a tin saucer of water.

She had brushed and repinned her hair by the time Phineas returned, chattering amicably with a tall, muscular man clad in a cheap suit and a bowler hat. Her gray woolen dress was rumpled for more reasons than Fancy cared to think about, and she tried in vain to smooth it.

"I was telling Mr. Stroble here about your act," her friend explained. "He's in charge of this magnificent show we see around us."

Fancy smiled, thinking what a truly good friend Phineas Pryor was turning out to be. Here was her chance to earn enough money to keep going until she could find more permanent circumstances. "How do you do, Mr. Stroble?"

Stroble harumphed and it was clear that he did not quite approve of Fancy. Very likely, he was a farmer or businessman, rather than a showman, and thus inclined to look down on people, particularly women, who earned their livelihood in such an unconventional fashion. "Pryor tells me that you sing and dance."

Fancy neither sang nor danced, when she could get out of it. Her voice was true but rather thin, and her dancing was downright awkward. "I prefer to perform magic," she said.

"Good," gruffed Mr. Stroble. "Country folks ain't much for singin' 'less it's gospel. Set up your tent, if you've got one, and you'll get two dollars for the day."

Two dollars was a small fortune for a day's work, and Fancy knew that if she performed well, she would earn that grand sum every day that the fair ran. "Thank you," she said.

"Do you have a tent?" demanded Phineas, the moment Stroble had marched away.

Fancy was fitful. Suppose Hershel failed her again? Suppose the few tricks she knew fell flat? "Of course not!" she snapped, instantly regretting her sharpness.

Phineas was not offended; indeed, he seemed to understand. "I've a small table in the wagon," he soothed. "It has a canvas canopy—you can use that."

"Don't you need it?" challenged Fancy.

"Only use it when it rains," disclaimed Mr. Pryor grandly. "I'll get it for you."

It was while Phineas was dragging the table and canopy out of the wagon that Fancy noticed the alarming grayness of his skin, the faint blue tinge around his mouth. Without thinking, she caught his elbow in her hand and cried, "Phineas—are you ill?"

He sighed, put one hand to his chest, and offered up a rather shaky smile. "On a grand day like this? Never!"

Fancy was unconvinced, but she knew that further questions would be pointless. "You've been so kind to me," she said softly. "I don't know what I would have done—"

Phineas smiled again and patted her upper arm. "You would have been just fine, Fancy. Just fine."

His use of her first name made her feel warm and sheltered, almost as though she belonged. She hummed as she made her way into a stand of fir trees, there to change into her star-spangled dress.

"She's gone, then?" guessed Keith Corbin, watching his brother's agitated pacing with mingled sympathy and delight.

Jeff ran one hand through already-rumpled, wheat-colored hair. "Yes, damn it—rabbit and all!"

"It's your own fault, you know," Keith observed cautiously, over the rim of his coffee cup. Standing at the sink, Alva flung him a red-rimmed look, while Jeff stopped pacing to glare.

"I know that!" he bellowed.

"So what are you going to do about it?"

The answer to that was another glare. Jeff stormed out of the kitchen and the screened door of the sun porch slammed in the distance.

"He loves Fancy," the housekeeper mused, scouring a frying pan.

"Yep," confirmed Keith. Then he drained his coffee cup, set it aside with a thump, and went off to his study to outline next week's sermon.

Fancy's act was going very, very well. The crowd of spectators who were gathered before her borrowed table oohed and ahhed appreciatively as she made fire dance from the tips of her fingers, then clapped with delight when she caused a simple wand to bloom with colorful silk flowers.

Confidently, she summoned a little, freckle-faced boy from the crowd and, with a proper flourish, drew a coin borrowed from Phineas from behind his right ear. The audience cheered and Fancy was so swept up in this success that she dared to produce the top hat, heretofore hidden beneath the table.

"You see before you, ladies and gentlemen," she sang out, "an ordinary hat. As you can also see, this hat is totally empty." She held the hat out and the spectators peered into it, mumbling.

Bravely, Fancy plunged her hand into the hat. "Remember, Hershel," she muttered, under her breath, "you can be replaced."

For the first time in weeks, Hershel came out of the black bag that hid him without incident. The audience was stunned at such a feat, and they not only cheered but flung precious pennies in a veritable frenzy of acclamation.

By midafternoon, Fancy was twenty cents richer and flying higher than Phineas's balloon. Again and again she had performed her act and it seemed that she and Hershel could do no wrong. For once, the tide of fortune was flowing with them.

But in the space of a heartbeat, everything went wrong. Fancy extended the hat for perhaps the tenth time that day, enjoining the rapt spectators to see for themselves that it was empty. Nothing there, no siree.

At which time Hershel leaped out of his hiding place and scampered into the crowd, dragging the black bag behind him for several feet before shedding it, like a second skin, on the grass.

Two old ladies fainted and a man in bib overalls grumbled fraud.

"Hershel!" Fancy shrieked, rushing after him and colliding with a rock-hard chest in her hurry.

She straightened, a queer premonition jiggling in the pit of her stomach, and saw what she had both hoped for and feared.

Jeff Corbin was standing before her, clad in brown trousers and the kind of flowing, open-throated shirt typical of a sea captain, holding a squirming Hershel in both hands. A grin quirked one side of his mouth. "If I were you," he said, "I'd start singing."

Chapter Five

A BITTERSWEET PANG STRUCK FANCY AS SHE REACHED out, her hands trembling slightly, to take the errant rabbit from Jeff's hands. She had gone to desperate lengths to avoid seeing him again, and yet she knew a certain joy that he had found her.

"What are you doing here?" she demanded, as the people who had been watching her act began to drift away.

The indigo eyes were unreadable, veiled. If Fancy had hoped for some statement of affection, she was bound for disappointment. "I saw the balloon," he said, gesturing toward Phineas's craft. It was aloft now, dancing in the breeze, bound to the earth by four separate ropes.

"Oh," said Fancy, biting her lower lip.

The sharp blue gaze sliced back to her face and Jeff

lifted his hands to his hips. "Did you think I came to swear my undying devotion?"

"Of course not!" she snapped defensively. But there was still the question of why he *had* come, and it crackled in Fancy's heart and mind like a bonfire.

He looked affronted. "Don't you believe me capable of such a noble emotion?"

Fancy was stung because she loved this man, wholly and irrevocably, and she hadn't planned to feel the things she was feeling, ever. "I cannot imagine you swearing 'undying devotion' to anyone. Undying lust is another matter!"

Jeff laughed and Fancy knew conflicting needs to slap him and hold him close. "That I will admit to," he said. "Where you're concerned, at least."

Mostly for dramatic effect, Fancy whirled and stormed back to her table, where she thrust the malcontent rabbit into his cage and slammed the door after him. Males! They were all alike—stubborn and self-centered and completely uncooperative! Why, the moment things were going well, one could count on men to snarl them up again!

When Fancy had secured Hershel underneath the table, she lifted her eyes to Jeff once more and was nettled to see that he had not been paying the least bit of attention to her flouncing umbrage. Damn him, he was watching Phineas's balloon with the rapt interest of a little boy.

"Go back to Wenatchee!" she hissed, furious. "I don't want you here!"

Now he turned to face her again. The thumb and forefingers of his right hand slid sensuously across his mouth in a motion she knew damned well was meant to remind her of things she didn't dare think about. "Don't you?" he challenged, in a voice that was little more than a gruff whisper.

"I hate you, you reprobate!"

"I could tell," he answered smoothly.

"If you think—if you think for one minute, Jeff Corbin, that you're going to—that I will—"

Without apparent upset, he walked away, leaving Fancy to stand there, beneath her borrowed canvas canopy, stammering like an idiot.

She stared after Jeff for a moment, then picked up the trick wand purchased in more prosperous days and flung it at his broad, impervious back. It struck him between the shoulder blades, burst into ludicrous bloom, and fell to the grass.

Jeff turned with an ominous laziness, arching one eyebrow. "Don't ever do that again," he warned. "If you do, I'll forget my principles and turn you across my knee."

"I could have sworn you didn't have any principles," muttered Fancy, furious but too afraid to challenge him further.

If he heard her, he did not respond. Phineas's balloon was gliding to the ground, the gondola swinging in a breezy seesaw motion as it descended, and Jeff strode off toward the craft.

Fancy went to where he had stood, picked up the flower wand in one shaking hand. The bright colors of the bouquet seemed to blur as she stared at them. Drat that insufferable ass, who needed him, anyway?

You do, taunted a little voice in Fancy's mind.

Phineas sat on a tree stump near his wagon, sipping coffee. His eyes were mischievous as they touched

Fancy's overheated face, clearly saying, "I told you he'd come."

Fancy risked one glance at Jeff, who was perched on the wagon tongue beside her, the top hat in his lap, a ponderous frown on his face. "You need either a bigger hat or a smaller rabbit," he observed, tugging poor Hershel out and then thrusting him in again. "He's wedged in here like pork in a sausage skin."

Stubbornly, Fancy refused to comment. Why couldn't Jeff Corbin just go back to where he belonged and leave her alone? In annoyance, she stood up, folded her arms across her chest, and walked around to the back of the wagon to fetch her valise. After taking out a bar of soap and a hairbrush, she started off toward the stream she'd visited earlier.

The water was ice cold, but Fancy stripped to her camisole and drawers and waded in to her ankles, determined. In the distance, she could hear the sounds of the carnival camp—laughter, the lowing and shifting of animals, the crackle of bonfires. A wounding sadness swept over her, a longing for a house with walls and windows and a roof.

Teeth chattering, Fancy bent to lather the soap cake in the frigid stream. To distract herself, she went on dreaming. There would certainly be a bathtub in her house, filled with hot, scented water. There would be beds with proper sheets and blankets and, best of all, there would be people.

"Oh, there's Fancy now," they would say to each other, if she chanced to be late returning from some errand. And if she didn't return, they would come looking for her.

Fancy waded deeper into the stream, the pebbled

bottom slick and icy beneath her feet, the water numbing her knees. When the creek gurgled around her stomach, she removed her drawers and camisole and flung them ashore, nearly going under in the process. With an industry born of almost intolerable cold, she washed her hair, scoured the rest of her body, and started back toward the grassy bank.

"Are you crazy?" demanded an all-too-familiar masculine voice.

Fancy stumbled backward, shuddering. The shrinking moon revealed the strong planes of Jeff Corbin's face, the breadth of his shoulders, the narrow power of his hips. "Not crazy enough to come out of the water with you standing there!" she sputtered furiously. "Go away!"

"I brought a blanket," he chimed in reply, teasing. "Don't you want it, Frances?"

"Leave it on the bank!"

Jeff threw back his head and his laughter thundered in the night, stilling the songs of crickets and frogs. "You dreamer."

Tears smarted in Fancy's eyes and goosebumps rippled over her bare skin. Her feet were so numb that she could no longer feel the stream bottom. "You bastard," she hissed, and then she stomped up out of the water and stood facing Jeff on the shore.

He chuckled as he draped her in the blanket. There was gentleness in the sound, as well as in the brief, warm touch of his hands. Leaving her to shudder inside the blanket, he bent to fetch her discarded underthings. With all the flourish of an experienced housewife, he gave them a brisk, snapping shake and hung them over a nearby bush.

"I can't leave them here," protested Fancy.

"Would you rather hang them by Phineas's campfire?" asked Jeff with tender sarcasm.

"Well—no—"

"You didn't plan this bath very well, did you?"

There was no arguing the point. Fancy had wanted to be clean and she hadn't thought beyond that point. If she had, she would have left her underthings on the bank in the first place or else brought dry ones along. "I didn't plan on seeing you here!" she snapped, hedging.

He sat down on a large, flat boulder at the streamside, drew his knees up, and wrapped his arms around them. "I'm sure you didn't," he said.

Fancy was at a loss. She wanted to put her dress back on and head for Phineas's campfire—Lord knew the warmth would be glorious—but something kept her there by the stream. "I should have known you wouldn't be gentleman enough to let me bathe in peace!"

Jeff laughed. "Yes, you should have. Come here, Fancy."

"Said the spider to the fly!"

The magnificent face sobered. "I promise not to touch you," he said, patting the rock's smooth surface with one hand.

Fancy believed him, though she couldn't for the life of her have said why. She picked her way to the boulder and sat down, keeping the blanket tucked tightly around her.

"Why didn't Temple Royce make love to you?" Jeff asked after several seconds of thoughtful silence.

The question, improper as it was, should have come as an insulting surprise to Fancy, but it didn't. "I wouldn't let him," she said softly, drawing her knees up and resting her chin upon them.

"Did you love him?"

"I thought I did." Fancy remembered Temple's pleasure over what he'd done to Jeff Corbin and ached with shame. "I didn't really know him, as it turned out." Any more than I know you, she added silently.

Jeff made no comment.

"Why did you follow me, Jeff? Why didn't you just let me go away? It would have been better for both of us."

"I'll grant that it might have been better for you," he said, on a long, ragged breath, as he leaned back to lie flat on the rock, his hands cupped behind his head. "For me it would have been the end."

Fancy sniffled and she wished that the water in that stream could have numbed her heart the way it had her toes. "I don't understand what you mean."

He shifted, so that he was facing her, his head propped up on one hand. "You changed everything, Fancy. I didn't want you to, but you insisted."

"I'm sorry," she said, confused, shivering in the chilling breeze that danced over the muttering stream.

"Sorry? Damn it, woman, you resurrected me! You made me laugh—you made me mad as hell—you made me—"

Fancy colored and covered her head with the blanket on the pretext of drying her dripping, tangled hair.

"You made me feel again, Fancy."

Fancy shot to her feet suddenly, nearly losing the blanket. "Well hurrah for me!" she shouted, all but strangling on a hoarse sob.

He caught her hand in his and pulled her back down beside him, irrespective of his promise not to touch her. "Marry me," he said gruffly.

That again. Anguish swept over Fancy, for she knew his reasons for proposing without his even stating them. He wanted to use her. "Damn you," she choked out, "why can't you just find yourself a whore and leave me alone?!"

His hand was strong on her chin, forcing her to face him. His touch made her heart tumble and skitter inside her, like a stone flung over a steep cliff. "I don't want a whore, Frances. I want you."

A tear trickled down Fancy's cheek and glittered like a jewel on the side of his thumb. "Why, Jeff? So you can forget Banner? So you can take something that Temple Royce wants?"

The hand tightened on her chin, fierce now, instead of tender. "What do you mean 'so I can take something Temple wants'?" he demanded, in a sharp undertone.

Fancy hadn't meant to say that, she hadn't even been aware that she was thinking such a thing. "Well—I mean—"

"Tell me!"

It was no use trying to evade him now, for he was not going to allow it, that was clear. "Temple has been looking for me," she whispered.

"What?!" Jeff was sitting bolt upright now and, mercifully, his hand slipped from her jaw. His eyes were demonic in the moonlight and the chill was back, reaching into the depths of Fancy's bones.

She lowered her head, ashamed and miserable and, now that she had permitted herself to think about it, scared. "W–When I was with Mr. Shibble's show, I had to hide sometimes. Men would come around, asking questions about me."

Jeff's hands closed over her shoulders, hurtful in

their strength. "You left without telling Temple?" he hissed.

Fancy nodded. There was more, of course—Temple wanted to silence her, so that she couldn't go to the authorities and tell them who had ordered the explosions onboard the *Sea Mistress*—but she couldn't very well explain that to Jeff. Not when he himself had been the captain of that ship, the object of the attack. "M–Maybe he's tired of looking for me—maybe he's forgotten—"

Jeff laughed and this time the sound was bitter, void of humor or warmth. "Temple? Woman, he'll dog you until it rains in hell! And I hope to God he finds you!"

Fancy blanched. "What?"

The reply was a raucous shout of triumph. "In fact, I intend to make *sure* he finds you!"

"No!" gasped Fancy, terrified at the prospect. Temple was not a man who took kindly to betrayal, and she would sooner have faced the devil than that man.

Jeff didn't seem to be listening; he was on his feet, wrenching Fancy after him. "We're getting married tonight," he announced.

"We most certainly are not!" sputtered Fancy, shivering inside her blanket despite the strange heat fostered by the idea.

It was then that Jeff caught the blanket in his hands and slowly parted it. It slithered off Fancy's naked shoulders and pooled around her feet.

Brazenly, Jeff cupped both her breasts in his palms, deliberately chafing the nipples to a state of throbbing response. Fancy groaned, helpless to escape, her mind swirling through a kaleidoscope universe.

"You belong in my bed," Jeff reminded her, in a soft, firm voice that seemed to deepen the treacherous trance. "And you will be there, tonight and every night, as my wife or my mistress—the choice is yours."

Some shred of dignity made Fancy whisper, "But we don't love—each other—"

"Maybe we have something better," he breathed, and his fingers were plucking at Fancy's nipples now, making them stand erect.

Fancy hadn't thought it possible to feel both misery and reckless joy, all of a piece, but it was happening to her then. Still, she argued. "Th–There isn't anything better than l–love—"

He made his counterpoint by bending his head to sip languidly at her right breast. "Ummm—so true—" he conceded, as shards of raw, jagged pleasure pierced every part of Fancy's trembling body.

As best she could, considering that Jeff was making a feast of her, Fancy thought about her predicament. She could not resist this man and there was no pretending differently. She loved him. If she married him, there was at least some chance that he might come to love her in return one day. And suppose she was pregnant? Suppose, even now, his seed was growing inside her? If she agreed to take his name, their child would have it, too, and a Corbin child would lack for nothing.

Jeff left her breast to stand straight again, though his hand still cupped the spoils of a gentle battle long since won. He seemed to be following the train of her thoughts with uncanny accuracy. "Think of your family, Frances," he urged quietly, deliberately. "Your father wouldn't have to work anymore. Your mother could have nice clothes, good food—"

"Stop!" Fancy cried frantically. "That isn't fair! Ever since I left home I've been giving and giving—"

He squeezed her breast and smiled at the obvious

electrical response that jolted through her. "Isn't it time that someone gave something back to you, Fancy? I have a lot to give."

Fancy blushed and swatted at his hand but it didn't move from her breast—it kept caressing, urging, stroking. "Jeff—" she protested in a distracted whimper.

"You could have everything, Fancy. Everything."

Reality descended on Fancy like a boxcar full of bricks. Temple Royce had said the same thing to her and for essentially the same reasons—he hadn't loved her, anymore than Jeff did. He had wanted her in his bed.

She leaned down, caught the blanket in her hands, and wrenched it around her like a woolen shield. "No, I couldn't!" she sobbed out. "I couldn't have a husband who didn't love me!"

Jeff was unruffled. He reached out and took the blanket and spread it on the grass. "All right, then," he said airily, "have it your way. Lie down, mistress, because I want you. Here and now."

"No!"

He arched an eyebrow and folded his arms. "No?"

Fancy looked with yearning at her underthings, which would be cold and clammy and wet should she put them on again. Her dress was out of reach and if she moved to fetch it, Jeff would get there first. She shivered and hugged herself and sobbed out, "I hate you, Jeff Corbin!"

He only gestured toward the blanket.

"Suppose I scream?" ventured Fancy, distractedly.

Jeff chuckled. "Everyone would come rushing to your aid and find you gloriously naked," he answered, in blithe tones.

Fancy gnawed at her lower lip, which, like the rest of her body, was blue with cold. "I–If I did agree to this—this proposal—where would we live?"

Jeff shrugged as though the conversation were perfectly normal. "We have a house in Spokane. We could go there until we decided on something more permanent."

He sounded so reasonable, so calm. As though he weren't forcing a freezing, naked woman to choose between marrying him and being ravished on a stream bank. Fancy wanted to tear his eyes out of his head. "I will never, never forgive you for this, Jeff Corbin."

"We'll see about that," he replied, with happy skepticism. "You've made your choice, I presume?"

Fancy nodded. "I'll marry you," she said, with a sort of broken elation.

"I have your word? No more running off in the night?"

Again, Fancy nodded. And, twenty minutes later, wearing a star-spangled dress with no underwear beneath it, she was wed to Jeff Corbin by a man who draped crawly snakes around his neck during the day. The ceremony cost one dollar and the bride and groom were assured by a pleased Phineas T. Pryor that it had been a legal proceeding.

It was just her luck, Fancy reflected, as her new husband's lips descended to claim hers, that the snakeman had to be a justice of the peace in the bargain.

They made their marriage bed along the banks of the stream, with blankets borrowed from Phineas. And despite a bittersweet ache in the shadowed regions of her heart, Fancy was happy. Sitting on the improvised bed, the light of real stars catching on those affixed to her dress, she tilted her head to one side and admired this magnificent man who was now her husband.

"You'll have to take a bath if you expect to sleep with me," she announced mischievously, as he shed his shirt with amusing haste.

"That water is cold!" Jeff protested, taken aback.

Fancy nodded, then shrugged. "All the same—"

Jeff opened his trousers and removed them, irritation visible in the swift motions of his hands. He looked so splendid in the moonlight, with muscles rolling under his taut flesh and the fine matting of golden hair covering him, that Fancy almost relented.

He cast one imploring look at her, his manhood rising slowly to power as if to bolster his case. "I'm clean, you know," he half wailed.

Fancy shrugged again, looking pained as she removed her dress.

"Son-of-a-bitch!" Jeff hissed, striding into the water and swearing again as its chill enveloped him. He splashed around, muttering, for all of a minute, then came storming up the bank toward Fancy.

There was a disturbingly evil leer on his face.

"Oh, no!" Fancy cried, suddenly understanding, but it was too late. He flung his icy, droplet-covered body down upon her warm one. His sodden hair dripped in her face and across her breasts.

She struggled, giggling, and, for a time, they were like children allowed to play outside after dark. They rolled off the blanket and into the grass, and then back onto the blanket again.

Suddenly, though, Jeff drew back from her, kneeling astraddle of her hips, and even in the darkness she could see the stricken look of wonder on his face. "You are so beautiful," he marveled, running just the tips of his fingers over her shoulders, her collarbone, her breasts.

Fancy's playful mood was instantly replaced with a passion of such measure that it staggered her senses. What was it about this man that enabled him to ignite such brutal needs in her with only a word, a look, a touch?

He lay down on his back beside her in a smooth motion. "Touch me, Fancy," he said quietly.

She sat up and felt enthralled by the stark, wholly masculine beauty of him. She touched his nipples, cosseted in their golden down, and reveled in the soft, strangled groan this brought from him. Strictly as an experiment, she bent and tasted one with just the tip of her tongue. He gasped and caught her still-damp hair in his hands and held her close and she felt a certain sweet triumph go through her. She suckled him, first at one delicious nubbin and then at the other.

It was sheer joy to know that he could be pleasured in much the same way that she had been when he'd enjoyed her breasts. As other parallels came to mind, Fancy began to kiss her way softly down over his hard stomach.

He choked her name as she reached the straining objective of her travels and flicked it delicately with her tongue.

Fairly bursting with the swell of this one small victory over him, she became greedy. His back arched and he gave a raucous gasp.

She nipped at Jeff with her teeth and rejoiced inwardly at his moaned, "God—Fancy—Fancy! Don't—"

"Don't?" Fancy teased, nibbling.

He writhed, groaning as if in delirium. "Don't—stop —my God—"

"Ummmm," boasted Fancy.

And Jeff laughed at her delicious audacity. "You'll pay for this," he moaned raggedly. "You'll pay."

Still she tormented him.

"W–Witch!" he gasped, after several feverish attempts at the word.

Fancy was a witch in those wild, unrestrained moments—she was all that was magic, all that was powerful, all that was triumphant. And his shuddering shout of glorified defeat echoed in the walls of her heart and became a part of it forever.

Still, Jeff had promised revenge and he extracted it with expertise, hurling Fancy past the moon itself on the wings of an exquisite frenzy, before wrenching her back to earth in dizzying spins. Finally, he fulfilled her, making the fevered journey in her arms.

Fancy lay dazed when it was over, her breath coming in short gasps, her eyes just beginning to focus on the moon and stars, on the shifting branches of trees that made a canopy for them. Making a low, growling sound of appeasement deep in his throat, Jeff sank to her breast, the moistness of his flesh mingling with hers.

They were still for a long time, listening to the nightcalls of an owl, the whispering song of the stream, the distant, settling sounds of the carnival camp.

"Do you suppose they heard us?" Fancy fretted when she could speak again.

"Who?"

"Phineas—the snake man—the fat lady—"

Jeff laughed against her breast and then licked teasingly at its rounded side with the tip of his tongue. "What a wedding party," he said.

Fancy was stung; suddenly, she was thinking of Amelie and Keith and the wonderful, elegant wedding they would have. Amelie would have a long white dress, a churchful of well-wishers, a bouquet to toss. There would be a tiered cake. . . .

"Fancy?"

She turned her head to one side, not wanting him to see her tears. But the effort came too late apparently, for he caught her chin in his hand and made her look at him.

"What is it?" he demanded gently—very gently, for a husband who did not love his wife.

Fancy permitted herself to imagine what this man's wealthy family was going to say when they found out that he'd married someone so far beneath him, and she was filled with horror. "You'll be ashamed of me!" she sobbed.

He kissed her, slowly, tenderly, his lips nibbling and drawing at her own. "Never."

Fancy was overwhelmed, and she lifted her hands to her face to cover it. Jeff immediately drew them away and held them, stroking her fingers with his own.

"Fancy, I—"

Her heart quickened, almost stopped. But Jeff's sentence fell away unfinished and the words that would have made everything all right never came.

The silence was unbearable, an aching void where there had been soaring passion only moments before. Fancy began to cry softly, in wretched misery.

"Don't," Jeff groaned, and she wept harder because he had used that word so differently during their lovemaking. "Please don't cry."

Fancy sniffled, honestly trying to cooperate. It wasn't often that she gave in to her emotions that way, but the events of the past few days were catching up with her and she simply couldn't be strong anymore.

Unexpectedly, with a tender, broken look in his eyes, Jeff stood up and then pulled Fancy up after him. He gave her a painless swat on the backside and then started toward the water.

Fancy dug in her heels. "No!" she protested.

Jeff wrenched at her hand and she was tumbling after him, into that chilly creek. She gave a shrill little cry at the insult to her passion-warmed body and tried to break free of her husband's grasp and scramble back to shore.

But Jeff held her. He kissed her and then began to wash her, his hands making slow, tender circles on her back, her breasts, her thighs. Soon, the cold didn't matter anymore.

Chapter Six

BIRDS CHIRPED HAPPY SONGS IN THE TREES AND THE stream hummed as it went on its merry way. Even before she opened her eyes, Fancy knew that Jeff was gone.

She sat up on the rumpled blankets and their grassy underbed, and smiled as she reached out for the drawers and camisole that had been carefully spread out, dry now, at her feet. She put them on and then the dress with its bedraggled stars.

Her hairbrush was where she had left it the night before, and she took it up and began the arduous task of working a night's tangles from her hair.

Phineas was alone at his campfire when Fancy approached it. She was careful to hold her chin high, though there was little she could do about the high blush that pounded in her cheeks.

He extended a cup of coffee and a gentle smile.

"Good morning, Mrs. Corbin," he greeted her, rising from his seat on the tree stump in a mannerly way and then sitting back down again.

Fancy allowed herself a moment of preening happiness at his use of her new title, but there were doubts gnawing at the edges of her mind as she sat down on the wagon tongue to enjoy her coffee. One casual, sweeping glance around the camp revealed that Jeff was nowhere in sight.

"He's gone into town," Phineas explained, obviously having looked beyond her attempt at subtlety and seen the fear. "Asked me to tell you that he'll be back before sunset."

Before sunset! Fancy was wounded. Was it customary for a groom to desert his bride so soon? For that matter, did Jeff intend to come back at all? It was entirely possible that he'd had second thoughts.

Phineas suddenly thrust a bowl of oatmeal into Fancy's hands, making her start. "Don't be borrowing trouble now," he urged softly. "Jeff loves you, Fancy. He'll be back because he's got no other choice."

There was no point in clearing up Phineas's misconception by telling him that Jeff didn't love her—he'd want to know why she had married him then and Fancy would have been too embarrassed to admit to the answer. Furthermore, annulling a marriage performed by a snake-man would probably be an easy matter for someone with Jeff's money and influence. "I knew a singer in Port Angeles who married a sailor," she reflected, after a while. "He went off to find a rooming house where they could live and never came back."

Phineas stirred the small morning fire and sat down again. That gray pallor she'd seen the day before was back in his face, and his lips had the same vaguely blue tint. "I don't think we're dealing with a man of that sort," he comforted quietly.

Fancy had forgotten all her own problems in her concern for her friend. "Phineas, you look wretched. You're ill, aren't you?"

"Just tired," he sighed. "To tell you the truth, Fancy, a few weeks of rest at my sister's house is sounding better and better."

Fancy took another sip from her metal cup, watching Phineas over the rim, then began to eat the oatmeal. "Does she live nearby?"

"Near enough," shrugged Phineas. "She teaches at a school for young ladies in Spokane."

Fancy looked down at her oatmeal and her coffee and was reminded of the debt she owed Phineas T. Pryor. If not for him, she might still be wandering the road. "I mean to reimburse you for all you've given me as soon as Mr. Stroble pays me."

"Nonsense," sputtered Phineas, and there was a flush under the grayness of his skin. "If one traveler can't help another, the world's in a sorry state."

"Some people say it is anyway," observed Fancy. "A preacher told me once that God was going to smite us all dead, except for the holy, of course. He said it would happen before this generation passed away."

Phineas chortled. "Every generation since the time of Christ has believed itself to be the last one ever. I think it's a sort of vanity—there are always people, you see, who can't imagine the world going on without them. There are others who'd like to see the judgment come because they're too lazy or too scared to live—they're afraid to fail, mostly."

Fancy pondered all the failures in her life and frowned. "I'm an expert at that," she reflected, without wryness or self-pity.

Phineas chuckled. "Better one grand, magnificent failure, I always say, than a lifetime of piddling successes."

Fancy was completely bemused by this remark. In any case, she had to feed Hershel, clean his cage, and get ready for another day of performing magic. After cleaning up the dishes—it was the least she could do, since Phineas was providing the food—she went about her tasks and tried not to watch the arriving crowds of carnival-goers for any sign of Jeff.

The morning went well, with no more rebellions on Hershel's part, and, at midday, Mr. Stroble came through the gathered spectators to pay Fancy her two dollars. His eyes kept dodging hers as he handed the money over, but she didn't give much thought to his curious manner for there were already people gathering to watch her next performance.

Late in the afternoon, a massive, thick-shouldered young man pointed to the signboard resting in front of Fancy's table. "That says you sing and dance, too. How come you don't sing and dance?"

Fancy's stomach tightened; if there was one thing she'd learned to recognize in her travels around the territory, it was trouble. She smiled broadly and went on with her act.

The young farmer meant to be persistent. "I want to hear you sing," he called out over the sea of calico bonnets and straw hats.

"Leave the lady alone, Rafe," put in a man's voice, from near the front. "She's doin' just fine."

"This here's fraud, that's what it is," argued Rafe

with a scowl, muscling his way closer to the canopied table. The pinkness of his round, plain-featured face testified that he'd been drinking.

Fancy took up the tiny, sulfur-filled vial that was easily hidden in her hand and made flames leap from her fingertips. The crowd in general was delighted, but Rafe was not appeased.

"I say she sings and does a jig or two!" he growled.

At that moment, Phineas came from out of nowhere, looking affable and guileless in his plaid suit and bowler hat. He approached the mountainous farmer without the slightest hesitation, his hands in his pockets, his smile broad. "What seems to be the trouble?" he asked.

Rafe turned toward him with a lumbering motion that chilled Fancy to the marrow of her bones. "I say it's a lie, that there sign. I paid good money to see this show and this lady ain't sung a note!"

Phineas was unruffled, his gaze shifting to a nervous Fancy. "Do you wish to sing, my dear?" he asked politely.

Fancy was terrified, but she shook her head.

"There you have it," shrugged Phineas, still smiling. "The little lady prefers not to sing today."

Rafe flung a dangerous, petulant look in Fancy's direction. "She'll sing," he said.

Fancy was just opening her mouth to comply when Rafe suddenly raised his meaty hands and gave Phineas a hard shove, sending him sprawling into the rocky dirt and trampled grass. Phineas winced and grasped at his chest with one hand.

"Phineas!" Fancy wailed, rounding the table to rush to her friend. "Phineas, are you all right?"

Phineas was not all right; his grimace of pain told her

that much, along with the absence of color in his face. "I'll be—just fine—"

Fancy looked up at Rafe, whose overall-clad frame loomed against the sky, blocking out the sun. "How dare you?" she hissed, furious beyond all good sense. She rose to her feet and advanced, and Rafe actually retreated a step. "Apologize this minute, you hulking beast!"

Rafe stopped. The realization that he was being backed down by a tiny woman, and in front of all his friends, to boot, dawned ominously in his face. He reddened and his bright little eyes narrowed. "No goddamned tramp travelin' with a freak show tells me what to do!" he spat.

"Rafe—" ventured some tentative peacemaker, from the gaping crowd.

Fancy had never been more frightened in her life, but she was prepared to fight if she had to. She crossed her arms over her bosom and waited.

Rafe bent toward her and she felt his fetid breath in her face, smelled it, even tasted it. Her stomach turned within her, but she stood her ground.

"What else do you do for a penny?" drawled the brute, smirking now. "Whatever it is, maybe you'll do it for me—in them bushes over there."

Fancy drew back her foot to kick him—the distance between them allowed her a target other than his thick shins—but before she could make contact at all, Rafe was spinning around, a surprised expression on his face. Peering around him, Fancy saw Jeff, and the look of white-hot rage in his eyes scared her more than Rafe ever could have.

"Would you mind repeating that?" Jeff drawled, in a

cold voice. A muscle leaped in the line of his jaw and was still again.

Rafe had had a moment to recover, and he squared his mule-strong shoulders in preparation for battle. Still, there was a tremor in his voice when he answered. "I just wanted her to sing."

Phineas had gotten back to his feet, and he caught Fancy's upper arms in both hands and pulled her backward, out of range. The crowd, silent now, drew back, too, making a thick circle around the two men.

Blood pounded in Fancy's ears and her heart nestled into her throat, fat and almost impossible to breathe around. God in heaven, did Jeff actually mean to fight with that monster of a man? That giant?

He did. Tired of waiting, he drew back one fist and then lodged it squarely in Rafe's fleshy middle. It made a thudding sound and the farmer's breath left his lungs in an angry whoosh.

With the hulking movements of a trained bear, Rafe swung one huge hand toward Jeff's head. Despite his own impressive size, Jeff was smaller than his adversary and Fancy closed her eyes, unable to watch.

The terrible sounds went on for an eternity, it seemed to Fancy, and she flinched at each grunt of pain, each muttered swearword, each thud of fist against flesh.

"Sweet Lord in heaven," marveled Phineas in an undertone, his hands still holding Fancy fast.

She opened her eyes at this and was surprised to see Rafe kneeling on the ground, blood trickling from his nostrils and making crimson patches in the dirt. His shoulders heaved with the effort to breathe and Jeff stood over him like an avenging angel, magnificent in his fury, unscathed except for a slight cut above his right eye.

Almost idly, he lifted one booted foot and placed it in the middle of Rafe's chest. With a desultory motion of his leg, he sent the farmer toppling backward to lie curled up on the ground.

Looking shame-faced and apologetic, several of Rafe's friends came to gather him up and lead him, stumbling, away. Jeff's furious indigo eyes sliced to Fancy and held, and the ferocity in their depths stunned her so profoundly that she couldn't move or speak. Why was he angry with her, she wondered wildly.

Phineas stepped around her rigid little frame to offer a congratulatory hand to Jeff. Some of the fury faded from Jeff's eyes as he hesitated and then accepted Phineas's handshake.

Throughout this brief exchange, Fancy stood still, hurting and defiant and wildly confused. She had done nothing wrong, nothing but try to defend her friend, and yet Jeff was clearly outraged. The look he flung in her direction as he listened to Phineas's raving skewered her with the piercing impact of a lance.

When Phineas wandered away to attend his balloon, Jeff approached her. Fancy averted her eyes, gnawing at her lower lip.

"What was that all about?" Jeff demanded coldly, standing so close that she could feel the power and strength of him in every fiber of her being.

Fancy lifted defiant eyes to his white, taut-jawed face. "The farmer started it all," she said.

"You could have been hurt!" Jeff retorted in a tight voice, and it was then that Fancy realized that he wasn't angry at all. He was frightened.

"I wasn't, thanks to you," she said lightly.

"Does that happen often?"

Fancy nodded reluctantly. "I'm afraid so," she admitted. "But it doesn't matter now, does it? It's all over."

His hands closed over her shoulders and he drew her close in a swift, almost desperate movement. She could feel just the hint of a tremor in his muscular frame. "Suppose I hadn't gotten here in time—"

Fancy laughed nervously, surprised that there were tears brimming in her eyes. "I would have started singing," she answered. She had never been rescued before, and it was a nice feeling, a touching feeling.

Jeff chuckled and caught her chin on the curve of his fingers, lifting. He kissed the tip of her nose and then held her close again, as though he feared to let her go. "What have I done?" he mourned, in an almost inaudible voice.

The magic of the moment was broken, as far as Fancy was concerned. The brutal fact was that, married to this man or not, she was still essentially on her own. Already he was regretting his association with her; the words he'd just uttered made that clear. "I told you that you shouldn't have married me," she said, hiding the sorrow she felt behind a thin wall of defiance.

His strong hands slid down from her waist to her round bottom, pressing her close. "Did you, now?" he teased, arching one golden eyebrow.

"Stop it—people will see!"

"I don't care," he replied, mischief dancing a weary jig in the depths of his navy blue eyes.

"Well, I do!" muttered Fancy, blushing. Though she'd thought otherwise, the things Rafe had implied about her morals smarted terribly in retrospect. She ached to be respectable.

Jeff gave her one more impudent squeeze and then let her go. "Shall I tell you what I plan to do to you when we're alone?" he drawled.

"No!" shouted Fancy, folding her arms across her breasts in an unconscious effort to keep him at bay.

He reached out and traced the outline of her jaw with one finger. "First," he said, as though she hadn't spoken at all, "I'm going to—"

Fancy whirled and stormed back to her table, Jeff's laughter ringing in her ears. When she looked back, though, he was gone and her moral outrage was all for naught. Considering some of the things he might be planning for when they were alone, she blushed hotly.

Mercifully, a new crowd was gathering in front of her table. She began her performance and only occasionally looked in the direction of Phineas's balloon.

Telling herself that it was stupid to be jealous of an inanimate object, Fancy wished devoutly that the damned thing would pop.

When nightfall finally came, Fancy was exhausted and petulant. She flounced and muttered as she tended to Hershel and repaid Jeff's amused perusal with a scowl.

He was sitting cross-legged in the grass, talking quietly with Phineas. Occasionally the two men laughed at some joke that Fancy couldn't quite catch, and that made her even angrier.

By the time Jeff produced the cold ham, biscuits, and cider that he'd brought back from town, she was ready to scratch his eyes out. She was hungry, though, having eaten nothing since the oatmeal at breakfast, so she sat down to share in the meal.

Looking a little less wan than he had that morning, Phineas was clearly enjoying the food. It occurred to

Fancy that his cider and Jeff's contained some element that hers lacked, but she dismissed the thought. She was just feeling fitful, that was all—it had been a hard, confusing day.

Still, Jeff and Phineas seemed to get merrier with every cupful of cider they drank. They laughed uproariously and Phineas told outrageous stories about his travels in that cursed balloon.

"Can't we talk about something else?" Fancy snapped, feeling left out.

Jeff slanted an unreadable look at her and asked Phineas an involved question about air currents. Phineas replied with a lengthy discourse and Fancy felt as though she'd been slapped. She set her plate down and scrambled to her feet, marching off toward the balloon.

Its hugeness shifted and whispered against the twilight skies, as if to taunt her. Drawing back one foot, she muttered an oath and kicked the wicker gondola soundly.

"You're acting like a child," observed a familiar voice from behind her.

Fancy whirled, the unaccountable tears that had been pressing toward the surface all day stinging in her eyes. "Talk about the pot calling the kettle black!" she cried.

Jeff smiled evilly and folded his arms across his broad chest. "You know what you need, Mrs. Corbin? A good, sound spanking."

Fancy turned her back on him, too angry to speak. Then, after one look up at the balloon, with its mysterious valves and ropes, she kicked the gondola again.

Steel arms immediately closed around her waist, startling her and then stinging her to fury. Jeff lifted her off the ground and carried her against one hip, as though she were no heavier than a valise.

Outraged and wildly embarrassed, she kicked and struggled against him. "You put me down—don't you dare—"

He strode on, chuckling. "It's time we had a little talk about who runs this family—darling."

Fancy squirmed as the woods bounced nearer and nearer. She could hear a nightowl calling, hear the silky rustle of the stream. If he really chose to spank her, there wouldn't be one wretched thing she could do about it, and the thought made her dizzy with fury. "If you lay one hand on me," she warned, in jerky tones, "I'll cut your liver out and feed it to Hershel!"

"Now, now, dearest," Jeff chimed in retort, "don't be vulgar."

Vulgar! Fancy was screaming mad now—what right had he to call her vulgar! *He* was the one that was making a scene! "You b-bastard—"

Jeff walked faster, deliberately making Fancy's unwilling ride that much rougher. Bushes snatched at her hair and clothes as they went closer to the stream. "I can see I'm going to have to take a firm hand with you," he said, with mock ruefulness. "I like spirit in a woman, but disrespect is another matter entirely."

He wasn't even winded, damn him, and Fancy could barely catch her breath. She gave a strangled cry of helpless rage and then was summarily flung down onto the blankets where they had loved so ferociously the night before.

Jeff dropped to his haunches and uttered a thoughtful "Hmmm," rubbing his chin with one hand.

Fancy half sat and half lay on the blankets, her breath tearing its way in and out of her lungs, scalded in her own fury. Had she the necessary power, she would have attacked him with both feet and both fists, but she was too undone even to move.

Meanwhile, Jeff went on considering her punishment. "I could give you a paddling you'd never forget," he speculated, his eyes on the trees and the pale, waning moon. Even though he was addressing his words to Fancy, she felt as though she'd suddenly become invisible. "Yes," he ruminated, "I could sit down on that stump over there, throw up your skirts and pull down your drawers and give you to understand who is the husband around here—"

Fancy's rage was settling into a heavy, delicious sort of terror. For all her brave words, she knew that his threat was not an idle one. "You w–wouldn't—" she struggled to say.

The indigo eyes met hers with cordial warning. "Oh, but I would. It runs in my family, you know. And I've done it for much less reason than you just gave me."

Fancy's eyes rounded. "You have?"

"Oh, yes. Of course, I was never actually married to the women concerned, and that sheds a new light on the situation."

Fancy hoped that light was merciful. "It does?" she choked out.

"It certainly does."

"Oh," said Fancy.

And suddenly he laughed.

Fancy knew then that he'd never intended to strike her, that he'd been teasing her all along, deliberately trying to scare her. The fact that he'd succeeded made her angrier than the threat itself. With a strength she'd never suspected she possessed, she bolted to her knees and thrust both her hands into Jeff's chest, catching him off guard and sending him rolling down the bank and into the stream. Of course the water wasn't very deep there, but he came up sputtering and wet all the same.

Fancy inched backward on the blankets as he strode toward her, his face hidden in the lavender shadows of deepening twilight.

"On second thought—" he rumbled, capturing her shoulders and halting her crablike escape in virtually one motion.

"No!" Fancy howled.

But Jeff wrenched her to her feet and in a twinkling, it seemed, he was sitting on the aforementioned stump and hauling a stunned Fancy across his lap. She felt a chilly breeze as he flung up her skirts, an aching vulnerability as her drawers came down.

"No," she said again, whimpering this time and squeezing her eyes shut in preparation.

But the stinging blow she'd expected never came. Instead, Jeff closed his hands around her waist and stood her upright. She stared at him for a moment and then reached down to pull up her drawers, her face flaming.

Jeff laughed at the inelegant little dance of the effort, and it was all she could do not to pull his hair out of his head. Only the realization that he might reconsider and spank her after all stayed her from doing just that.

She was tying her drawer strings in angry, jerking motions when his hands reached out to close over hers and stopped them.

"You didn't think you were going to get off as lightly as that, did you?" he asked.

Fancy dropped her hands to her sides in a defiant sort of obedience, oddly powerless to do otherwise. She shivered helplessly as he undid the frayed strings again and slowly slid her drawers down over her hips and thighs. They came to rest around her ankles; Jeff ordered her to step out of them and she did.

One of his hands bunched her skirts at her waist, while the other stroked the inside of her thigh. "Spread your legs, Fancy," he commanded gruffly.

"I—oh—"

Jeff chuckled and his fingers parted her. The pad of his thumb was administering a sweet punishment, making her heart leap inside her while her groin ached in grinding submission. "I am the husband," he reminded her, and she could feel the warmth of his breath as well as his marauding thumb. "And you are . . .?"

Fancy shuddered and a whimpering sound rattled its way out of her constricted throat.

He nipped at her, sending rivers of fire raging through every part, every hidden place. "Fancy," he prompted.

"The w–wife!" she managed, in splendid defeat.

Jeff burrowed deeper into her moistness and warmth, groaning softly as he plundered her. And between forays calculated to drive her insane, he lectured her.

She tangled her hands in his hair and whimpered as the breathless climb began. His name came repeatedly from her lips, making pleas, confessing defeat, vowing rebellion. He chuckled and punished her with a series of soft kisses. As he rolled the captured treasure between his tongue and his teeth, Fancy's control shattered.

Suddenly, she was caught in an inner inferno, battered and shaken by its burning force. She shuddered and cried out in throaty, glorious despair.

Jeff stroked the bare, glowing flesh of her bottom until she was inside herself again. When she was, he gave her a patronizing pat and pushed her gently away, as though she were a good meal and he'd had his fill.

"I brought you some things from town," he said, indicating a parcel resting a few feet away, on their blanket-bed.

Fancy was still trembling, and her eyes were wide and questioning as she watched him run one hand through his hair and glance in the direction of the camp. Wasn't he going to stay? Wasn't he going to make love to her, to finish what he'd started?

"Sleep well," he said affably, dashing all her hopes.

"Wh–where are you going?" Fancy managed, hating herself for letting him know she cared.

The powerful shoulders lifted and fell again in an off-handed shrug. "Just go to sleep," he said, in a dismissive tone.

Fancy felt a flood of crimson pass her erect nipples and flow into her face. "Sleep?" she echoed in a small and stricken voice.

He was leaving her, actually walking away. "Good night, Fancy," he said.

Fancy boiled and then went chill. She wanted to lunge after him, wanted to batter him with her fists. This urge was rivaled by yet another—the impulse to plead for the fulfillment he was withholding.

She hugged herself and bit down hard on her lower lip to keep from doing any of those things. When he was completely out of sight, however, she stumbled back to the blankets, fell down on them, and alternately cursed and cried until she slept.

Jeff did not return at all that night and, when Fancy woke up, she scowled at the still-wrapped parcel he'd mentioned the night before and kicked it away with one bare foot.

Still, her eyes went back to the packet several times as she dressed and groomed herself for another day. She hadn't had a gift since she was a child, and resisting that one was almost more than she could manage.

All the same, Fancy did not tear away the brown paper and the tightly drawn string, even though her fingers ached to do it. He could keep his geegaws and his—well, he could just keep everything.

The first thing Fancy noticed when she reached the carnival camp was that hateful balloon. It was aloft, doing its colorful sky dance, straining arrogantly at its ropes.

And inside the gondola was Jeff, one arm draped reassuringly around the shoulders of a buxom farm girl. She was laughing up at him, that trollop, and even from the ground Fancy could see the glow in her plump cheeks. No doubt there was a corresponding invitation in her eyes.

Fancy looked darts at that balloon, but it didn't pop as she hoped. On the contrary, it seemed to stay up in the air far longer than the ten-cent fee would have justified.

Chapter Seven

THEY WERE ALL GATHERED AROUND THE KITCHEN TABLE, Melissa, her mother Katherine, and Banner, prattling with delight. Dr. Adam Corbin, just back from his morning rounds, paused in the doorway for a moment, letting the sound soothe away some of the tension aching in his neck and shoulders.

Banner looked up and saw him a fraction of a second later, her shamrock eyes sparkling. "Darling, look—read this!" she cried, waving a yellow sheet of paper.

"Jeff's married!" blurted Melissa, his young sister, before he could take the telegraph message from his wife's hand.

Adam muttered an exclamation and snatched the paper from Banner's fingers to see for himself. Sure as hell, Jeff had wed a young woman by the name of Frances Gordon and even though they had been reduced to print, there was a lilt of happiness in his words.

Adam closed his eyes, relieved. Like the rest of the family, he had despaired over Jeff's decline into emotional withdrawal, railed inwardly at his own helplessness to reach his brother. Ever since last December's holocaust aboard the *Sea Mistress,* there had been pain, not just for Jeff but for everyone who loved him.

"Hallelujah," Adam breathed, and his arms went naturally around Banner's waist, pulling her close.

"Yes," she agreed, and there were tears of joy in her voice.

In another Port Hastings house, not so far away, a man with caramel hair and eyes of exactly the same color read a similar message from a telegraph communiqué of his own.

LAST NIGHT I MARRIED FANCY JORDAN. YOU OVERLOOKED ONE SLIGHT DETAIL, TEMPLE, BUT DON'T WORRY—I TOOK CARE OF IT FOR YOU.

REGARDS,
JEFF CORBIN

Temple Royce crumpled the crackly yellow paper in one hand, seething. He'd known Jeff was alive, of course—everyone in Port Hastings had rushed to the scene the night of the explosion, including Adam and Banner Corbin. Adam had spotted Jeff in the water and brought him ashore, near dead. Somehow in that crummy little hospital of theirs, the Doctors Corbin had managed to keep the patient alive.

Temple hadn't a hope of getting to Jeff then; with the finger of suspicion pointing in his direction he didn't dare try. Later, when Jeff was well enough to travel to the central territory and languish away in his younger brother's house, he hadn't found it necessary to strike again. Everyone knew that Jeff Corbin was willing himself to die and, knowing the will of that man as well or better than anyone else, Temple had been content to let nature take its course.

A sick rage swept through him, swirling in his stomach, pounding in his head. He grasped the mantelpiece over his study fireplace in white-knuckled hands. Things were different now—very different.

Obviously, Jeff had recovered. And damn the luck, he'd married the one chit in the world who knew for a positive fact that Temple had been behind the attack. If Fancy chose to testify, he could hang in payment for the deaths of the dozen or so crewmen who had not been so fortunate as their captain.

Temple drew deep, ragged breaths, trying to steady himself, trying to think. He'd had men looking for Fancy all this time, but to no avail. Had they brought her back, as ordered, he would have had to kill her or marry her, in order to keep her from going to the authorities.

Now, unfortunately, one of those two choices had been eliminated.

Temple looked at the top line of the telegraph message and saw that it had been sent from a town called Colterville. He knew it was a small place, not far from Wenatchee. And he knew he was going there.

Grimly, because he'd never felt any desire to hurt Fancy, he went out to summon his men.

It turned out that the farm girl's name was Jewel Stroble, the daughter of the man who had been overseeing the Colterville Fair.

"You'll want to watch that one, Fancy," observed Phineas cryptically after Jewel had paid for her third ride in the balloon. Obviously, he had been through these parts before.

While Fancy certainly felt no affection for that bovine creature in the tight calico dress, she was nettled that all the responsibility for morality should rest on Jewel. After all, Jeff was a grown man and he had to know the significance of the wedding vows—didn't he? "I don't see why you're letting him operate the balloon anyway," she pouted.

"We have an arrangement," said Phineas, and though his regard was as friendly as ever, he was watching Fancy with a measure of curiosity.

Jeff flashed a perfect white smile at Jewel as the balloon ascended into the skies again and Fancy, standing forgotten on the ground, was jarred anew. Her husband had been gone all night. Had he spent that time, perchance, with Miss Jewel Stroble? She had assumed, until now, that he'd slept beside Phineas's wagon.

She cast one look at Phineas and found that she was too proud to ask whether or not she had assumed rightly. If Jeff had been elsewhere, her friend would instantly guess what had happened. He would pity Fancy then and that would be too dreadful to bear.

"I've got work to do," she said, with false brightness, turning away in a rustle of star-speckled skirts.

Phineas said nothing at all.

At noon, Mr. Stroble appeared with another two dollars in wages. As he handed the money to Fancy, he reddened and repeatedly cleared his throat. Again, he seemed reluctant to meet her eyes.

Fancy tucked the coins into her dress pocket, and bit her lower lip to keep from demanding his daughter be kept under proper restraint.

The afternoon dragged by with hellish slowness, and Fancy's performance, while without incident, was lackluster. She had not once looked in the direction of the balloon, fearing what she would see. When it was time to tuck Hershel back into his cage and gather up her other props, she was grateful.

Phineas would be preparing supper at the fire, she knew, but food held no appeal for Fancy that evening. Despondently, she tended to Hershel's needs, put her things away in the back of the wagon, and went off to the stream bed to be alone.

Kneeling on the blankets there, which were now littered with twigs and leaves and much in need of a good shaking, she assessed the wrapped parcel through blurred eyes. Despair twisted in her throat. How could things change so much in so short a time?

She reached for the package with shaking hands and then drew back.

"Why don't you open it?"

Fancy stiffened. She had not laid eyes on Jeff since morning and now, suddenly, he was standing directly behind her. She didn't think she could bear to look at him and see the mockery in his eyes. "Wouldn't you rather give it to Jewel Stroble?" she retorted, in a small, tight voice.

The reply was a throaty chuckle. "If I'd wanted to do that, I would have."

Fancy dashed away the tears that were streaking down her dust-smudged face. How could such a tender lover as Jeff be so cruel and unfeeling? "Thank you very much, but I don't need anything from you."

"I see. Don't you want your supper?"

Supper. Fancy squeezed her eyes shut and swayed slightly, praying that he would go away, yet yearning for him to stay. "I'm not hungry," she said.

She heard twigs snapping beneath his boots as he approached. When she opened her eyes, he was crouching before her. He dropped to his knees, took up the package, and silently held it out.

Fancy didn't want to accept it, but she did. As her fingers awkwardly undid the string and folded back the paper, she sniffled once.

"I'm sorry, Frances," Jeff said softly.

A deceptive shrug bunched Fancy's shoulders. Unable to think of anything to say, she fixed all her attention on the presents inside the package.

There was an ivory nightgown of elegant, embroidered silk, a small bottle of perfume, and a dress of the softest blue lawn. Fancy had never owned such fine things and she was overwhelmed.

Jeff captured her chin in his hand, forced her to look at him with her tear-stained, swollen face. "Don't you like them?"

It was too much; the sobs Fancy had been holding back solidified into one echoing wail. "They're beautiful!" she cried.

Jeff shook his head, marveling. "Then why are you crying?"

Fancy couldn't answer that, so she shook her head and sniffled again, and then scrambled to her feet, holding the glorious blue dress up in front of her. "Do you think it will fit?" she stammered out.

"It will fit," he answered, with gruff certainty and a measure of tenderness.

Suddenly, Fancy had to know. Forgetting that there was a man present, she shed her old dress and shimmied into the new one. Jeff did up the row of tiny buttons at the back with swift, warm fingers.

"You look wonderful," he said, turning her around to face him.

Fancy did look wonderful, she knew it. The dress fit and it was beautiful and she wasn't afraid of strumpets like Jewel Stroble.

Jeff smiled, a little sadly, Fancy thought, and his hands came to rest on the sides of her face. She saw a pulse leap in the muscular column of his throat.

"Fancy," he said, and while he'd only uttered one word, it was as though he had given some long and poetic avowal of love.

She stepped back and swirled about, suddenly merry. He laughed and drew her close again, planting a brief, noisy kiss on her mouth.

Fancy's heart quickened and she stepped back from him, solemn again. "Were you with Jewel Stroble last night?" she whispered.

"No," he replied flatly.

Fancy searched his face and knew in that instant that he was telling the truth. He was a blunt man, woundingly so at times, and if he had spent the night with Jewel he would have said so. Probably without apology. "Y–You'll never take a mistress?"

"I can't promise you that, Fancy. Right now, though, I can't imagine needing anyone else but you."

"Not even Banner?"

"Banner is my brother's wife!" he spat, apparently appalled by the suggestion.

"But you don't get along with your brother, do you? Keith told me that there was a rift between you and—and—"

"Adam," supplied Jeff sharply. "His name is Adam." He looked away, toward the shadowy sky, and Fancy saw his jawline grow taut and then relax again. "My brother kept something from me," he said finally. "Something I had a right to know. I was and am angry. But Adam is still my brother and I love him."

"What did he keep from you, Jeff?"

His hands were resting on her shoulders now, squeezing in reaction to some emotion that Fancy knew had nothing whatsoever to do with herself. "I can't tell you, not now."

"It concerned Banner, didn't it?"

"No. It concerned my father. Now let's go back to camp and get something to eat—I'm starving."

Fancy knew that there was no point in arguing and, now that matters had smoothed out a little between Jeff and her, she was ravenously hungry. She smoothed her hair and the soft skirts of her dress and then bent for the perfume bottle. "I'll be along in a minute," she said. "I want to freshen up a little."

He laughed and hugged her, his strange mood of moments before wafting away on a spring breeze. "So you plan to make an entrance, do you?"

"If I'm going to be a lady," responded Fancy in airy tones, "I'd best start acting like one."

Jeff frowned with mock disapproval and swatted her lawn-covered bottom with possessive hands. "Not too much of a lady," he warned.

"My good sir, are you implying that I am ever otherwise?"

"Yes. You're a hellion in bed, and I want you to stay that way."

Fancy blushed, not knowing whether to rejoice or be insulted. "You are no gentleman!"

He kissed her in a way that could only be called suggestive. "We've already established that, haven't we?" he muttered, and then he left Fancy alone to wash her face, redress her hair, and dab on a few drops of the frightfully expensive perfume.

She was just starting up the path toward the camp when an enormous man stepped in front of her. Fancy's light heart grew heavy with fear as she recognized Rafe, the farmer Jeff had battered senseless the day before.

Fancy's fear was equal only to her outrage. She knew that it would be sensible to scream, but her throat had drawn shut and she was momentarily incapable of sounding any sort of alarm.

"Don't you look fine, now?" murmured Rafe, staring at Fancy as though he couldn't quite believe she was real. "Don't you look right fine?"

Fancy thrust out her chin, but she had stopped breathing. Just stopped. Still unable to speak, she retreated a step.

Rafe's meaty hands closed over her shoulders; she could feel their heavy warmth through the delicate fabric of her dress. His moist mouth was moving toward Fancy's, and she realized with jolting horror that he planned to kiss her.

She gave a strangled cry and squirmed out of his arms. Her breath burned in and out of her lungs, so hot and harsh that she could hardly bear it. But she was vocal now. "If you touch me again," she managed, "my husband will kill you."

"All I want is a little kiss," complained Rafe petulantly.

Fancy closed her eyes and a scream swelled up into her throat, pressed its way past her lips. Rafe turned and lumbered into the bushes like a retreating bear.

Jeff appeared only moments later, followed by a pale and frightened Phineas.

"What happened?" demanded the former, clasping Fancy's shoulders in hard hands.

"Rafe," she choked out. "He was—he wanted me to k–kiss him—"

Jeff muttered a lethal word and released his wife, his fierce indigo eyes scanning the trees and bushes.

"No harm done, now," soothed Phineas quickly. "No harm done."

Jeff sighed and a quiver of suppressed anger moved through his frame. "Is that right, Fancy? Are you hurt?"

Fancy shook her head. She'd been frightened, but, as Phineas said, no actual harm had been done. In fact, she felt rather foolish now. "H–He startled me, that's all. Wh–when I screamed, he ran away."

Phineas seemed determined to brighten the situation. "Aren't you a page from *Godey's Lady's Book*?" he sang out, admiring Fancy's new dress and carefully styled hair.

Fancy smiled, understanding. Phineas wanted no more trouble and she was in hearty agreement. "Thank you very much," she said, in the ladylike way she'd been mentally practicing almost from the moment Jeff had given her the dress. "Will you please be so kind as to offer your arm, sir?"

Phineas complied with a doffing of his hat, a dashing bow, and a suave extension of his elbow. "Shall we dine?" he said.

"Christ," muttered Jeff, his eyes still fixed on the bushes that had swallowed the amorous Rafe.

Fancy took Phineas's arm and lifted her skirts in her other hand, the very picture of feminine deportment. "Leave us leave," she said.

Phineas laughed and so, however reluctantly, did Jeff.

"Please?" pleaded Jeff, all the more appealing because the bright morning sun was shimmering behind his wheat-gold head.

Fancy looked at the balloon and crinkled her nose. "Suppose the ropes came unfastened?" she ventured doubtfully.

"Would that be so terrible?" Jeff retorted with a good-natured shrug. "We would soar—"

"Or crash to the ground," Fancy broke in, brow furrowed.

"The ropes are secure, Fancy."

Fancy gave the ropes a careful scrutiny. While the idea of flying was singularly terrifying, it also had a certain dashing appeal. And Jewel Stroble hadn't been afraid to go up in the balloon, had she?

"All right," blurted Fancy.

Jeff lifted her inside the wicker gondola and then sprang in to stand beside her. He reached above his head to pull at the handle of a valve and there followed an unnerving, hissing sound.

"Oh, God," whispered Fancy as the gondola toppled slightly and began to lurch heavenward. If Jewel Stroble hadn't been standing less than a dozen feet away, she would have slid down to her knees and closed her eyes.

Up and up the balloon went—when would those damnable ropes reach their limits?

Fancy looked at the ground—Phineas and the others and the wagons looked so small—and then swung her gaze to Jeff's face. He was smiling at her.

"You are very brave, Mrs. Corbin."

"B–Brave?"

"Yes. Courage isn't an absence of fear, you know—it's going ahead and doing whatever you're afraid of."

Fancy's shoulders squared and her chin came up. She'd never thought of herself as courageous, but Jeff was right—she was. She'd gained something by meeting this challenge, however small, something lasting and good. And she could see for an incredible distance. "Look—there's the river. And there's Colterville."

Jeff laughed. "This is better than sailing," he said to himself and Fancy and the blue, blue sky.

Fancy looked down, without a qualm this time, and waved at Jewel Stroble. Even from that height, she could see the guarded rancor in the woman's round face.

A sudden and stiff wind struck the balloon, making a crackling, silky sound, and the gondola rocked precariously. Fancy paled, her courage waning a little. But Jeff's arm was quick to encircle her shoulders and it seemed that some of his fathomless strength flowed into her.

"How do you make this thing go down?" she demanded, through a clenched and rigid smile.

Jeff chuckled, letting go of her to pull a cord near the valve that had made them rise. The strange vessel wafted slowly to earth. Phineas secured it as Jeff leaped out, lifting Fancy after him.

Jewel sidled over, her hands coquettishly caught behind her back so that her ample bosom was thrust forward. The way she smiled at Jeff made Fancy feel as though she'd suddenly turned transparent, and she was having none of that.

"Don't you have to milk a cow or something?" she snapped, stepping directly in front of Jewel, thus forcing the woman to acknowledge her.

Jewel's brown eyes widened, then snapped with challenge. For a moment, it appeared that she was going to argue and Fancy hoped for that, yearned for it.

But Jewel reconsidered and turned in a pool of calico to stomp away.

"What was that all about?" asked Jeff, with an innocence too guileless to be false.

"Territorial rights," snapped Fancy, catching her skirt up in her hands. With Jeff's chuckle reddening her ears, she went off to tend to Hershel and dispense another day's magic.

Jewel came to watch her last performance and it was clear that, while she'd backed down earlier, she did not consider herself defeated. Her eyes followed every move Fancy made, and they were bright with skepticism and malice.

Fancy was gathering up the pennies tossed by her admirers when Jewel approached the table in that sidling motion designed to display her voluptuous femininity.

"I'd hate to have people throw money at me," she

observed, in sugar-sweet tones that nonetheless smarted. "It must be sort of—well—demeaning."

Fancy was determined to keep her temper. After all, she was going to Spokane soon and she would be expected to behave as a lady. There was no better time to start than the present. "I seriously doubt that anyone will ever throw money at you, Miss Stroble." Chamberpots or bricks, maybe, but not money, Fancy thought uncharitably.

"Are you Jeff's woman?"

"I am his wife," Fancy said evenly.

Jewel did not look the least bit disturbed. "How come you don't wear a wedding ring?"

The jibe had hit home, but Fancy was careful not to reveal the fact. "We decided to marry rather . . . suddenly," she said, in dulcet tones.

"I see." Jewel paused, drawing a long breath that lifted her melonlike bosom. "Papa and I have known the Corbins a long time."

This was news to Fancy; Jeff certainly hadn't mentioned a long-standing friendship. Still, she was circumspect and mannerly. "Congratulations," she said.

"Do you have just that one dress?" pressed Jewel, as Fancy set Hershel's cage on the tabletop with a telling thump and shoved him inside.

Fancy had reached the end of her rope. Being ladylike was one thing and being stupid was quite another. "What exactly do you want to say to me, Miss Stroble?" she asked, with acid patience.

Jewel curled the fingers of one plump hand and inspected the short, uneven nails as though they had just been expertly manicured. "They're Catholic, you know. The Corbins, I mean."

This, too, was news to Fancy. There were so many things she didn't know about Jeff, so many things he hadn't bothered to tell her. She remained silent, waiting for the next parry.

It came within seconds. "Jeff's family won't recognize a marriage made outside the church, you know. As far as they're concerned, people who aren't married by a priest just plain aren't married."

Fancy felt just a bit sick. She knew little about the Catholic religion, having been raised as a Presbyterian herself, but she did know how the Catholic Church felt about secular wedding ceremonies. Jeff had to know, too, and that was what hurt.

Before she could say anything, Jewel saved her the trouble with an airy, "Of course, it will be easy for him to annul the arrangement once he's tired of you. And he will get tired of you, Fancy Jordan."

Fancy's control was costly; in fact, she had never paid a higher price for anything. "The way he got tired of you?" she asked.

Some of the rosy color drained from Jewel's plump cheeks. Her lush mouth moved as though she might say something, but then she turned suddenly and stormed away.

Fancy felt anything but triumph. It had been a terrible mistake to marry Jeff Corbin—that was the one thing in the world she was certain of at that moment. She should have guessed that a man like him would not enter into a long-term relationship with someone like herself, someone poor, someone who picked up pennies off the ground and wore the same stupid dress day after day.

Hot tears streaked down her face as she gathered her props. Maybe the snake-man wasn't empowered to perform marriage ceremonies at all. Maybe Jeff had tricked her. The advantages to be gained by such a deceit were obvious enough.

Ten minutes later, Fancy found her "husband" helping Phineas secure the balloon for the night. She thrust the awkwardly rewrapped package containing the dress, nightgown, and perfume into his arms and turned away.

As she had half expected, as she had both hoped and dreaded, Jeff immediately dropped the parcel to the ground and caught her arm in one hand, staying her dramatic departure.

"Wait a minute!" he rasped.

Phineas walked away, whistling, his hands in his pockets. Other members of the show, however, were not so obliging, and Fancy was aware of their interest in the forthcoming scene. For that reason, she tried to speak calmly and quietly.

"Let go of me, you lecherous wretch, before I have you arrested for every sort of debauchery."

Jeff stared at her, his blue eyes at once puzzled and angry. But his hand fell from her arm. "What now?" he wanted to know.

"You are a Catholic," Fancy seethed. "Why didn't you tell me you were a Catholic?"

"Does it matter?" snapped Jeff defensively, annoyed now.

Fancy's control was slipping, and fast. Her voice rose a pitch when she spoke again and suddenly she didn't care that the fat lady and the elephant trainer and the man with tattooes were looking on. "Your brother is a *Methodist minister*, for God's sake, and you didn't tell me that you're *Catholic?*"

"I didn't have time for semantics!"

"No, you were too busy defiling me!"

"Defiling you?!" bellowed Jeff with no regard whatsoever for the scandal that would ensue. "Is that what I was doing, Fancy? Defiling you?"

The crowd laughed but Fancy only half heard them; it was as though they were standing beyond some pulsing, invisible veil. "Yes!" she screamed.

"Well, you sure as hell enjoyed it, didn't you?!" shouted Jeff, his hands on his hips now, his nose only an inch from Fancy's.

"I endured it!" she shrieked, to the delight of the onlookers. "But no more! This farce of a marriage is over and I'm leaving!"

"Good!"

Fancy had been prepared for an argument. Now that Jeff had agreed to her going, she was at a loss. "I never want to see you again!"

"Wonderful!" came the immediate and scathing reply. "Just exactly where do you plan to go?"

"Anywhere where you aren't, you—you trickster! You debaucher! You—"

Jeff's right eyebrow arched ominously. "Yes?"

Fancy could bear no more. She flung herself at him, fists flying, feet kicking, tears of rage and humiliation flowing down her face. "You only married me—if it *was* a marriage—to get me into your bed!" she screamed, in unbridled hysteria.

"You tell him, honey!" cheered the fat lady.

Chapter Eight

"YOU STAY OUT OF THIS!" JEFF BELLOWED, AND THE FAT lady stepped back, chins trembling. His menacing gaze swung back to Fancy's face. "Come with me," he bit out, grasping her elbow in one hand and half propelling, half ushering her toward Phineas's wagon.

"Why did you have to yell at Eudora like that?" complained Fancy, as she double-stepped along. "She has problems enough, what with her weight and people paying money to stare at her!"

"She doesn't have half the problems you're going to have," Jeff retorted in a snapping undertone. The back of Phineas's wagon was open and he lifted her up to sit on its floor, her feet dangling. "Now what is all this talk about Catholicism and leaving me?"

Fancy couldn't meet his eyes. "You lied to me," she accused miserably.

"How?"

Fancy sniffled. "For one thing," she muttered, "you didn't tell me that you knew Jewel Stroble before."

"Jewel." Jeff sighed the name and Fancy saw him run one hand through his hair in exasperation, though she was pretending not to look at him. "I should have known she had something to do with this."

"You've been intimate with her!"

"So has every other man in the territory. Besides, I was sixteen at the time and hardly in full possession of my senses!"

"I think your senses were probably just fine, Captain Corbin!" Fancy paused and sniffed indignantly. "I don't appreciate being confronted with your former mistresses at every turn."

"Every turn? How many others have you met, Fancy—besides Jewel?"

"There are probably dozens!"

"At least," Jeff said promptly.

"Beast!" flared Fancy.

"Enough. I will not stand here and be harangued for something that happened years ago. And if you ever make a scene like that again—"

Fancy arched an eyebrow and stiffened her shoulders. "Yes?"

Jeff swore and shook his head in annoyance. "Why were you going to leave?" he persisted, after an interval of considerable inner struggle.

"Because you lied to me!"

"Back to that, are we? And just exactly how did I lie?"

"You didn't tell me that your family is Catholic."

"Fancy, I really don't understand why that bothers

you so much. Have you got something against Catholics?"

"Of course not!"

"Well, then?"

Fancy's emotions were churning; she was beginning to suspect that she'd made a fool of herself. Again. "I believe Catholic marriages are generally performed by priests, rather than snake men!"

Jeff stared at her, incredulous. Then, after long moments, he laughed. "You think the ceremony was a fake, don't you?" he demanded.

"Was it?"

"You saw the certificate. You signed it. What do you think?"

"I think, Mr. Corbin, that it would be easy for you to annul such a marriage, even if it was legal!"

Angry wonder played in his magnificent face. "You think I would do a thing like that? You actually believe—"

"I do!"

"All right, then have it your way! I set it all up! It was a joke, a fraud! And when I get tired of you, I'll find myself a nice, nubile Catholic girl and haul her before a priest—with no thought of you or your goddamned rabbit!"

Fancy was bruised by his words, but she lifted her chin and willed the tears throbbing behind her eyes not to fall. "I only married you for your money anyway," she lied. In actuality, she had never given much thought to his fortune, except where it could make life easier for her family. But now she wanted to hurt him as cruelly as he had hurt her.

To her mingled remorse and triumph, she saw that

she had succeeded. He turned away, his head tilted back, his face to the brassy sky. "So be it," he breathed.

"You'll go back to Wenatchee, then?" Fancy dared, her voice trembling. Suddenly, the pain she had dealt him was doubling back on her.

"No," he replied, in tones of dry, dusty gravel, without turning to look at her. "And neither will you, my dear."

"I had no intention of—"

"From now on," he snapped, "your intentions don't matter in the least. You married me for my money. That's fine. But the price for all that luxury and influence may be much higher than you bargained for, Mrs. Corbin." Now, he turned to face her, his eyes brutal and distant. "Much, much higher."

"Jeff—"

He held up one hand to silence her. "No more. If I've bought myself a bride—and it appears that I have—then be assured of one thing: I'll get my money's worth."

With that, he turned and started to walk away. Fancy scrambled down off the wagon and caught one of his arms in a frantic hand.

"Jeff, what are you saying?"

His eyes were averted, fixed on, of all people, Jewel Stroble, who seemed to be waiting for the drama to end. No doubt, she planned an epilogue of her own. "You'll find, Mrs. Corbin, that I'm not such a bargain," he replied coldly. "Now, gather your things because we're going to town."

"Going to—"

"Town," he put in, savagely condescending now.

And then he walked off toward a grinning Jewel, without so much as looking back.

Fancy was torn between running after him and running away. She watched in anguish as he draped one arm around the waist of the simpering Jewel and disappeared with her into the woods lining the stream. Their stream.

"Bastard," she sobbed, biting her lower lip and wishing that she knew a worse word.

After a few minutes, Fancy had managed to summon up a façade of composure, and she went to fetch the parcel she had thrown at Jeff near the balloon. She was about to get Hershel and her other props and start down the winding, rutted road toward Colterville when Eudora Strittmatter, the fat lady, halted her with a gentle, "Miss Jordan?"

Fancy paused, letting her misery show in her face, partly because hiding it was too great an effort just then and partly because she knew Eudora understood pain. "Yes?"

"You're not going to leave, are you, and let that strumpet have your man?"

"She has him already," mourned Fancy, looking toward the hidden stream and speculating on what was probably going on there right at that moment.

"No," argued Eudora. "He's just trying to nettle you—don't you see that?"

To Fancy, one thing was as bad as the other. Whether Jeff was just trying to make her jealous or whether he was actually availing himself of Jewel's favors, he had done her an injury she could not deal with. "He's succeeded then," she said, and after a short farewell to Phineas, she left.

Phineas had not accepted the money she had offered him for her keep these past few days, and he had not tried to talk her into staying, either. She was grateful on both counts.

The walk into Colterville was longer and more difficult than she'd expected, especially carrying a valise, the parcel, Hershel's cage, and her few props. The sun was setting and her feet were burning when she finally reached the edge of town.

Colterville was obviously a place of limited prospects. There were two saloons, a feed store, a mercantile, and a few ramshackle houses—that was the extent of it.

With a sigh, Fancy approached the largest house, which was within a hundred yards of the railroad tracks. A hand-lettered sign was propped in the window of what was probably the parlor, reading, ROOMS TO LET.

She climbed the steps, weary to the depths of her soul, and rapped disconsolately at the door. There would be no jobs in Colterville, that much was clear, but perhaps she could get train passage out of town without too much delay. In the meantime, she would take a room, have a bath, try to sleep, and try *not* to think about what Jeff and Jewel Stroble were probably doing.

A heavy woman came to the door and assessed Fancy with swift, narrowed eyes. "You travelin' folk?" she demanded, looking wary.

Fancy squared her shoulders. "Please, ma'am—when does the next train leave?"

The woman relaxed a little, though she made a point of inspecting Fancy's star-spangled dress, her props, and her rabbit. "Tomorrow, if you're going east—next day after if it be west. Rooms are twenty-five cents the night and you can't have that critter in there."

Fancy dared to hope a little. "I can rent a room, then?"

"Cash in advance, missy. And if you want a bath and supper, it's fifteen cents more."

Fancy nodded. She had just over three dollars and that decided her on going east. It would save her one night's room rent. "Thank you," she said, and then, on orders from the woman, she put Hershel in the wood-shed around back, giving him some dandelion greens and a jar lid full of water.

Her room was on the second floor and hot as the devil's breath, even though the window was open. Flies buzzed in the close, musty air and crawled on the narrow bed.

Resigned, Fancy closed the window.

"I'd be for bathin' when it's cooler, were I you," said the proprietress. There was a stain on the bodice of her colorless calico dress and she scratched inelegantly at her protruding middle.

Fancy had a headache and the beginnings of a sour stomach. "Yes," she agreed, mostly to get rid of the odious woman. "I believe you're right."

"Forty cents," she reminded Fancy.

Fancy counted out two dimes and four nickels and placed them in the woman's outstretched hand. When she was alone, she immediately checked the bedding and the seams of the mattress for cooties.

Remarkably, the bed was clean. She sighed and sat down on it, bending to unfasten her high-button shoes. It was going to be a long night, she reflected as she lay down to rest, and, without Jeff, a long lifetime.

But she was not going to think about Jeff Corbin, not

ever again. If there were to be any sanity for her, she would have to forget him once and for all. Write him off, like a fizzled magic trick.

Lying back on pillows that smelled faintly of a man's hair oil, Fancy tried to make plans for the future. She would head east, on the next train—to Spokane, maybe. It was a growing city, in the center of the wheat country, and bound to offer some sort of opportunity.

She could wait tables there, or perhaps work as a servant in a fine home. Like Jeff's?

Fancy turned over fitfully, trying to shut out thoughts of Jeff. She wouldn't encounter him again, not in a city as large as Spokane—he probably wouldn't even go there now, for that matter. He'd be too busy with Jewel.

A tear squeezed past Fancy's squenched-shut eyelashes to slide, tickling, down her face. Jewel. Jeff. Their images, entwined and naked, tortured her, despite her resolve not to consider them. Were they making love on those dear, lumpy, leaf-littered blankets by the stream? Were they bathing each other, laughing and cold, in the water?

Fancy turned her face to the pillow and gave a muffled howl of protest and hurt. For the first time, it occurred to her that Eudora might have been right. Maybe she shouldn't have left; maybe she should have stayed and explained to Jeff that she'd spoken in angry haste—that she hadn't married him for his money but because she loved him and hoped that, someday, he would love her, too.

But she couldn't have done that. He would have laughed at her.

Fancy cried until her throat ached and then fell into a fitful sleep. When she awoke, there were shadows creeping across the dusty board floor and someone was knocking impatiently at the door. Stumbling a little, disoriented and headachy, she made her way across the tiny room and released the bolt. Probably, the proprietress had brought her bath water.

She was only half-right. Her bath water was being delivered, steaming in two large kettles, but its bearer was Jeff.

"Madame," he said with a suave bow, stepping around her and into the room before she could recover enough to slam the door.

"Get out," she managed impotently, as he set the kettles down on the floor and assessed her with bold blue eyes.

"I will. I've got two more kettles and a tub to carry up," he said as though they had never quarreled. As though he had not spent the afternoon tumbling in the grass with Miss Jewel Stroble.

"Thank you, but I'd rather you left entirely," Fancy declined with remarkable dignity.

At that moment, the proprietress of the seedy little railroad roominghouse arrived, carrying a huge, round tub and another kettle of water. She gave Jeff a beaming smile. As she was leaving the room, she pointed out that towels and a new bar of soap could be found under the washstand.

"I didn't think anyone could make that woman smile like that," marveled Fancy, momentarily distracted. "Not even you."

Jeff shrugged with feigned humility. "I try to be humble," he demurred.

"You have never tried to be humble in your life!" countered Fancy furiously, coloring now. "Get out of my room!"

He simply folded his arms. "Our room, dear."

Mocking him, Fancy folded her arms, too. Since she was incapable of brute force, there was only one other way of getting rid of Jeff Corbin, and she was desperate enough to make use of it. "I told you that I only married you for your money," she said.

Jeff arched one butternut eyebrow. "And I told you that I intend to have my money's worth," he replied. And then, cool as a cucumber picked in the shade, he closed and bolted the door and began filling Fancy's tub with clean, singularly inviting water.

"Take your bath," he said finally, sitting down on the edge of the bed in the attitude of a spectator.

"You'll have to leave first."

"That water will ice over before I do that."

"Fiend!"

He lay back on the bed, stretching his long frame out with a hearty sigh, cupping his hands under the back of his head. "I could use a little sleep before we go to dinner," he said.

"I've made my own arrangements for dinner, thank you very much!" sputtered Fancy, glaring at him.

He closed his eyes and, despite her scathing gaze, he did not stir again. After several minutes, he snored.

Fancy didn't trust him, but the bath water was growing colder by the moment, and everything within her craved its comfort and solace. She stepped closer to the bed and peered into Jeff's face. "Are you asleep?" she whispered hopefully.

Breathing deeply and evenly, he seemed to be in genuine repose. As if to prove this, he snored again.

Fancy made haste to get out of her dress and underthings and into the bath water. When she looked in the direction of the impossibly narrow bed, she saw that Jeff was watching her, his head propped up on one hand.

"You are beautiful, Frances Corbin," he said, unperturbed, apparently, by his own deceitfulness.

Fancy sank deep enough to cover her breasts. "My name is not Frances Corbin, you hateful man!" she bit out, taking up the soap and lathering it.

Jeff only laughed.

"What are you doing here, anyway? Is Jewel indisposed?"

"I think she's milking a cow or something."

Fancy stretched one leg out and covered it with soap suds. "How fitting," she said.

"How are we both going to sleep in this bed? It isn't long enough for me, let alone wide enough for both of us."

"Don't worry about that, Mr. Corbin. *We* are not going to sleep in that bed—I am."

Jeff grinned and, with that audacity so peculiar to him, came to kneel beside Fancy's tub. He took the soap and sponge from her and began to methodically scrub her back. "You're probably right," he conceded. "I doubt that we'll sleep."

Fancy closed her eyes, trying not to succumb to the feelings spawned by the totally innocent washing. "Why are you here?"

"Because my wife is here," he answered, and set aside the sponge and soap for a moment to repin her tumbling hair.

"Am I really your wife, Jeff?" she dared to ask after a very long time. "Was that ceremony real?"

"Absolutely."

"But your family—"

"My family didn't marry you, Fancy. I did."

She couldn't argue with him anymore, not tonight, for she had neither the strength nor the spirit to prevail. She said nothing at all, in fact, as he lifted her effortlessly to her feet and completed the bathing process, leaving no part of her unattended.

Just when Fancy was ready for him to make slow, sweet love to her—yes, in spite of everything, she wanted that—he swatted her bottom, handed her the towel, and said, "Get out of there. I want a turn."

Fancy watched in amazement as he stripped off the clothes he'd been wearing ever since he arrived at the carnival camp and stepped into the tub she had just left. He sang a bawdy saloon song as he washed, ignoring his startled wife completely.

Befuddled, Fancy dressed herself in her spare camisole and drawers, then put on her new lawn dress. She was brushing out her hair before a cracked little mirror affixed to the wall when Jeff finished his bath and took up her discarded towel to dry himself.

"Hurry up," he said, for all the world like a long-time husband. "I'm hungry."

Fancy shrugged. "You can't very well eat naked," she observed, putting the finishing touches on her coiffure.

"I can do almost anything naked," he replied, in sunny tones, as he dressed again. "In fact, some of my favorite activities are things that I do naked—"

Color ached in Fancy's cheeks, even though she knew that he was teasing her, deliberately maneuvering her into just such a reaction. "Preferably with bosomy milkmaids," she declared acidly.

Jeff laughed, his shirt still gaping open to reveal a broad expanse of muscular midriff matted in a golden tracery. "Next time you shop for a husband, my love, you might want to be a bit more choosey."

"I might want to be a *lot* more choosey!" snapped Fancy, too angry to tell him the truth. Let him go on believing that she'd married him because he was wealthy. What did it matter?

He sat down on the edge of the bed and, in a lightning-quick motion, he caught Fancy's hand and pulled her onto his lap so that she was straddling his thighs and looking away from him. "I do have my redeeming virtues," he breathed against the bare, tingling flesh along her neck.

"I have yet to see them!" hissed Fancy, scrambling to rise. But he held her fast, his hands sliding up to cup her breasts in a bold display of mastery.

"Let me refresh your memory," he enjoined gruffly. And then he undid the buttons at the back of Fancy's dress and drew downward on the front, causing her breasts to spill out, covered just to mid-nipple by her camisole. This, too, was easily removed.

"Jeff," Fancy choked out, in dazed protest.

He was stroking her, at once soothing her and setting her afire. "Is it really such a bad bargain, Fancy?"

"Jeff, I didn't mean—I don't think—"

"Hmmm?" He turned her with idle strength so that she was lying on the narrow bed, looking up at him. And then he lifted her skirts.

Fancy struggled. "No—not now—you've got to listen—"

"I have something else in mind." He made short work of her drawers, then knelt on the floor. She could not close her legs for he was blocking them with his body.

A jolt shot through Fancy as he parted and then tasted her. "Damn you—is this—what you did to Jewel?" she rasped, already caught up in sweet anguish.

"No. But it is sure as hell what I'm doing to you, lady." He enjoyed her for a while, idly, and then went on, his strong hands pressing her knees farther and farther apart. "Furthermore, I intend to go on doing it. In carriages, on trains, wherever the mood strikes. And when I do this"—he paused, running the fingers of one hand across his lips—"it means that I plan to exercise this particular pleasure at the first opportunity."

"That is"—Jeff came back to her, with savage hunger, and Fancy had to pause to cry out—"despicable!"

"Nevertheless," he replied presently between kisses that made her writhe and toss on the narrow little bed, "that's the way things are, Mrs. Corbin. God, you are a sweet—delicious—little morsel—"

"Oooh," Fancy cried, shuddering even as her back arched in a spasmodic, furious surrender. Again and again her body buckled, and it was a very long time before Jeff allowed her to descend to that little room again.

They ate their supper alone in a little café down the street. There were dusty potted palms everywhere, and the windows were fly-speckled, but the food was surprisingly good. Fancy devoured her Swiss steak, mashed potatoes, and peas, not only because she was hungry but because it gave her a brief respite from all the contradictory thoughts and emotions inspired by the man across the table from her.

"I didn't notice this place when I arrived," she said over strong coffee and peach pie.

Jeff grinned. "You were too full of righteous wrath to

look around you, no doubt," he replied. "What a pity that it was all unfounded."

"You went off into the bushes with Jewel Stroble!" Fancy blurted. Of course, the sole waiter's attention was immediately drawn by this unfortunate remark.

"Must you shout the scandalous details to the world?" retorted Jeff, not seeming particularly upset. "And I did not 'go into the bushes' with Jewel Stroble."

"You did so! I saw you!"

"I meant, you thick-headed little wench, that I did not figuratively—"

"Figuratively?!"

Jeff sighed, looking pained. "Damn it, I'm trying to say that we didn't do anything there. I just wanted to make you mad, that's all."

Fancy was skeptical and wildly hopeful. "Then how come it took you so long to get here?" she demanded.

"Phineas was sick."

The glorious rage Fancy was working up instantly deflated. "What? What's the matter with him? What happened?"

"One question at a time, sugarplum. He's resting comfortably now in the back of his wagon, but I think we should get him to Spokane, where he can rest. He has a sister there."

"W–What about his wagon—his balloon and everything?"

Jeff looked away momentarily, then met Fancy's eyes again. "I bought the balloon."

"You what?!"

"I bought it." He was defensive now. "Any objections?"

"As long as you don't expect me to fly in it, none at all!"

"Good. Then can we get back to the subject of Phineas's health, please?"

Fancy was properly shamed. "Do you know what's wrong with him?"

"I'm no doctor, but I'd say it's his heart. I've seen some of my brother's patients with similar symptoms."

"We should leave right away!"

"Wrong," Jeff immediately replied. "He needs to rest first. Spokane is several days' journey from here and it will be hard in a wagon."

"Couldn't we send him ahead on the train?"

"I suggested that, but Phineas wanted no part of the idea."

"What are we going to do, then?"

Jeff smiled over the rim of his coffee cup. "Finish our supper, go back to the roominghouse, and make love. I've never had you in a real bed, you know, and I do find the prospect intriguing."

"How can you even think of something like that when Phineas is so gravely ill?"

"Bemoaning our friend's condition won't change anything. Besides, life is a fleeting thing, Fancy, and it can be gone"—he snapped his fingers—"like that. In my opinion, we should take advantage of every opportunity to enjoy the pleasures at hand."

Fancy blushed. "And in my opinion, you are positively shameless. In fact, you're a libertine!"

Jeff lifted his coffee cup in a mocking toast. "Get used to it," he said.

"I will not!" hissed Fancy, leaning across the sugar bowl to make her point. "I didn't bargain for this!"

"All the same," he answered smoothly, "you did bargain. You sold yourself to me, Fancy, and—"

"I know, I know. You intend to get your money's worth!"

"And more," crooned Jeff. Then he rose from his chair and solicitously helped Fancy out of hers. After he'd paid their check, he escorted her out onto the narrow board sidewalk.

Fancy tried to pull her hand from the crook of his elbow, where he had firmly placed it, and found that it was stuck there. "Let go of me!"

"Not on your life, dear."

"You have no right to treat me like this—as though—as though I were a slave! I don't have to follow your orders, Jeff Corbin!"

"Of course not, my dear. For that matter, you needn't sing, you needn't dance—" He paused, sighed philosophically, and kissed the tip of her nose. "Just do magic."

Chapter Nine

THE SOUND OF A TRAIN WHISTLE DREW JEFF UP FROM THE depths of a drugged sleep. A train. There was somewhere he should be going, something he should be doing.

It was cool in the small room due to a soft breeze wafting in through the window. Fancy lay across his chest, her hair tickling his chin. He smiled and entangled one hand in the honey-colored tresses, careful not to awaken her.

She made a kittenlike sound in her throat and stirred. Their flesh was bonded together by the fever of the night, it seemed to Jeff, and he wished that they could remain this way forever.

Again, the train whistle sounded, nearer this time, intrusive. Jeff closed his eyes and held onto the moment, knowing that the sweet peace of it would soon be gone, driven away by the din from the nearby railroad tracks and by facts that would demand to be faced.

Fancy wriggled and then stretched, and Jeff ached with love for her. He should tell her how he felt, he knew that, but the act required more courage than he'd been able to muster up. Another announcement like the one she'd made yesterday would devastate him.

The arrival of the eastbound Pacific Central shook the roominghouse and the flimsy cot. Fancy lifted her head, looked at Jeff with befuddled violet eyes, and murmured, "Good heavens, what's that noise?"

Jeff smiled sleepily. "Noise?" he asked with feigned surprise as the cot began to dance and jiggle beneath them. The keening shriek of a steam whistle muffled her reply.

He slid his hands down her satin back to her bottom, nipping at her earlobe.

She squirmed against him, igniting fires that burned away his doubts. He turned her, placed her beneath him. "I love you," he said at her breast.

Fancy could not hear him, he knew. But her body arched toward his in heated welcome and, minutes later, when their frenzied need was satisfied, their cries of despairing triumph went unheard for the clanging of the conductor's bell.

They lay still in the aftermath, clinging together, struggling for each breath as though they were one entity. Desire, now sated, ebbed and flowed over them in warm waves.

Jeff closed his eyes and shuddered, certain that should he ever care more deeply for Fancy than he did at that moment, he would not be able to bear it. The feeling coursing through him now was startling in its intensity.

"Jeff?" She spoke his name softly; it was only then that he realized that the whistling clatter of the train had died away.

He could not speak; if he did he would do something stupid and unmanly. He would cry.

Fancy tangled a finger in the hair at the nape of his neck. "Darling, what is it?" she pressed.

Jeff clenched his teeth together, the flesh on his face seemed to stretch taut over his cheekbones and the bridge of his nose. She married you for money, not love, he reminded himself savagely. If you forget that for one minute, you're a fool. "Fancy," he said despairingly, his voice muffled by the pillow.

"We'd better get back to Phineas, don't you think?"

The cool practicality of that remark sobered Jeff, allowing him to lift his head without fear of disgrace. "Yes," he croaked out, careful not to look directly into those lethal violet eyes. "You're right—"

She cupped her hands on the sides of his face and made him look at her. "Jeff," she insisted softly. "What's the matter? D–Didn't I please you?"

With a strangled exclamation, Jeff thrust himself out of her arms, off the cot. He wanted to batter the wall with his fists, wanted to shout and rail. Instead, he let his forehead rest against the cracked plaster and struggled for some semblance of control. His shoulders heaved with the effort.

He heard quiet desolation in her voice. "I'm s–sorry," she said.

Jeff whirled, unconcerned now with the tears that were glittering in his own eyes, blurring his vision. "Sorry?!" he rasped. "God in heaven, Fancy, *for what?*"

She was crouched in the middle of that miserable, rumpled, sagging excuse for a bed, her fingers knotted in her lap, her face wan. "I–It would seem that I've upset you—disappointed you—"

Heedless of his nakedness, Jeff stared at her in frank amazement. "Disappointed me?" he echoed.

Fancy bit her lower lip and nodded. A tear streaked down her face and fell away into the twisted sheets.

"No," he protested hoarsely. "No."

She drew a deep, quivering breath. He knew that she was attempting to be brave for some reason, and it wounded him that she felt the need. "Yesterday, when I said I only married you for your money, I was lying," she announced, in a tremulous voice. "I l–love you, Jeff."

Jeff felt as though he'd just had a bucket of ice-cold water poured over his head. God, if he could only believe her! He reached for his trousers and wrenched them on. Believe her? Why should he, when she'd been nothing but trouble from the first? She had left him twice. She had accused him of betrayal and even of falsifying his own wedding. Furthermore, she had associated with Temple Royce.

"Right," he rasped, pulling on his shirt, averting his eyes. "Get dressed."

"Don't you believe me?" Fancy persisted with dignity as she climbed off the bed.

"I believe you," he lied. "I just don't care, that's all. This is a business arrangement. Let's keep that in mind, shall we?"

She was crying; Jeff knew that but he steeled himself against it. Another trick, another tactic. Petunias would bloom in hell before he fell for that again.

"So far," she began, her voice quivering with rage and hurt, "the advantages of this 'arrangement' have all been on your side! When do I benefit?"

When he could bear to, Jeff met her gaze. "Get dressed," he ordered with a coldness completely unrelated to what he was feeling. "We'll talk about your 'benefit' when we get to Spokane."

Fancy stepped back from him as though he'd slapped her. He almost relented, almost made an ass of himself and told her that he loved her, wanted her, needed her. Had it not been for the crisp knock at the door, he would have.

"Don't you dare open that door!" Fancy hissed, lunging for her clothes.

"Just a minute!" Jeff snarled.

"I've got all day," sang Jewel Stroble, from the hallway.

Fancy knelt beside Phineas's pallet in the wagon, forgetting her own concerns as she noted the deep blue smudges of pain beneath his eyes, the pallor of his skin. "Do you want me to get a doctor?" she whispered.

"No," replied Phineas with surprising briskness. "I most certainly do not. Did you and that husband of yours manage to talk to each other, Fancy?"

Fancy swallowed hard. For a time, it had seemed that she and Jeff might be able to converse sensibly. Lord knew, their bodies had been in accord. But when Fancy had worked up her courage and declared her love, Jeff had flung it back in her face, just as she had feared he would. "Oh, Phineas," she whispered, "it was a disaster."

Fatherly concern shimmered in his eyes. "Why?" he wanted to know.

"I t–told Jeff yesterday that I married him for money. I didn't really do that—I was just speaking in anger—but he's convinced that I meant what I said."

"Oh," said Phineas, and the expression on his face urged her to go on.

"I told him that I loved him and he—he said he didn't care, that all w–we had was a business arrangement."

"A business arrangement, is it?" chortled Phineas. "That kind of arrangement makes babies, if memory serves me correctly."

Fancy blushed and looked away. "Yes," she choked out.

"Are you in the family way, Fancy?"

The question was put so kindly that Fancy couldn't be offended. "I don't know. It's too soon."

Phineas groped for one of Fancy's hands and held it tightly in his own. "Jeff loves you, Fancy. You remember that. You stay by his side, no matter what, and you go on loving him. The day will come when he'll be able to get past all the barriers he's set up to protect himself."

"Protect himself? From me?" Fancy was truly startled. "I couldn't hurt him!"

"You've done that already, Fancy—twice that I know of. I'd say Mr. Corbin is afraid to love you the way he'd like to. That would put a terrible weapon in your hands and men are shy of such things."

Fancy bristled. "Well, he certainly isn't shy of Jewel Stroble!" she argued, forgetting Phineas's illness for a moment. "That woman had the audacity to knock on our door and ask Jeff to have supper with her tonight!"

Unbelievably, Phineas chuckled. "She's a brassy piece, that one. And did she invite you, too?"

"Of course not! The bold thing—it didn't even matter to her that I was standing right there!"

"And what did Jeff say to her?"

Fancy couldn't help smiling. At least, out of all her defeats, there had been that one minor triumph. "He told her to stop behaving like a trollop and leave us alone."

"There, you see?"

Fancy's glory was short-lived. She colored at the memory of what had happened next. "He swatted her on the bottom!" she marveled angrily.

"Jewel's got that sort of bottom," observed Phineas.

"Phineas Pryor!"

"Well, she does. Not being a man, you wouldn't understand."

Fancy understood, all right. One woman wasn't enough for Jeff Corbin. Even though he'd spurned Jewel's attentions, he hadn't been able to keep his hands off her. Drat it all, she'd seen the glimmer in his eyes as he assessed the bottom in question. "Is there anything I can do for you, Phineas?" she asked stiffly, tucking the blankets more closely around him and touching his forehead to check for fever.

"You can find that man of yours and you can tell him you love him. Tell him until he listens, Fancy."

Fancy nodded distractedly, but she had no intention of laying herself open for another brutal rejection. If Jeff wanted to believe that she'd married him to assure her own comfort, then let him.

Smiling at her own cleverness, Jewel bent over as far as she could to place that hussy's rabbit, cage and all, in the gondola of the balloon. Then she stepped aside, folded her arms, and waited. Jeff Corbin would come to her house for supper that night, all right. And for a lot more, if Jewel had her way.

Soon enough, Jewel saw Fancy approaching, her purple eyes flashing fire just the way her fingertips did when she was performing magic tricks. If it hadn't been for that Jeff Corbin-sized ache inside her, Jewel might even have liked Fancy. As it was, she couldn't afford to do that.

"Afternoon, Mrs. Corbin," she sang out.

"Eudora said you took my rabbit!" accused Fancy, ignoring the neighborly greeting. "Where is he?"

Jewel thought she'd burst with glee, but she managed to point to the gondola and say, "In there."

Fancy gave her a scathing look, then sprang quite deftly over the side of the big wicker basket. Jewel immediately released the ropes that kept the balloon on the ground, and it began to rise.

Mrs. Jeff Corbin clutched the gondola sides with white-knuckled hands and peered down in terror. She could have jumped, but she seemed too shocked to try it.

Jewel was already beginning to doubt the wisdom of what she'd done, when Jeff came bolting through the crowd and sprang into the air, just managing to catch hold of the gondola's jutting brim before the vessel rose in earnest. It was about ten feet in the air, Jewel supposed, when Jeff managed to scramble over the side and join his petrified wife.

"Fancy?" Jeff was there. Everything would be all right. One of his arms slid around her shoulders and supported her. "Fancy!"

She drew a deep breath. "Down," she said, with dignity. "I want to go down."

Instead of complying, Jeff swore. Fancy opened her

eyes, looked at him, then looked at the ground. She trembled and grasped the edges of the gondola even harder than she had before.

Temple Royce was standing in the grass, gazing upward, grinning. In his right hand a nickel-silver pistol caught the bright spring sunshine.

"Go ahead and shoot," Jeff prompted with a responding grin. "With all these witnesses, old friend, you'll end up where you belong—at the end of a rope."

Temple's toothy smile faded to taut-lipped grimness. "Corbin, you son-of-a-bitch, come back here!"

Fancy slid to her knees and the gondola rocked sickeningly at the motion. "Oh, God," she whimpered.

"Corbin!" Temple bellowed.

Jeff stood straight and tall while Fancy cowered. The way he smiled and waved one hand, reminded her of a politician making a speech from the back of a railroad caboose. "Do you remember the lady?" he called, as the balloon bobbed higher and higher. "She sings, she dances and, believe me, Temple, she does magic!"

"Get down here!" screamed Temple. Even from that height, he looked apoplectic.

"Sorry," Jeff sang back. "Another time, another place."

Fancy groaned. She couldn't bear to look anymore. "Jeff—the balloon is loose—" she reminded her companion frantically.

"Yes it is," he exalted.

They were soaring through the blue skies, free and, for the time being, safe, but Fancy couldn't find any joy in the adventure. Still, if given a choice between this rash method of escape and facing Temple Royce in his present mood, she would certainly have chosen the balloon flight.

Somewhere over the Columbia River, she grappled to her feet. Jeff was too busy pulling the valve that released gas into the balloon to help her. "W–We got away," she said, smiling thinly.

"For now," replied Jeff. "He'll follow, of course."

Fancy hadn't thought of that. "How do you suppose Temple found us in the first place?" she choked, sickness scalding the back of her throat. The fields below were like squares on a patchwork quilt, the river no wider than a ribbon.

"I told him where we were," Jeff answered blithely.

Fancy hung her head over the side of the gondola and threw up.

They drifted for hours, it seemed to Fancy, sometimes brushing the lower borders of heaven itself, sometimes coursing along a few dozen feet off the ground. The great undulating shadow of the balloon spilled before them, rippling over rocks and bushes, making oblong circles in fields, flowing over the tops of barns and houses.

Finally, at sunset, they came down with a jarring thump in a field of new wheat. Fancy sprang out of the gondola and fled.

Jeff howled with laughter, but he did not pursue her. Over the pounding of her own blood in her ears, she heard a familiar hissing sound and knew that he was letting some of the hydrogen gas escape the balloon. She ran on, clods of rich earth breaking under her shoes.

Eventually her breath failed her and she stumbled, landing on her hands and knees in the dry dirt. Scrambling back up again, gasping, she turned to look back and saw that Jeff was hauling huge rocks from the edge of the field and placing them inside the gondola.

"You idiot!" she screamed, clenching her fists. "What are we going to do now? You tell me that! What are we going to do now?"

"I'm going to secure this balloon and you're going to stop carrying on like a fishwife!" he yelled back.

"A fishwife?!" Fancy shrieked, stomping back toward him. Her hair was falling down around her shoulders and her dress was filthy and God only knew what would happen to them now. "How dare you call me that?"

"Shut up," growled Jeff, still filling the gondola with stones.

Now that she was on the ground again, Fancy dared to take umbrage. "Don't tell me to shut up, you pebble-brain! It's your fault we're in this mess!"

He stopped and glowered at her, his big, dusty hands resting on his hips. "What did you want me to do—stay there and let Temple Royce blow my brains out?"

"I didn't know you were afraid of Temple," she taunted, keeping her distance just in case.

Jeff stormed toward her and bent to snarl into her face. "I'm not afraid of Temple or anybody else! But he had a gun and a dozen men and all I had was a goddamned rabbit!"

"If you hadn't baited him like that, there might not have been a problem!" cried Fancy, tired and sick and totally undone. "I'm not stupid, you know! I clearly understood what you meant when you said I do magic! You were referring to our intimate relations!"

He grinned obnoxiously. "Yes."

"How dare you?!"

"You keep asking me that. 'How dare I this, how dare I that.' Well, I'll tell you—I do whatever I damned well please and you might as well know it!"

"In that case, would you please jump off the nearest cliff?!"

Jeff grinned again and touched his mouth in that impudent signal he had warned Fancy to expect. She was so furious that she slapped him across the face, then turned in a huff to stomp away.

Blinded by tears, Fancy nonetheless managed to find her way out of the seemingly endless wheat field. She came upon a little stream, perhaps the same one that ran past the carnival camp, and knelt beside it to wash her face and hands. Looking up from that task, she saw a small flour mill on the other side, its wheel still and glistening with water-dappled spiderwebs.

Jeff came up beside her and set Hershel's cage down on the grassy ground with an irritated briskness. "I am not afraid of Temple Royce," he said evenly.

Fancy bit back a smile and turned her face so that he couldn't see the effort involved. "You haven't the sense to be," she said in gentle tones.

He sat down beside her and the scent of the grass was the sweeter, the lusher, for the crushing it had suffered. "But you were right about one thing," he admitted, after a long pause. "I'm an idiot."

Fancy laughed, her legs drawn up, her arms wrapped around them. It was safe to look at him now and reveal her amusement. "What accounts for such a major concession?" she teased, resting one cheek against her knees.

Jeff glared up at the sky, annoyed. "You're my wife. I promised to protect you. And here we are in the middle of some god-forsaken wheat field with night coming on and a choice between starvation and eating the family pet!"

A sweet tenderness swept through Fancy, for she

loved the little boy in Jeff as well as the man, and the former was so visible now. "I doubt that we'll perish for missing one or two meals," she comforted, reaching out, without thinking, to smooth his rumpled hair.

"It really did you a lot of good to marry a rich man, didn't it, Fancy?" he drawled, lying prone on the grass now. There was no rancor in his voice, at least none directed at her.

"Do you think Temple will find us here?" she asked, ignoring his question.

"He might. That balloon is sure to draw his attention if he's anywhere near."

"But we drifted miles—"

"And Temple has horses."

Fancy shuddered. "Oh, Jeff, why did you have to let him know where we were? Why?"

He sighed. "It seemed like a good idea at the time."

Shadows were dancing on the stream as twilight flung itself, in shades of maroon and gray and lavender, over the mill and the little patch of ground where they rested. Fancy swallowed further criticisms and concentrated on the sights and sounds around them.

Frogs and crickets began their chorus and the breeze rustled in the young wheat. Jeff sighed again and stretched out his long legs, the heels of his boots almost in the water.

Suddenly, despite everything that was wrong in her life, Fancy was brimming with mischief. She undid her shoebuttons, kicked off her shoes and plunged into the stream to wade, shivering deliciously at the cold.

Jeff sat up and stared at her as though she'd gone mad. She laughed at the expression on his face as she bent to scoop up icy water in her hands and fling it at him.

He bellowed a curse, bolted to his feet, and then plunged into the water after her, boots, trousers, and all. A water fight ensued that left them both drenched and weak with laughter.

Fancy's black dress clung to her, sodden, clearly revealing her turgid nipples and the smooth curves of her hips. Her hair escaped its pins and cascaded down her back, wild and tangled and free.

And Jeff stood stock-still in the rushing water, his blue eyes darkening. In an easy motion, he lifted Fancy up into his arms and carried her across the stream and through the sagging doorway of the mill.

There were rats there, no doubt, and fallen beams stretched across the dusty floor. But the place might have been a palace, for all Fancy knew.

She stood silently as Jeff slowly undid her dress with its water-dulled silver stars. She remained still as he removed it and then the drawers and camisole beneath. She was proud of her nakedness. Before this one man, she was proud of it.

He bent his head and kissed her, and her lips, shivering and blue from the cold of the stream, immediately parted for his warm conquest. Their tongues battled briefly and then caressed. A moan filled the musty little building, a moan that might have come from either one of them.

Finally, Fancy pushed Jeff away, with a gentle thrust of her palms, and then unbuttoned his wet shirt. He groaned and closed his magnificent eyes as she slid the garment away from his skin.

With surprisingly deft hands, considering the numbing cold that possessed them, Fancy proceeded to unfasten his trousers.

He gasped and drew her close again, kissing her,

consuming her, and at the same time lowering both of them to the floor. They knelt, facing each other, on Fancy's discarded dress, neither noticing, neither caring.

Fancy escaped the dazzling kiss to nibble at his neck and the muscular planes of his chest. His nipples were still wet from the spirited water battle in the stream and she made them wetter with her tongue. A throaty rumble came from his chest as he surrendered fully, his head thrown back, his eyes closed in ecstasy.

Fancy bit and nibbled her way down over his hard stomach, her hands preparing him for a fuller conquering. "What I need is a signal," she teased in a whisper. "Something to let you know that I mean to do this to you at the first opportunity."

The answer was a fevered gasp, the tangling of strong hands in her hair.

Having thus repaid him, Fancy proceeded to pleasure him, fully, shamelessly, and with love.

He made a growling sound low in his throat, and shuddered. "I'm going to—oh, God, Fancy—please—"

She was noisy, even greedy, and his pleasure became her own. His grating cries and hoarse pleas only made her bolder; she felt strong and pagan as he fell back to grant her full surrender, bracing himself with his hands. His powerful body strained to be conquered, every muscle was taut and strong.

He shouted in lusty defeat and still she suckled, refusing to let him rest, plundering without mercy. She wanted, she demanded, she took, and the feeling of glorious victory she enjoyed was almost a release in itself.

Jeff finally fell away, his eyes sightless in the shadows, his chest rising and falling in a harsh rhythm. Spotting an old pail, she rose from her knees and went outside to fill it with water.

Bringing it back, she smiled because, for all his delirium, he'd managed somehow to finish undressing. His boots and trousers were nowhere in sight.

Fancy knelt again and soaked her camisole in the water she'd brought. And then, despite his gravelly, half-audible protests, she washed him. The bath was a tender one, beginning with his face, progressing to his neck, his chest, one unblemished arm and then the scarred one. She bathed his hips, his thighs, every part of him.

It was obvious that the cold of the water had long since stopped bothering Jeff; he watched her with dark wonder in his eyes. Only when she began to attend his slowly rising shaft did he attempt to stop her.

She pushed his hands away, gently but firmly. "This is my night," she said, "and I will love you as I please."

His willingness to surrender was the measure of his fathomless strength. His eyes glittered as she washed him.

Fancy set aside the cloth and began to stroke him, now almost tickling, now taking firm command. Jeff whispered her name, over and over again, and it was a harsh yet gentle sound, beautiful to hear.

"I love you," she said, clearly and without shame.

Jeff was writhing, his head moving back and forth in a delirium of need. "Let me—take you—Fancy, please —let me—"

"No," Fancy said, powerful in her triumph, dizzy with the magnitude of the love she bore for this man. Tomorrow she might feel shame, anger, remorse. Tonight, she felt victorious.

She bent and reprimanded him with a nibbling kiss

that drew a gutteral cry from the depths of him. Tonight, at least, he was hers and only hers. She would enjoy him, savor him, bear him to the heights and depths of passion.

The golden fingers of dawn were reaching across the floor of the mill before Fancy granted her captive the merest measure of mercy.

Chapter Ten

TEMPLE ROYCE HAD GONE TO SLEEP IN ECSTASY, AND HE awakened to more of the same. Damn. If it weren't for Jeff, he'd be content to lie there forever on the banks of that ice cold creek, letting Miss Jewel Stroble have her way with him.

Alas, Jeff had to be dealt with. It was a matter of honor.

He sat up and Jewel drew away, pouting. Temple laughed, caught her plump face between his hands, kissed her forehead. "Another time," he said, standing up and righting his trousers in a simultaneous motion.

"Do you mean to hurt Jeff Corbin?" Jewel asked, smoothing her grass-stained calico skirts, but making no attempt to rise from the blankets spread out on the ground.

Temple was rolling down his sleeves, refastening the

cuff links. "Jewel, Jewel," he reprimanded smoothly, "don't tell me that you love another man!"

Jewel knew that he was mocking her and she was respectably angry. "Jeff's—well, Jeff is real special, that's all. I don't want you to hurt him."

Temple shrugged and bent to fetch his round-brimmed hat from the grass. "I see no reason to lie to you, dearest. When I find Jeff Corbin, I'm going to make him wish he'd been stillborn."

Jewel gnawed at her lower lip, plucked at the dew-moistened grass with the fingers of one hand. "I wouldn't have—I wouldn't have been with you, if I'd known."

"The fact that I wanted to shoot him and his damned balloon right out of the air should have given you a clue, sweetness," replied Temple, shaking out his suitjacket and shrugging into it.

"This was where they slept," Jewel announced distractedly, frowning at the blankets. "Jeff and that woman, I mean."

Suddenly Temple's smooth manner was gone. "Here?" he rasped.

His agitation clearly pleased Jewel; it was balm to her wounded pride. "Here," she confirmed, with a broad smile. "You want her, too, don't you? You want Fancy."

"What makes you say that?" snapped Temple, uncomfortable and annoyed. He didn't "want" Fancy; he had to shut her up, that was all.

"You called me by her name last night, that's what. Twice."

Temple cursed. Fancy Jordan had been a diversion to him, an amusement. Trying to seduce her had been a pleasant game and nothing more. If he'd suffered after she disappeared—and he had—it was only because he hated losing. Now, he looked at the blankets on the ground and seethed.

Defeat was bitter, but defeat at the hands of Jeff Corbin was intolerable. "Jesus," he muttered. And then he turned away, his determination to finish the chase and close in for the kill renewed. He'd been a fool to stay here, indulging with the likes of Jewel Stroble, letting his quarry quite literally fly away.

"He can make her beg for it!" Jewel hurled after him, with crude relish. "Ask anybody."

Temple paused, caught in the clutches of a hot, squeezing fury. "Shut up," he breathed.

"Jeff could make any woman do that," persisted Jewel, blithely unruffled by Temple's rising wrath. "He's all man, that one."

Temple turned and doffed his hat in a manner that was meant to be insulting. His smile was deliberately cruel. "I'm sure you know what you're talking about, Jewel. How does he compare to the rest of the men in the territory, now that you've tried us all?"

Jewel uttered a cry of outrage and scrambled to her feet, her round face red, her teeth bared. She shrieked an Anglo-Saxon epithet and Temple laughed as he strode through the trees.

The small carnival was just coming to life, and his men were gathered into a tight little group, more than ready to get on with the business at hand. They had even saddled his horse.

Grinning, Temple mounted, realigned his hat, and took up the reins. At peace with his body, thanks to the tender attentions of Miss Jewel Stroble, he could now turn his thoughts to the exquisite misery he planned for Jeff Corbin.

Fancy rose, yawning, from the bare, dusty floor. Because Jeff was still sleeping, she helped herself to his shirt, put it on quickly, and crept outside. Her dress and underthings, hastily rinsed out in the stream just after dawn, were draped over a blackberry bush a few yards from the mill's entrance.

The garments were still damp, but Fancy was resigned to wearing them anyway, having no other choice. She smiled wryly as she hurried back into the mill and put them on. When she was fully dressed, she nudged Jeff with the toe of one shoe.

He stirred, grumbling, and then sat up. "What—"

"Get dressed, you waster," Fancy ordered good-naturedly. "We've got to get out of here."

Jeff gave her a look and then fetched his trousers and boots, his shirt and his wits. "You're right about that," he conceded, rather grudgingly. "God, I'm hungry. Do we have time to fry Hershel?"

Fancy giggled, tossing her unbound, tangled hair back over her shoulders, grooming it as best she could with her fingers. Her hairpins were lost now and she had no hair brush, having left the carnival camp in such haste. "Sorry," she sang.

"I'd like to know what the hell good it does me to be rich," grumbled Jeff, making his way out of the mill and into the bright morning sunshine. Fancy followed, smiling.

He stopped so suddenly that she collided, hard, with his back. Her heart leaped into her throat and she peered around his right arm, fully expecting to see

Temple Royce. Instead, she was met with the annoyed glare of a grizzled old farmer.

There was a shotgun resting easily across his thick, meaty arms. "I hope you folks got a real good reason for mashin' down my wheat with that contraption yonder," he imparted.

Jeff spread his hands in a conciliatory gesture, and Fancy stepped up beside him, seeing in a sidelong glance that he was grinning. "Don't you remember me, Eustis?"

The farmer squinted, bending forward, loosening his hold on the shotgun just a little. "Jeff? Jeff Corbin? Jesus and Mary, it *is* you!"

There followed an exchange of jovial greetings and blustered cusswords.

"Why, last time I seen you," raved Eustis, "you was no higher than your daddy's belt buckle! I heared the youngest feller got religion!"

Jeff was solemn for just the merest flicker of time, and Fancy couldn't tell whether it was the mention of his father or Keith's ordination as a minister that had dampened his good spirits.

"How's Daniel?" Eustis rushed on, with gruff good humor. "Is your mama still the same pretty little spitfire she used'ta be?"

"Papa died," Jeff answered quietly.

"Daniel?" Eustis's weathered farmer's face contorted a little. "That's right bad news. I'm sorry to hear it."

A muscle leaped in Jeff's jawline, but was visibly subdued. "You look good, Eustis," he said, and it was clear that his cordial manner required an effort. "Is Isabella well?"

"Fat as a hen and got all her teeth yet!" chortled Eustis. "Who's this little gal?"

Jeff stiffened and Fancy knew that he'd forgotten her presence until that moment. He glanced at her and the guarded warning she read in his eyes stung even more than the knowledge that she could slip his mind so easily. Was he ashamed to present her, with her mussed hair and damp, star-spangled dress, as his wife?

"Eustis, this is Frances. My wife."

Frances. What was wrong with 'Fancy'? She extended her hand to Eustis and smiled warmly. "Everyone calls me Fancy," she said.

Eustis returned her smile, took the offered hand in a strong grip. "I'm real pleased to meet you, ma'am," he replied. "Come along now, and I'll have Isabella rustle up some breakfast for you."

Jeff nodded gratefully, but when Eustis turned to lead the way to his house, his gaze sliced three inches into Fancy's heart.

Certain now that he was ashamed of her, even ashamed of her name, Fancy glared up at him in silent defiance.

"Everyone calls me Fancy!" he mimicked in a brutal undertone as they followed the unsuspecting Eustis along the creek bank and into an ocean of wheat.

"Perhaps you'd like me to change my name to Jewel," Fancy hissed in furious response. "Or maybe Banner!"

Jeff paled and his jaw was clamped steely hard. Indigo sparks flared in his eyes and then dimmed to cold disgust. He pressed one hand into the small of Fancy's back and propelled her onward.

It wasn't until they reached Eustis's weathered frame house that he pretended to like her again. Fancy wasn't fooled by the warm smiles, the loving gestures, the careful introductions. Despite all those amenities, the cool disdain still glittered in his eyes.

Fancy smiled and ate the hearty breakfast Eustis's Isabella provided, but inside she was broken and bruised. She would have liked nothing better than to throw herself down on the nearest bed and sob her heart out, but that luxury would have to wait.

When Jeff and Eustis went out to look at the balloon, however, she relaxed a little. Isabella Ponder was a warm, plain-featured woman, easy to be with.

"I never!" exulted the older woman, standing at the window over her iron sink. From there, the slightly limp balloon was clearly visible. "Trust one of Daniel Corbin's boys to carry his bride away in a blamed contraption like that!"

Fancy might have smiled if she hadn't felt so much like crying. Isabella would probably talk about Jeff and the balloon for months, maybe even years. "Did you know the Corbin family well?" Fancy asked, mostly to make conversation.

"Well as could be expected. They weren't at the Wenatchee place much, 'cept in the early years."

"What are they like?" Fancy was surprised at the smallness of her voice.

Isabella turned, her broad face gentle. "Why, child, don't tell me you haven't met them?"

"Just Keith," replied Fancy, her coffee cup shaking in her fingers. She set it down with brisk awkwardness.

"That Jeff! What was he thinkin' of, marryin' without his kin there to celebrate with him?"

Fancy lowered her eyes. She couldn't very well tell Isabella that he probably had no wish to show off such a bride. Like as not, his family would be furious when they learned of the marriage. "I–It was sudden," she managed, covering her left hand with her right in an effort to hide the finger where a wedding band should have been.

There was a short, poignant silence; Fancy could almost hear Isabella going over the reasons for a marriage to be sudden and settling on the most scandalous one.

"I'm not pregnant!" she blurted out, before she could stop herself.

Isabella chuckled warmly and patted Fancy's hands. Before she could say anything, however, Jeff spoke from the doorway.

"Only a matter of time," he said, with a roguish grin.

Startled, both Isabella and Fancy jumped in their chairs.

"Land, I thought you went with Eustis!" trilled Isabella fondly. "Did you come back to take your pretty bride away before we could even have our chat?"

Jeff was looking at Fancy with fondness, though that subtle rancor still chilled his eyes. "I'm afraid we'll have to leave as soon as possible. I just came back to tell you that it will be a few minutes before the balloon is ready."

Fresh despair filled Fancy; she'd forgotten about the balloon. "I–I'll have to fetch Hershel—" she stammered, unwilling to voice her fear of flying in that awful vessel again.

Jeff shook his head. "I'll get him," he said. And then he was gone again and Fancy dissolved in tears.

Isabella was all motherly concern. She fussed and patted and commiserated, but she didn't question, and Fancy was grateful for that.

Half an hour later, Fancy had recovered. She was sipping hot coffee and listening to Isabella's chatter when Jeff strode back into the farmhouse kitchen, looking frustrated and annoyed.

He muttered a swearword and Fancy looked up at him with puffy, questioning eyes. A flame of fear leaped in a secret part of her heart. "Temple?" she whispered.

There was a scathing reprimand in Jeff's gaze. "Nothing so dramatic," he snapped, now making no effort at all to portray the devoted husband. "The hydrogen tank is empty. The balloon is deflating now and Eustis and I are going to put it in the barn."

Fancy felt a degree of relief, though she didn't dare show it. "Oh," she said, distractedly.

"We'll spend the night here—" He paused, sparing a deferential nod for the lady of the house before continuing. "If that's all right with you, Isabella."

"You know it is!" beamed Eustis's wife, delighted at the prospect of company. Living in relative isolation as she did, she was probably lonely. "My goodness, of course it is!"

"Thank you," Jeff said, and then he went out again.

Isabella was instantly out of her chair, her face alight. "We'll just fix you a nice bath, Fancy, and then we'll wash and iron that dress of yours, proper-like." She paused and gave a sympathetic chortle. "For that matter, I reckon you'd like to curl up in the spare room and have a nap. The shadows under your eyes tell me that man doesn't let you rest much!"

Fancy colored and averted her eyes. Actually, her lack of rest, where the previous night was concerned anyway, was strictly her own fault. She couldn't very well point that out, of course.

While Fancy bathed, hidden away in the cinnamon- and coffee-scented pantry, Isabella laundered her clothes. A warm wrapper, much too large, was provided, along with a towel and a brush for her hair.

Finally, groomed and scrubbed, Fancy padded gratefully into the spare room and collapsed onto the bed. She remembered the wicked, wonderful things she had done with and to Jeff on the floor of Eustis Ponder's mill house and ached. He had been so beautifully vulnerable then, submitting to her love, reveling in it.

Why couldn't he return it?

Tears pricked Fancy's eyes and slid down her cheeks. She curled up in a tight little ball and stifled the hurting sobs that kept rising into her throat.

Beyond the open doorway, Isabella sang happily as she worked. There was a certain comfort in her presence and Fancy gradually stopped crying. After all, she'd had a bath and a good breakfast and now she was going to have a badly needed nap. It had been a long, long time since she'd felt so pampered and safe.

After one muffled sniffle, Fancy closed her eyes and let sleep overtake her.

"Don't you bother her!" scolded Isabella in a hushed voice as Jeff lingered in the doorway.

Lying there on the spare room bed, Fancy looked like an angelic child, her spun-honey hair trailing out over the pillows. She was practically lost in the flannel wrapper Isabella had loaned her, but the luscious tip of one breast peeked invitingly from its folds.

Jeff considered closing the door and sampling the sweet morsel, but immediately dismissed the whim. After all, that would lead to other things, things Eustis and Isabella wouldn't be able to help hearing.

"Come on back here and have some pie with Eustis," Isabella insisted, still keeping her voice low. "That child is plumb wore out."

A reluctant grin curved Jeff's lips. Considering the night that "child" had had, Isabella was very likely right. He stepped back and closed the door carefully.

After pie and coffee with Eustis—this following an enormous supper—Jeff excused himself and went out to the barn to see to Hershel's welfare. After feeding the rabbit, he looked at the once-grand balloon, now tucked ignobly into its gondola, and shook his head. How brief is glory, he thought wryly.

He went back to the house, borrowed soap and a towel, and set out for the creek, having politely turned down Isabella's offer to heat water for his bath. He needed to be by himself for a while and, with the sight of a sleeping Fancy warm in his mind, he needed the bracing chill of the stream.

While bathing, he tried to think clearly. Even though the balloon was out of sight now, it was still possible that Temple would stumble upon them. While Jeff ached for a confrontation with his enemy, he didn't want it to happen when Fancy was around. The best thing to do, he decided, was get her to Spokane as soon as possible—once she was installed in the house there, he could backtrack and find Royce.

Jeff climbed out of the stream, teeth chattering with cold, and dried himself with the borrowed towel. Then, gingerly, he put on his dirty clothes again. Lord, he wouldn't mind reaching Spokane himself. He could get a new wardrobe there, as well as one for Fancy, and good food would be a matter of course, rather than one of luck. Best of all, he could bed his wife in chambers reserved for the purpose, rather than on the ground, on narrow roominghouse cots, or on the dusty floors of deserted flour mills.

Just imagining it lifted his spirits. Silken sheets. Candles. Brandy in crystal snifters. And Fancy.

Jeff walked faster, entered the house, and headed for the spare room.

"You throw them filthy clothes of yours out here and I'll wash 'em," Isabella ordered.

Jeff cast one baleful look at his slumbering wife and shrugged. Why was he hurrying? He didn't dare touch Fancy, not with his friends sleeping just on the other side of a thin wall. Behind the door, he took off his clothes and tossed them out.

He went to the bed and slid beneath the covers, achingly conscious of the warm, silken figure beside him. Nervous, he sat up, straightened his pillow, then sank back onto it again. The bed squeaked at the motion and Jeff closed his eyes, determined to sleep.

But Fancy stirred and the scent of her pulled at him. He cupped his hands resolutely behind his head and reminded himself that he was furious with Fancy. Hadn't she deliberately thrown Banner in his face that very day?

Banner. Jeff could think of her now without hurting. He could think of her fiery hair, her clover-green eyes, her womanly figure. He hoped that she and Adam would be happy together, always.

With a sigh, he turned onto his side, propping his head up in one hand. For a long time, he watched Fancy sleep—what a wonder she was, with that crazy tangle of golden hair, that angelic face.

Jeff swallowed a laugh and a fierce desire to touch her, both at once. Some angel. The night before, she'd nearly killed him.

The memory made Jeff stiffen and he moaned, rolling over onto his stomach, willing himself to sleep, sleep, sleep.

But he was wide awake.

He shifted so that he was facing away from Fancy, and thus from temptation. He rolled onto his back and counted cracks in the ceiling.

A sudden and alarming thought struck him. Good Lord, Fancy had been sleeping most of the day! What if she were sick?

He touched her forehead and found it cool. Satiny smooth. Jeff wrenched his hand back and resumed his study of the ceiling.

Just beyond the bedroom door, he could hear Eustis and Isabella in the kitchen talking in hushed, companionable voices. End of the day voices. A tender sort of envy squeezed Jeff's heart. Would things turn out that way for Fancy and him? Would they grow old together, share laughter and confidences in the night?

Presently, the sounds from the kitchen ceased, only to be replaced by noises from the other side of the wall. "At their age?" he muttered.

A giggle from the clump of moonlit hair and Fancy-scented flannel next to him was the reply.

Jeff drew back his hand and swatted her soft derrière. Springs began to creak in the next room and there were muffled words, groans.

Fancy giggled again, the sound muted by the blankets. "This is worse than that train in Colterville," she whispered.

"What train?" Jeff teased. "I didn't hear any train."

"It shook the bed!"

He laughed, a low laugh that felt good in his chest. "Is that what that was?"

A small fist punched him in the side, then opened to move up and down his stomach, stroking. Fingers tangled mischievously in the hair on his chest, circled and taunted his nipples.

The wall reverberated and the bed springs in the room next door reached an impressive crescendo.

"My God," said Jeff.

"Don't be such a prude," reprimanded Fancy, her lips following the same path her fingers had. "You've had a bath—you taste so good—"

"Fancy, stop."

She did, and Jeff wasn't sure how he felt about that. Damn the wench, she didn't know when to be obedient and when to rebel. "Why?" she asked, innocently.

"Because—because I'm chapped, that's why."

Fancy's laughter pealed like a bell. "Chapped?" she almost shouted.

"Shut up, for God's sake!" Jeff hissed. "You don't have to tell the whole world!"

She covered her mouth and nose with the blankets, bunching them under her eyes with both fists, and her flannel clad shoulders shook with the effort of restraining her glee.

Jeff scowled at her. He meant to lecture her. Instead, to his own surprise, he found himself saying, "Fancy, I love you."

She stared at him and the blankets slowly fell away from her face. "What did you say?"

He reached up, traced the outline of her cheek with one finger. "I said I love you."

With a completely startling squeal of absolute fury, she drew back both of her feet and pushed Jeff out of bed. He landed on the floor with a painful thump.

"Why did you do that?" he asked, too startled to be angry. Yet.

She knelt in the middle of the bed, her arms folded. The wrapper gaped open and Jeff saw a tangle of curls, the faintest curve of one breast. "I don't like being lied to, that's why!" she declared, in a scathing whisper.

Jeff's mouth fell open. "Lied to?" he echoed.

"Yes, lied to! I should have known that as soon as we ended up in the same bed—"

He got up and shouldered his way furiously between the sheets, though Fancy was doing her best to block his way. "You think I want to make love to you?" he rasped, with dramatic amazement.

She grasped the evidence in one angry hand. "I know you do!"

Briskly, Jeff displaced her fingers. "Well, you're wrong, Mrs. Corbin. I must say, however, that this is hardly the reaction I expected—"

She was scrambling over him, as though he were a hurdle or an obstacle. "I'm quite aware of what you expected!" she railed, in a grating whisper, opening the bedroom door.

Jeff sat bolt upright. "Where do you think you're going?!" he demanded.

"To the barn!"

"The hell you are!"

"The hell I'm not!" she replied, and there was laughter on the other side of the wall. Jeff devoutly hoped that Eustis and his wife were sharing a private joke.

"Get back here!"

Fancy stomped out, letting the door click shut behind her. Jeff flung back the covers and then realized that he couldn't give chase—his clothes were still wet from Isabella's washing them. He cursed and lay down again, willing himself to sleep.

But Fancy had been gone for too long. What did she want in the barn, anyway? By God, if she slept out there, he'd blister her in the morning.

Only minutes could have passed, but it seemed like forever to Jeff. Maybe Temple had found the place somehow, maybe he'd waylaid Fancy between the house and the barn. . . .

Not having had much sleep the night before himself, Jeff was suddenly tired. He yawned and closed his eyes. He was worrying for nothing—Fancy was probably in the privy.

Soon, Jeff was resting soundly and having a very pleasant dream in the bargain. The blankets slid down, cool air washed over him. And he was being—well, he was being soothed in the most delicious way.

Suddenly, he was wide awake. He tried to sit up and a hand pressed him back again. "What the hell—" he muttered, his words breaking off because he didn't have the breath to sustain them.

"Bag balm," said Fancy solicitously. "You said you were chapped so I went out to the barn and found this. I think Eustis uses it for the cow."

"Christ," said Jeff.

And Eustis and Isabella shouted with laughter.

Chapter Eleven

ISABELLA WAS UP AND ABOUT; FANCY COULD HEAR HER humming in the kitchen, clattering pots and pans in melodic activity. She slipped out from under the inert weight of Jeff's left arm and smiled to see her dress hanging neatly from a wall peg just inside the bedroom door. It looked clean and crisp; the stars that had been loose were now stitched neatly back into place.

There was water in the pitcher on the night stand, and Fancy performed quick but thorough ablutions, careful not to awaken Jeff. The rigors of the coming day would consume him soon enough, so he needed his rest. She smiled again, with mischief. Yes, indeed, he needed his rest.

Feeling strong and refreshed, Fancy gave her waist-length hair a brisk brushing. She could not pin it up, but that didn't matter—the weight and softness of it felt very good.

Jeff stirred and muttered something and Fancy's heart twisted within her. Now that the magical night had passed, would they be enemies again? Would he be cold and uncommunicative? Would she, despite her best intentions, end up baiting him?

Fancy bent and kissed the bridge of his aristocratic nose. There was so much she wanted to say to him and so much that she didn't dare voice.

The moment she entered the kitchen, Isabella presented her with a cup of hot, fresh coffee. Eustis had eaten and gone about his work, but Fancy could smell breakfast in the warming oven.

After the events of the previous night, she had a little trouble meeting Isabella's eyes. The woman set a plate of sausage, scrambled eggs, and toast before her with a good-natured thump.

"No need to be shy," she said. "Me and Eustis sure ain't."

Fancy looked up with an effort, a blush in her cheeks, and Isabella laughed a happy, chortling laugh.

"No shame in a man and a woman loving each other," the farm woman imparted.

Fancy couldn't quite bring herself to comment on what she had heard through those thin bedroom walls, what Eustis and Isabella had probably heard, too. "Thank you for laundering my dress," she said, taking up her fork. "You've been so very kind."

"That's all right," said Isabella brightly. She was bustling around the kitchen again, and Fancy looked up to see that she had been pressing Jeff's shirt and trousers on a board near the stove. "Truth is, it's a joy for me to have somebody to fuss over. Our girls are all grown and gone, don't you know."

There followed an interval of comfortable chatter,

with Isabella telling Fancy about her three daughters. All had husbands and families of their own, all lived at considerable distance from their parents.

Fancy had just finished her breakfast when a gruff call sounded from the bedroom.

"Frances!"

Isabella smiled and thrust the clean trousers and shirt into Fancy's hands. "Reckon he wants these," she chimed.

Fancy was nettled. "Why can't he call me Fancy, like everybody else?" she muttered, more to herself than to Isabella.

"That's easy," came the prompt reply. "He wants a name for you that nobody but him will use, Jeff does. If the rest of the world called you Frances, he'd say Fancy."

Fancy grinned. "You're right!" she whispered, and then she took the freshly laundered clothes to her husband.

He was grumpy, sitting up in bed, his hair tousled. "What took you so long?" he demanded.

Fancy bent and kissed the top of his head. "Good morning to you, too, darling," she chirped.

Jeff's mouth twisted in a reluctant grin. "Darling, is it? Last night I told you I love you and you kicked me out of bed. What a contradictory creature you are, Frances Corbin."

"I was—overcome with emotion."

He laughed and swatted her off-handedly and there was a softness in his eyes. "I'm sure," he replied, in a mocking drawl. Then, in the space of a heartbeat, his voice became serious. "Your hair is beautiful that way."

Fancy soared; she felt wild and sensuous. "Thank

you very much, my good sir," she said, with a stiff formality they both knew was pure pretense. "Now, will you please put your clothes on?"

Deep blue mischief frolicked in Jeff's eyes. With slow, measured movements, he flung back the covers, stretched, and then sat up. He was so totally, shamelessly male that, despite all their past intimacies, Fancy was moved to wonder.

She bit her lower lip to keep from telling him outright that she thought he was magnificent. "A–Are we going back to the carnival camp or what?" she asked, in a small voice.

Jeff slid languidly into his trousers, taking an inordinate amount of time, it seemed to Fancy, to fasten them. "We're going to Spokane," he said, and the simple words seemed fraught with sweet intrigue.

Fancy took a few steps back. "How?"

He put on his shirt, buttoned it to the middle of his chest, then opened his trousers again to tuck it in. The color flooding Fancy's carefully composed face inspired him to grin. "By train. We'll be there by tonight."

"Stop looking at me that way!" Fancy hissed, unaccountably flustered.

Jeff arched one eyebrow and moved closer to her. "What way?" he countered smoothly. He was standing only inches away and Fancy was conscious of his damnable virility in every smidgeon and whit of her body.

"L–Like I'm a piece of ripe fruit or—or something!" gasped Fancy. Here it was, broad daylight, Isabella singing happily in the very next room, and surges of incredible heat were pulsing through her, melting her.

Jeff chuckled, bent his head, and nuzzled through her hair to touch her earlobe with his tongue. "Tonight," he said in a rasp, and that one word positively reverberated with wicked intentions.

Fancy didn't wait to ask how they were going to find a train out here in the middle of nowhere, what they were going to do about the balloon, or anything. She scrambled out of the bedroom, fighting for every breath.

Jeff followed almost immediately, of course, and all the while he ate his breakfast and chatted with Isabella, he watched Fancy, delighting in the reactions she couldn't hide.

She tried not to acknowledge his gaze, or meet it, but the truth was that she could feel it. He was preparing her, making silent promises, and Fancy was caught between outrage and a scandalous yearning for night to come.

Soon enough, it was time to leave. Fancy had a brief respite in the business of thanking Isabella and saying good-bye. The exchange was a tearful one.

Hershel, being their only baggage, was loaded into the back of Eustis's wagon, content to munch dandelion greens in his cage. They drove through the nodding wheat to the railroad tracks; to Fancy's surprise, there were other people waiting for the train, too.

Jeff thanked Eustis, helped Fancy down from the hard wagon seat, and collected Hershel. The approach of the train was audible now, a metallic clacking sound mingled with those of escaping steam and a shrilling whistle.

The locomotive stopped beside them with a smoky clatter and the two calico-clad women waiting with their husbands finally stopped staring at Fancy's free-falling hair and outlandish dress. She boarded the train with help from both Jeff and the attentive conductor, and then the train was moving again.

Jeff grinned as he settled into the seat beside hers, Hershel having been consigned to the baggage car. "What's the matter with you?" he asked. "You're blushing."

"Those women were looking at me," Fancy replied, folding her hands in her lap and keeping her eyes down.

"So were their husbands," said Jeff with a shrug in his voice.

Fancy shifted her gaze to the wheatlands waving beyond the train window. "I hate it when people stare at me," she whispered. Now that they were actually on their way to Spokane, she was feeling intimidated. Her life there would be different from anything she had ever experienced before, and she wondered how she could possibly be equal to it all.

Jeff caught her chin in a gentle hand and turned her to face him. "Frances, people look at you because you're beautiful."

Tears suddenly blurred her vision. "Because I'm strange, you mean!" she whispered fiercely. "Because I'm wearing a stupid dress with stars on it, b–because I couldn't pin up my hair—"

"You're scared, aren't you?" Jeff broke in, with tender clarity.

There was no point in lying. Fancy nodded her head and sniffled in an attempt to regain her composure.

"Why?"

"I'm not a lady, that's why! People will say, 'Whatever possessed Jeff Corbin to take such a wife?'!"

Jeff chuckled and kissed her forehead. "No. They'll say, 'Damn it, why does he get all the luck?' " He paused to smooth her hair back from her face. "You'll have everything you want, Fancy—I'll see to that. Jewelry, clothes, anything."

Pain stretched itself from Fancy's solar plexus into every extremity. Did he think luxury was what she wanted and needed? What about his love? What about children?

It was silly to suffer such doubts when he had told her just the night before that he loved her, but Fancy could not shake them.

"I want to have a baby," she ventured, just to test the waters.

Jeff grinned. "I've been doing my best," he said, looking comically wounded. Then, in an easy gesture, completely disregarding the other passengers aboard that train, he draped one arm around her shoulders and pulled her close.

Fancy tried to look forward to reaching Spokane—no doubt the house would be grand. There would be good food and probably a bathtub big enough to languish in. There would be books and entertainments, pretty clothes, new people, parties.

And gossip. It wouldn't be long before society figured out that Frances Marie Corbin wasn't one of their number. "Jeff Corbin married a show woman," they would say. "She was actually wearing a dress with stars on it!" others would trill.

Fancy turned her face into the hard strength of Jeff's shoulder and wished that she'd been born a lady. Still, echoes from the near future assaulted her . . . "It will never last, you know—she's not good enough for him—she was born in Newcastle and her mother is a washer woman—you did notice, didn't you, that she isn't wearing a wedding ring?"

Somehow, the cacophonous rhythm of the train put Fancy to sleep. The voices followed, taking on disapproving faces.

"Jeffrey Corbin, it *is* you!"

The trilling exclamation at first seemed to be part of Fancy's bad dream. When she opened her eyes with a start, however, she found that the speaker was all too real.

A gloriously beautiful woman with titian hair had materialized in the seat facing Jeff's, wide green eyes all but devouring him.

"Hello, Meredith," Jeff said evenly.

The lush Meredith rewarded the greeting with a blinding smile. Fancy felt about as much a part of the gathering as the ugly rose cabbage pattern of the train seats. *"Tell* me you're on your way to Spokane, darling!" the vision enjoined.

Jeff's arm didn't hold Fancy quite so close as before, it seemed to her. "All right, Meredith," he answered. "We're on our way to Spokane."

Meredith's eyes widened; it was clear that she hadn't noticed that Jeff wasn't alone until that moment. Surreptitiously, her gaze dropped to Fancy's bare left-hand ring finger before it could be hidden. "I'm Meredith Whittaker."

Fancy sat up very straight. "Frances Corbin," she replied. The look on Meredith's face was a delight.

"You're married?" she asked of Jeff, looking wounded.

Jeff simply nodded. Fancy might have wished for a more enthusiastic response, but she had to be content with the fact that he had, at least, acknowledged her.

Slightly pale, Meredith took in Fancy's cascading hair and star-spangled dress. "I don't believe it," she murmured.

"Believe it," said Fancy.

Jeff gave her an amused, sidelong look but said nothing.

Meredith was more than willing to fill the breach. "I hear that Adam is married now, too," she said quickly and with some surprise. "What's her name again? Something odd—"

"Banner," Jeff replied shortly. Fancy instantly tensed at the name. Merciful heavens, she had yet to meet her sister-in-law and already she hated her.

"That's right," sang Meredith. "Banner. Mother met her when last she saw Katherine in Port Hastings, and she was very impressed."

"It's impossible not to be impressed by Banner," Jeff answered, and Fancy was stung anew.

Meredith seemed to be at a loss, too. She stood up, looking a mite nervous, and excused herself with a few polite words and a promise to come calling as soon as Jeff and "Frances" were settled.

"Whoopee," breathed Jeff, removing his arm from around Fancy's shoulders and sitting back in the train seat in an attitude of unperturbed relaxation.

"What does she look like?" Fancy asked, in a small voice.

Jeff closed his eyes and sighed. "Who?"

"Banner."

His jawline tightened momentarily, but his eyes remained closed. "She has red hair and green eyes," he answered in weary tones.

"Like Meredith?" dared Fancy.

"Meredith pales by comparison."

"Oh," mourned Fancy, turning to look out the window. The wheat fields were far behind now, having given way to a rocky, desolate terrain.

After a time, Fancy slept again. She dreamed that she had just borne Jeff a child, a healthy daughter. "Look," said the doctor, who had no face. And Jeff and Fancy looked, seeing their baby girl wearing a tiny black dress with stars affixed to it.

Fancy was glad to awaken until she realized that the train was approaching Spokane and she was alone. Panic, partly spawned by her silly dream, swelled into her throat.

A scarecrow-thin woman across the aisle noticed her distress and promptly added to it, clearly disapproving of Fancy. "If you're wondering where your man went," she imparted with relish, "he's up in the next car with that society lady."

Though she was wilting inwardly, Fancy would have died before letting the crone know it. "Thank you," she said, turning to look out the window.

Spokane was a good-sized city, though not as big as Seattle by any means, and it sat down in a valley. There were many evergreen trees, even though the community was surrounded by prairie, and, as the tracks descended, Fancy could see a river sweeping through the center of town.

An impressive brick tower with a clock in its top rose up out of the railroad yard, but the other buildings were mostly of wood.

The thinly cushioned train seat gave a little as Jeff sat down next to Fancy. She pretended rapt interest in the view and bit back all the questions she wanted to ask about what he'd been discussing with Meredith Whittaker in the next car.

He seemed to read as much from the set of her shoulders and the determined upward tilt of her head. "Frances," he said quietly.

Fancy ignored him. So Meredith resembled Banner, did she? No wonder he'd been so anxious to spend time with the woman.

"Turn around and look at me."

She turned, her eyes bright with angry tears. Tears she had not even realized were there. If he asked her what was the matter, she was going to scream.

"You're tired," Jeff said sympathetically. "After what you've been through in the past few days, I'm not surprised."

Fancy clasped her hands together in her lap. "Temple didn't catch us, at least," she said, trying to look on the bright side. She did have something of a tendency to let her emotions run away with her, where this man was concerned, anyway, and she was determined not to make that mistake again.

"Don't assume that we won't have to deal with him," Jeff warned in response. "If I've learned one thing in the last twenty years, it's never to underestimate Temple Royce."

Fancy closed her eyes. And, unbidden, the memory of Temple gloating over the destruction of Jeff's ship came to her mind, filling it to the breaking point. "Jeff," she began shakily, "I—in Port Hastings—"

She could feel Jeff's sudden alertness even before she looked and saw it in his face. "Yes?" he prompted gravely.

"I—" Fancy paused, swallowing hard. "Temple—"

The train whistle shrieked suddenly and there was a sensation of impending collision as the wheels were thrust into reverse, screeching along the metal tracks. Before Fancy could regroup her meager forces and go on, Meredith lurched elegantly up the aisle.

"My carriage is here," she said, her green eyes warm

as a caress on Jeff's face. "Won't you let me drop you off?"

Jeff's lips moved in an inaudible curse, but he stood up and favored Meredith with a cordial nod. "Thank you," he bit out. "That would be convenient."

Fancy's intention to confess what she knew about the sinking of the *Sea Mistress* was washed away on a tide of fresh humiliation. How could Jeff have agreed to let that woman escort them home in her carriage? Fancy was embarrassed enough by her appearance—now she would have to collect Hershel and explain why she happened to have a rabbit in her possession!

"A *rabbit!*" cried Meredith when Jeff had fetched the caged creature and brought it to the fore. "Good heavens, what do you want with a thing like that?"

Standing there in the railroad yard of a strange city, Fancy closed her eyes for a fraction of a second and blushed for considerably longer. By this time tomorrow, every socialite in Spokane would have heard about Mrs. Jeff Corbin's pet rodent.

Jeff laid a reassuring hand on Fancy's shoulder. "Why does anybody have a rabbit, Meredith?" he asked, stalling.

"Why, indeed?" Meredith pressed.

Fancy wanted to cry. Again. She was too tired and too undone to hide what she did for a living, social acceptability be hanged. "I—"

Jeff's arm was a steely support around her waist. "Hershel is a pet, Meredith," he said, his tones brooking no further questions. "If you object to his riding in your carriage—"

"Oh, no—of course not!" Meredith cried quickly. "There it is, over there. Herbert! Oh, Herbert!"

Fancy, grateful for the rescue, followed Meredith's

gaze and saw a glistening black carriage attended by a driver. Herbert, no doubt, she thought wearily.

Jeff was standing beside her, and he jolted her out of her lethargy by giving her bottom a surreptitious squeeze and whispering, "This too shall pass. I promise."

Fancy laughed in spite of herself and managed an affronted scowl. "Keep your hands to yourself," she whispered.

He pinched her again as he handed her up into the elegantly appointed carriage after Meredith. Hershel had already been consigned to a compartment in the back.

"I've got so much luggage, Herbert!" wailed the sweetly weary Miss Whittaker. "Come back for it later, won't you?"

"Yes, ma'am," came the desultory reply, from the carriage box.

Jeff got in and sat down beside Fancy, looking innocent and yet mischievous. He folded his arms across his chest and sighed. "That's the advantage of traveling light," he remarked, to no one in particular. "You just pack up your rabbit and you're off. It does save wear and tear on the servants, too."

Meredith looked confused, as though she didn't know whether she was being mocked or not. Fancy smiled, knowing that she was.

As they drove out of the noisy and bustling railroad yard, Fancy silently berated herself for being nasty. She had no real reason to dislike Meredith, and taking pleasure in her discomfort, however moderate, was wrong.

Meredith recovered quickly. "I told Herbert to stop at Corbin House," she informed Jeff, "but won't you reconsider and come have supper with us? Mother will be perishing to meet the new Mrs. Corbin and—"

"No," Jeff broke in, with polite firmness. "Not tonight."

A vague, heated memory was triggered within Fancy. She looked out at Spokane, busy even in the gathering dusk, and instead of buggies, board sidewalks, telegraph poles, and buildings, she saw Jeff putting on his trousers that morning in Isabella's spare room. *"Tonight,"* he'd said, giving the word scandalous meaning.

Fancy shivered with a sort of delicious dread. No matter how many more Merediths she had to face, no matter how intimidating the august "Corbin House" turned out to be, she did have the unsettling comfort of knowing that Jeff would soon be loving her, with his body if not his heart.

As if to acknowledge these unspoken thoughts, Jeff casually squeezed her knee. An anticipatory jolt went through Fancy and he seemed aware of that, too.

The inside of that carriage fairly crackled. Blessedly, Meredith hadn't noticed; her chatter went on and on, and Fancy, looking ahead to the night, paid scant attention. She wondered how Hershel was faring in the compartment, but not with much interest. She was too conscious of the man sitting next to her for that.

"Yes," Meredith went on, her words finally penetrating Fancy's distracted and bedazzled mind, "I know just the dressmaker for you, Frances. She'll take you in hand and you'll be presentable in no time!"

Presentable! The word struck Fancy with the force of a blow, but she had no time to respond to the remark because Jeff beat her to it.

"My wife is already 'presentable,'" he said, putting a cold and measured emphasis on the first two words.

The carriage was lurching and shifting up a steep hill. Fancy found herself hoping that Hershel would throw up in the luggage compartment.

Meredith was quick to regroup. "I didn't mean that the way it sounded," she said sweetly.

The lie was obvious, but Fancy didn't see a need to point that out. Jeff's glare said he knew it already.

"Well, you did ask me to help her along!" Meredith wailed, sounding put upon.

Fancy was suddenly rigid, her gaze boring into Jeff's face. He wouldn't look at her, and his jaw was rock-hard, imperious. "You asked her to what?!" she demanded.

Now, Jeff met her eyes. His face was taut and his gaze freezing cold. "Meredith is familiar with Spokane," he replied reasonably, "and you are not. Therefore, I thought it would be a good idea if she introduced you—"

"If she 'helped me along,' you mean!" Fancy broke in, seeing the warning in his face and ignoring it all the same. "You can't have me going around witlessly buying more dresses with stars stuck all over them, now can you?!"

"That," Jeff said evenly, "will be enough."

Remembering Meredith and how gleefully she would recount this episode, Fancy subsided. "I will deal with you later," she said, with tremulous dignity.

"Not in the way you think," Jeff replied.

Meredith was fairly bursting, but she tried to look as though she hadn't heard any of the conversation. In fact, she spoke as though the entire incident had never taken place at all. "Blue would be a wonderful color for you, Frances—"

"I hate to be called Frances," Fancy put in. It was a small defiance but the taste of it was sweet.

She felt Jeff's gaze touch her; it seared her flesh and then, conversely, raised goosebumps. One very long minute later, the carriage lurched to a sudden halt and Herbert was jumping down to open the door.

"I'll thank you to remember your principles," Fancy said to her husband in a terse whisper when they had both alighted and Jeff had reclaimed Hershel.

"Good-bye, Frances!" sang Meredith, from the interior of the carriage. "I'll see you tomorrow!"

Seething, Fancy put out her tongue at the retreating vehicle.

"You'll thank me to remember what principles?" Jeff drawled furiously, as he gripped her elbow in one hand and propelled her toward a sprawling two-story frame house with green shutters and windows spilling squares of golden light onto the lawn.

Fancy knew that she was on dangerous ground, but the knowledge that Jeff had thought her incapable of buying clothes without Meredith's advice stung so badly that she didn't care. "What principles, indeed?" she snapped. "I'm quite sure you don't have any!"

"Some of them are a little strained at the moment!" Jeff snarled back, settling Hershel's cage down on the front porch and turning the bell knob with a furious twist of one wrist. "Particularly the one about beating you!"

The front door swung open before Fancy could reply and a middle-aged woman filled the golden gap, peering out in surprise. "Jeff? Good heavens, is that you?"

"I think so, Miriam," Jeff replied crisply, "but, at the moment, I'm not entirely sure."

Miriam laughed delightedly and stepped back. "Walter!" she shouted, as Jeff literally flung his bride over the threshhold. "Look who's here! Little Jeffrey!"

Despite the obvious perils of such an act, Fancy couldn't help laughing. "Little Jeffrey," she mimicked, giving the giant beside her a scornful look.

With frightening speed, Jeff wrapped one arm around her waist and lifted her off her feet. Once again, she found herself pressed sideways against his hip. Fancy was mortified and she gulped miserably as he started toward a nearby stairway, his strides ominously long.

"Jeffrey Allen Corbin," Miriam interceded with crisp dispatch, "you put that young lady down this instant!"

To Fancy's eternal surprise, Jeffrey obeyed.

Chapter Twelve

FANCY WAS A LITTLE UNCERTAIN ON HER FEET, AND SHE looked anxiously from Miriam to Jeff. Saying anything more could only get her into trouble again, so she bit her lower lip and remained silent.

"Now," said Miriam, imperiously, her hands on her box-shaped hips, "what's going on here?"

Jeff looked furious, but he answered in civil tones. "Miriam, this is my wife—Frances."

"Fancy," dared said wife, though only in a whisper.

"Wife!" Miriam literally clapped her hands. "And all this time we thought you were married to the sea! Walter! Walter, Jeffrey's married!"

Jeff rolled his eyes heavenward and Fancy permitted herself a giggle. Walter, a white-haired man with a marked limp and clear blue eyes, stumped into the entryway. "What's that you say?" He paused. "Why, it's Keith!"

"No," corrected Miriam patiently. "This is Jeffrey. And here's his pretty bride, too! Isn't she a sight for sore eyes, Walter?"

"Bride!" boomed Walter with glee. "See, Miriam? I told you the Corbin boys was all too much like their daddy to stay single!"

Fancy stifled another giggle, but she couldn't resist darting one sidelong look at Jeff. He was fuming.

"We're hungry," he bit out, taking Fancy's elbow in a firm grip and double-stepping her toward the stairway. "Please prepare something immediately."

"Certainly, Jeffrey," sang Miriam, clearly unintimidated. "Land sakes, imagine you married."

"Imagine," muttered Fancy, grinning.

Jeff's grasp on her arm grew more forceful. "It is amazing, isn't it?" he hissed, in retaliation. Then he squired Fancy up the stairs, into a hallway, then through the open doorway of the grandest room she had ever seen in her life.

The bed was a gigantic four-poster and there were three floor-to-ceiling windows covered by blue velvet draperies. There were bureaus and armoirs and two beautiful, fan-shaped rattan chairs facing a small, ornate ivory fireplace.

Best of all, though, behind a gilt-trimmed changing screen, there was a bathtub. Not one that had been carried in from the kitchen or storage shed, either, but an impressive marble affair large enough to accommodate not just one person, but several.

Fancy blushed and turned away, only to collide immediately with an amused Jeff.

"Watch," he said, and then he strode over to the tub, knelt on its tiled edge, and bent to secure a plug in the bottom. That done, he turned two faucets simultaneously and steaming water began to flow from an elegant spigot.

Fancy was enthralled. Temple had a tub like this in Port Hastings, but she'd never used it, of course, nor had even seen it in operation. The Evanstons, the people she'd worked for right after leaving home, had only aspired to such luxury. Even Keith's house in Wenatchee boasted nothing remotely comparable.

Jeff idly began to unbutton his shirt. "Will you join me, Frances?" he asked.

The temptation was too great. Hot water, and all she wanted of it. Were those bath salts, those pink granules in that apothecary jar on the tub's broad edge? "Of course I will—Jeffrey."

Jeff paled slightly. "Don't start calling me that!"

"Why not? You insist on calling me Frances."

"That's different!"

Fancy turned, so that he could help with the fastenings of her dress. "Is it? Why?"

Jeff gave Fancy a little push instead of an answer and then announced, "You'd better hurry, my dear, unless you want the devoted Miriam to come prancing in here and find us in the altogether."

"She'd do that? Walk right in?!"

"Of course she would," he replied, stripping off his shirt and trousers before Fancy had even progressed to her underthings. He climbed into the wonderful bathtub and sank, with a sigh, to his chin.

Fancy scrambled to join him. His steady regard made her uncomfortable, so she turned away, kneeling in the deliciously hot water, to add some of the pink bath salts. "Ummmm," she said, drawing in the floral scent.

"My sentiments exactly," drawled Jeff.

Fancy cast one look at him over her bare shoulder, and realized that the anticipated 'tonight' had finally arrived . . . with a wallop. "Don't you dare think what you're thinking!" she hissed.

"Why not?" replied Jeff in a husky tone born of utter contentment.

"Because—because Miriam is going to arrive at any moment, that's why. You said so yourself."

"Yes, but even she can't see through that screen, and she'll only be here long enough to leave our dinner."

"And hear us!" flared Fancy, sitting down with a plop and stretching her legs straight out in front of her. Even then, her feet didn't reach the other end of the bathtub.

Jeff laughed and pulled her backward so that she rested against his chest. She would have drawn away but for the fact that his arms closed around her, forestalling any such motion. "The way we heard Eustis and Isabella last night?" he drawled. The palms of his hands were on her breasts now, circling. Kneading. Claiming.

Fancy moaned. "I should have pinned up my hair," she despaired. "Now it will get wet—"

Jeff's fingers were attending her nipples, sending piercing shards of desire stabbing through her. "It will dry," he pointed out.

At that moment there was a bold knock at the bedroom door and Fancy tried to sit up, only to be restrained again. Jeff continued to caress one imprisoned nipple, but his other hand glided under the water and over Fancy's stomach. "Come in, Miriam!" he shouted good-naturedly, as though they were playing chess instead of sprawling, naked, in a bathtub.

There was a rattling sound and Miriam hummed, beyond the wide screen, busy for the most appalling length of time.

Meanwhile, Jeff was stroking Fancy, slowly, skillfully, into a fever of need. Helpless, she pressed her head back against his hard chest and submitted, her legs spreading wide of their own accord. Her hips began to rise and fall; she could not stop them. And still Miriam worked in the main part of the room.

Dishes and silverware chimed. The night was cool and Fancy heard wood being laid in the fireplace, a blaze catching and then crackling.

The motion of Jeff's marauding hand accelerated and Fancy arched, biting her lower lip to keep from crying out in the first throes of a lengthy release.

"Just roll the cart back out into the hall when you're finished," Miriam sang out from somewhere in the spinning storm of sensation that surrounded and pervaded Fancy.

Jeff chuckled, still attending his shuddering wife, as a door clicked shut in the distance. "Are we finished, Mrs. Corbin?" he asked, in a wicked undertone that whispered past her ear.

Fancy hadn't the breath to answer and he damned well knew it, the wretch. To express her rebellion, she clawed the length of his bare leg with her toenails.

He laughed and rose out of the water with a thrusting rush, like some great beast of the sea, hauling an unsteady Fancy with him. "Supper awaits," he reminded her, after patting her tingling bottom once and then thrusting an enormous towel into her hands.

Red to the roots of her hair, she flung the towel back at him and stomped, stark naked and beaded with scented water, around the changing screen. By the time he followed, the towel wrapped casually around his middle, Fancy was shivering before the fireplace.

Jeff arched one eyebrow and favored her with a mocking grin. "Eat," he said.

Having had nothing since the hearty breakfast at Isabella's, Fancy couldn't afford to decline. She sat down in one of the big wicker chairs, took a plate from the rolling cart between them, and began to fill it from the covered dishes thereupon.

"You're going to have a plaid backside, you know," Jeff observed as she began to eat. When she didn't reply, he went to the bed, took up one of the pillows, and extended it to her.

Fancy balanced her plate in one hand, grudgingly taking the offered pillow and tucking it beneath her. "You'd think rich people would at least put cushions on their chairs," she muttered.

Jeff laughed and sat down to have his own supper. "You're the mistress of this house, Fancy. If you want cushions, buy them."

She ignored him, concentrating on adding a dollop of butter to her mashed potatoes.

"Why are you so angry?" Jeff asked after a long time.

Her hunger sated now, Fancy met her husband's gaze, glaring. "Miriam was right here, in this room! And you just kept—you just kept right on—"

"She didn't see us," he reasoned patiently. "And she didn't hear anything, either."

"That was God's own wonder!" spouted Fancy.

"You liked it. That's what infuriates you. You can lie from now till the Second Coming, but you liked it."

"I did not!"

Jeff set his plate aside with an ominous leisure. "Shall I prove that you did?"

"No!" cried Fancy, too quickly.

"Will you admit it, then? You might as well because your body has already confessed, Fancy."

Fancy scowled at him; it was a defense and she knew it, but she couldn't seem to stop herself. "Have you no shame? I swear, you're as bawdy as Eustis and Isabella!"

Jeff laughed. "At least they're honest," he said. "Sex is a natural thing and they aren't shy about it. Why should they be?"

Fancy couldn't think of an answer to that for the life of her, so she took a second helping of thinly sliced roast beef and kept her peace. She probably would have gone on eating all night just to protect herself, if Jeff hadn't calmly taken away her plate and then returned the serving cart to the hallway.

When that task had been attended to, he turned back to face her. The light of the small fire on the hearth danced on his broad, furred chest and flickered in his eyes.

Fancy swallowed a lump of mingled excitement and dread and was suddenly very conscious of her nakedness.

There was a long, pulsing silence, during which neither of them moved. Then, slowly, surely, Jeff crossed the room. Standing in front of the crackling fire, he removed the towel from around his waist and bent to spread it on the plush rug, just inches from the hearth.

Fancy watched him in bemusement. She wondered what it was in her that always made her want to resist this man when she knew that there was no doing that. When he offered a steady hand, she took it with one that trembled.

"I've been thinking about this ever since we decided to come to Spokane," he said, his lips not an inch from hers and already working their compelling magic.

"A–About what?" whispered Fancy, even though she knew the answer already. Something wanton within her needed to be told.

"Making love to you, Fancy. Right here, in front of this fireplace." His hands resting on her shoulders now, he pressed her downward until they were kneeling on the damp towel, facing each other. He caressed her neck, his thumbs moving softly in the hollows beneath her ears, then pushed her hair back over her shoulders. "It will be a long, long time before I let you sleep, Fancy," he went on in husky undertones. "And even then I'll wake you up and have you at my leisure."

Fancy shivered, entranced by his words, knowing and not caring in the least that he would do just that. She tilted back her head and sighed as his hands came inevitably to her breasts, stroking them, caressing, but denying the throbbing nipples the attentions they craved.

He made her ask. And ask again.

She crooned, her fingers tangled in his damp, gleaming hair, as he cupped one warm mound in his hand and nipped at its peak with careful teeth.

Even then, he taunted her with broken, husky words, muttered between plays of his tongue and sucklings that were too brief. "I wanted—this—on the train today," he said. "Next time—Mrs. Corbin—we're going to have a private—compartment. And you are going to—attend me properly."

Fancy moaned, soaring on the wings of her own femininity, as he turned his head to the delights of the other breast. "A–Attend you properly?"

He drew at her noisily, beautifully, and then stopped to reply, "I told you once before. When I want a breast, you will bare one."

His words were outrageous and arrogant in the bargain, but Fancy didn't care, not then. She was honest enough to know that if Jeff demanded suckle, regardless of the circumstances, she would nurse him willingly.

He pressed her back to lie prone on the towel, stretching her hands high above her head and holding them there. Assessing her breasts with molten indigo eyes, he breathed, "And I assure you, I will want them often."

Fancy moaned as he again took sustenance, now greedily, now at leisure. She writhed and the bud of her womanhood grew hard and moist with wanting, raging at its neglect. "W–What about me?" she choked out, wanton in her desire. "W–Will I be p–properly attended?"

Jeff chuckled, understanding, kissing his way down over her glistening, taffeta-smooth stomach. "Until you beg for mercy," he assured her, in a throaty rumble.

Minutes later, she was doing just that.

While Fancy lay quivering and sated on that bright hearth, her skin warmed to luscious comfort by the heat of its blaze and by Jeff's lovemaking, he disappeared from the blurred edges of her vision. Moments later, she heard the clinking of crystal, and then he was back, sitting beside her, offering her a glass of shimmering Burgundy wine.

"Have you no—conscience at all?" she struggled to

say, managing to sit upright only because he helped her.

Jeff lifted his own glass in tender deference. "None at all."

Beyond the door, Miriam could be heard collecting the dinner cart and humming. "Do you suppose she heard us?" Fancy whispered.

Jeff grinned. "What do you mean, 'us'? You were the one making all the noise, my love."

"How ungentlemanly of you to point that out!" hissed Fancy, over the rim of her wineglass.

"We've been over this ground before—where my being a gentleman is concerned, I mean. I don't claim to be anything other than a salacious rake."

"At least you're honest," replied Fancy with a saucy toss of her head. Then she took her first sip of wine and found it pleasant. Eventually, a sweet warmth began to spread through her, following the paths that still celebrated her passion.

She set aside her glass and then took Jeff's, putting it with the other. Laughing, he got to his knees and made to reclaim it. When he reached, leaning forward, Fancy took instant and scandalous advantage.

Jeff was trapped; he moaned in protest and Fancy enjoyed him with abandon. He had no choice but to brace himself with his hands and endure the pleasures in store for him.

Fancy held him fast, her hands on his flexing hips, her heart soaring as he groaned in fierce, reluctant surrender. She began to experiment, nipping at him, kissing him softly, tonguing his magnificent length to a state of sheer splendor.

"Woman," he warned, his voice rumbling above Fancy like thunder in a stormy sky.

Still, Fancy tormented him, and when he uttered that same word again, it had the tone of a plea.

Suddenly, she felt him stiffen. The muscles in his hips grew taut and then rippled, and a low, growling cry of wondering defeat escaped him. When he collapsed to the floor, breathing in ragged gasps, Fancy smiled and patted his hard stomach. "Have you been properly attended?" she teased.

He emitted a gasping chuckle, though his eyes were still closed and his chest was still heaving. "Oh, yes," he breathed. "Quite properly."

Meredith Whittaker assessed Jeff Corbin's wife with carefully hidden dislike. Sitting there in that wretched, star-dappled dress, her cascading pale hair almost silver in the morning sunshine, she looked like some elfin creature from a fairy tale. The smudges of fatigue beneath her eyes and the velvety shine of satisfaction inside them nettled Meredith, made her want to cause pain.

"What do you mean you don't want to go out shopping today?" she asked pleasantly, following this with a steadying sip of her tea.

Frances shrugged, curled up in the big barrel-backed chair facing Meredith's. In another part of the parlor, Miriam Carrington dusted industriously, pretending not to listen in. "I'd rather rest."

Meredith smiled. With an effort. "Long night, Frances?" she asked cattily.

"My name is Fancy," replied the sprite with an answering smile. "And, yes, it was a long night."

Harlot, Meredith thought, uncharitably. But then she remembered that she'd spent a few nights in Jeff

Corbin's bed herself. A delicate blush moved up over her breasts and tingled on her cheekbones. "Very well, Fancy," she said, placing an emphasis on the ridiculous name. "If you want your husband to be ashamed of you—"

Fancy tensed in a very satisfying way, and there was a wounded look in the depths of her lavender eyes. Before she could speak, however, Miriam bustled nearer, feather duster in hand. Though the servant didn't look at Meredith, she felt as though she'd been warned in a most threatening way.

"Oh, dear, I do seem to be tactless today," she chimed anxiously, reaching out to pat Fancy's hand and ignoring Miriam as best she could. "I just meant that—well—you've obviously lived a very different sort of life than Jeff has. Certain—certain things are expected—"

"Like what?" demanded Fancy with bravado.

Meredith drew a deep breath. "Like not wearing that dress," she replied in a rush.

"I like this dress."

"Well, it's hardly proper!" cried Meredith, at the end of her patience. She wondered if Jeff would be faithful to this creature, then dismissed the thought. Of course he wouldn't. He was too virile. Too sophisticated.

All she had to do was wait.

Meredith set aside her tea cup and stood up with dignity, smoothing the skirts of her soft blue gown. "Have it your way—Mrs. Corbin. I'm sure your husband will have a few things to say about your recalcitrant and unfriendly manner."

Fancy simply looked out the window, her eyes wistful, and said nothing.

Once the front door had slammed behind the indignant Meredith, Fancy let the tears she'd been holding back well up in her eyes.

Miriam refilled her tea cup and extended it with gentle insistance. "You mustn't mind Miss Whittaker. She's just jealous of you, love."

Fancy could well imagine why. "H–Has Jeff been in Spokane a lot?" she dared to ask after taking a steadying gulp of her tea.

"Enough," said Miriam reluctantly.

The word confirmed Fancy's suspicions. "And Miss Whittaker was his mistress," she said. Somehow, Meredith was far more threatening than Jewel Stroble had been.

Miriam didn't offer confirmation, at least not directly. To do that would have been presumptuous and Fancy had already learned that, her familiar manner aside, Mrs. Carrington was very conscious of her proper place. "Nothing that permanent," she answered, eyes averted.

Fancy sighed and wiped away her tears. If she was going to cry every time she met a woman who had been intimate with the man she loved, she'd get nothing done for weeping. "It doesn't matter," she lied firmly.

Miriam's gentle manner said that it did, but her words were more discreet. "My sister sews, Mrs. Corbin, and right well, too. It's true you'll need more clothes and I thought—perhaps—"

Fancy smiled. "Would you send for her? I–I didn't really want to go out in public, looking like this."

"You'd be surprised how nice you look," Miriam responded briskly, "but I understand. I'll send my Walter for Evelyn right now."

Twenty minutes later, Evelyn, who might have been

Miriam's twin, so greatly did she resemble her, arrived burdened with copies of *Godey's Lady's Book* and dozens of squares of sample fabrics.

These were being spread out on the dining room table for Fancy's perusal when Jeff returned, wearing a dapper suit and carrying a number of parcels wrapped in brown paper. Fancy's heart caught at the sight of him; he'd said he wasn't a gentleman, but he surely looked like one. Was she lady enough to hold him?

He kissed her briefly, paying no attention at all to Miriam and Evelyn. "Order one of everything," he said.

Fancy shivered because even the nearness of this man had such a staggering effect on her senses. Always a reticent person, she was shaken by Jeff's ability to turn her into a shameless wanton with only a look, a touch, or a caress.

"I think Mrs. Corbin is a little overwhelmed," observed Miriam respectfully.

That subtle rescue won her a place in Fancy's heart forever. "I wouldn't know what to buy, or how much—"

"See that my wife has everything she could conceivably need," Jeff said to the two older women. Then he kissed Fancy again and disappeared, taking the parcels with him.

Fancy spent a bedazzling, confusing, exhausting afternoon being measured for everything from capes to camisoles. She chose styles from the *Lady's Book,* fabrics from the samples. There were silks and lawns, rich velvets, cottons, and cambrics.

By the time Evelyn bustled out, clutching all her notes and paraphernalia, Fancy was quite undone. Declining Miriam's offer of something to eat, she went upstairs to lie down for a while. Perhaps she could make up for some of the sleep she'd lost the night before.

Entering the master bedroom, she was confronted with the reason for her lack of rest. Jeff was sitting in one of the wicker chairs, his back to Fancy, looking out the window toward the west. He had taken off his suit coat, and one of his booted feet was braced against the windowsill.

Fancy wondered what he was seeing there in the distance, and again felt a tugging ache in her heart. Maybe he was yearning for Banner, or the sea. It wouldn't be unnatural for the former captain of a clippership to dream of sailing again.

Feeling bereft, Fancy was about to back out of the room when he suddenly turned and smiled at her. It was a sad, distant smile. "Stay," he said softly. "Please."

Fancy drew a deep breath and worked up a smile of her own. Crossing to the bed, she sat down and made a great business of undoing her highbutton shoes and then removing them. Because she knew she would have a disgraceful fit of weakness if she didn't occupy herself, she chattered nonstop about all the wonderful things she'd chosen from the fashion book.

Jeff watched her, listening in tolerant silence. She knew she wasn't fooling him, but still she rushed on.

Finally, he extended one hand and said in a low voice, "Fancy, come here."

Fancy knew the dangers of that. "I'm too tired!" she protested.

He laughed. "So am I. I only want to hold you."

She went to him and he drew her down onto his lap,

cradling her head against his strong shoulder. His vest and white linen shirt felt soft under her cheek, and he smelled pleasantly of clean air and sunshine. She began to cry.

Surprisingly, Jeff did not demand to know why. He simply held her, sheltering her in his arms, stroking away the occasional tear with the side of his thumb. Fancy wondered how she would bear the pain of loving him and wailed with the grief of knowing that she always, always would.

His embrace tightened, strong but not crushing, and he propped his chin on the top of her head.

Fancy went on crying—it seemed impossible to stop—and Jeff finally lifted her and carried her to the bed. Gently, he helped her out of her dress and then tucked her under the covers.

She looked up at him and sniffled. "I've mussed your new clothes," she said.

Jeff shrugged and then bent to kiss her forehead. "Rest," he said hoarsely.

"Will you hold me?" she persisted in a small voice. "Please?"

Slowly, he undid the string tie at his throat, the buttons of his vest, his shirt. When he was finally naked, he slid into bed beside Fancy and drew her into his arms. His body was strong and warm and completely undemanding, and Fancy allowed herself to feel safe, to imagine that he would never leave her. With her head propped on his shoulder, she slept.

The room was shadowy when she awoke, and a fire danced on the hearth. She stretched languidly, feeling rested and composed, and then realized that she was alone. She sat upright, her heart in her throat.

"Jeff?"

He laughed and she heard water splash. "Can't a man take a bath in private around here?" he teased.

Fancy was so relieved that he was there that swift tears smarted in her eyes. She dashed them away, drew a deep breath, and bounded out of bed. Rounding the folding screen, she put her hands on her hips and assumed a stern look. "Absolutely not!" she answered.

He grinned a sultry, teasing grin and settled back in the huge marble tub, his hands behind his head in an attitude of total relaxation.

Fancy approached intrepidly, shedding her camisole and drawers as she went. This gentleness, this caring—without passion—was a new element in their relationship. Plunging into the bathtub, she kicked water in Jeff's face and he bellowed with affronted laughter.

They played that night, like happy children, and there was no lovemaking. Or was there? After a spirited water fight and supper in front of the fireplace, after more laughter and quiet talk, Fancy fell asleep in Jeff's arms feeling exalted.

Chapter Thirteen

FANCY STOOD STARING AT THE CLOCK ON THE STUDY WALL, waiting. During the past week, it had often made odd noises, always just before or just after she entered the room, or as she passed in the hallway. The enigma of it was too much for her; she was determined to learn its secret.

She held her breath as the hands moved into position and a strange whirring sound came from the intricately carved timepiece. It looked like a little house, and the weights hanging beneath it resembled pine cones . . .

Fancy's face was now within inches of that of the clock. Suddenly, a tiny door in its upper part creaked open and a little bird leaped out at her, shrilling, "Cuckoo, cuckoo, cuckoo!"

Startled, Fancy jumped back, gasping. "Thundera-tion!" she choked in amazement.

A masculine chortle sounded behind her, and she

whirled, red in the face. Jeff was standing there, a mug of coffee in one hand, a huge cylinder of rolled paper under his arm. Ink-blue amusement sparkled in his eyes.

"Don't you dare laugh at me!" she hissed, smoothing the skirts of her new gingham gown to keep from flailing her hands in wild emphasis.

"I won't," he promised solemnly, but the tremor in his broad shoulders betrayed him.

"I've never seen such a clock!" railed Fancy, embarrassed.

"That's obvious," replied Jeff, more soberly. "You almost jumped out of your bustle."

Fancy reddened again. "What's that?" she demanded, pointing at the paper under his arm.

There was a sort of closed look in Jeff's eyes, and within the space of an instant, too. "Just a design," he answered, turning away, settling at his desk with a dismissive air.

Fancy was having none of that. She hated secrets and there were too many of them in this family—such as whatever it was that had happened between Jeff and his brother Adam. She sidled around to stand behind her husband's chair.

"Don't you have something to do?" he asked, in moderate and somewhat distracted irritation. Jeff clearly didn't intend to unroll that "design" in her presence, and she was annoyed.

"I could take the trolley car downtown," she suggested, knowing full well that Jeff would not permit that. In some ways, her life was restrictive—she was not allowed to go out alone.

"Wrong," said Jeff, a muscle knotting in his jaw. "We've been over that. The fact that we haven't heard from our friend Temple doesn't mean that he isn't around."

Fancy bit her lower lip. Again, her instincts urged her to tell Jeff what she knew. Then Temple could be legally prosecuted for implementing the explosion aboard the *Sea Mistress* and he would undoubtedly go to territorial prison. How could he be a threat if he was jailed?

But she was afraid. If Jeff's anger should turn in her direction—and there was every likelihood that it would —she would lose him.

"Go feed Hershel or something," he said, and Fancy was so insulted that she forgot her dilemma again.

She folded her arms, lifted her chin, and glared off into space, demonstrating her defiance. She would stand there all afternoon if she had to.

But Jeff suddenly swiveled in his creaky chair and, in an instant, she found herself in his lap, half reclining, staring into his amused face with wide eyes. "What—"

He was unbuttoning the front of her brand new dress, maddeningly casual as he went about it.

Fancy stiffened, outraged but filled with contradicting needs, too. "Stop that!" she gasped, squirming now, though to no real avail.

A gold cuff link winked up at her as Jeff slid one hand under her satin camisole and brazenly cupped it around a pulsing breast.

Fancy wriggled. "You insufferable—"

He laughed low in his throat, and the side of his thumb stroked the captured nipple to aching obedience.

"This is the study!" Fancy reminded him in a breathless gasp.

"Broad daylight, too," agreed Jeff, lowering her

camisole so that the breast he had chosen was completely bared. He was turning her, pressing on the small of her back so that her bounty was arched helplessly toward him.

Mischievously, he tongued the nipple into a piercing response.

A shudder of delight went through Fancy, mingled with that familiar rage at her own helplessness. Was there no limit to this man's insolence? "Jeff Corbin—"

He laughed and then took full and greedy suckle.

Fancy's face flamed and because words of protest were suddenly beyond her, she kicked her feet. It was a hopeless rebellion.

When he tired of that one breast, Jeff availed himself of the other. He was leisurely with it, unconcerned, it seemed, that the study door was open and Miriam or Walter might wander in at any second.

Desperation gave Fancy strength. She bounded out of his lap and stood at a distance of a few feet, breathing hard and glaring down into that imperious, aristocratic face.

"Shut and lock that door," he ordered in even tones, and his navy blue eyes darkened with both amusement and desire.

Marveling at herself all the while, Fancy obeyed. She was standing with her back to the door before she realized that her dress was still open and her breasts, moist from their recent tribute, were bared to his gaze.

Damnably handsome in his dove-gray trousers, matching silk vest, and pristine linen shirt, Jeff pushed the chair back from the desk but made no attempt to rise from it. "Come here," he said.

Fancy hesitated. Everything within her urged her

back to him, but there was such a thing as pride, after all. Such a thing as dignity.

"Frances," he reiterated firmly.

She closed her eyes and her breasts, warm under his steady gaze, rose and fell with the quickness of her breathing. Her grasp on defiance was a tenuous one, but it was sweet, adding somehow to the splendor of the inevitable.

When Jeff said her name again in a throaty, insistent whisper, she was lost. Like a sleepwalker, she went to him, resigned to her fate. Glorying in it.

Instead of drawing her back onto his lap, however, he stood her between his chair and the desk. His hands rose to caress her breasts, to pluck gently at their peaks, and a piercing fever was born in the depths of her womanhood, gradually spreading to all parts of her.

Presently, he began guiding her heavy skirts upward; they bunched on the surface of the desk behind her. She gasped and braced herself against its edge as his fingers came boldly to the ties of her drawers. "What are you—doing?" she choked out, full of a sweet and familiar misery.

"I think you know," he replied, and her drawers were going down, smoothly, over her hips and her thighs. Her flesh was cooled by this exposure, but an incomprehensible heat surged beneath.

"Oooh," Fancy groaned, as he maneuvered her backward. "Jeff—"

She was lying across the desk now, completely vulnerable to him, uplifted for his access by her own skirts, now gathered beneath her bottom like a pillow. "Sweet," he said, his breath fanning against the tangle of golden curls. A pulse point hidden within leaped at his approach.

As he took possession, Fancy gave an animal cry, beyond caring who might hear or see, beyond all but the strange, spasmodic passions he had induced. He became greedy and one hand rose to fondle a breast, to ply its nipple. He continued to enjoy her while he attended the other breast in exactly the same way.

Fancy writhed and twisted, whimpering his name, tangling frantic fingers in his hair. When the explosion came, she gave a lusty shout of satisfaction and lay trembling as he led her back to sanity with soothing words and tender strokes of his hands.

"Wretch!" she said, buttoning up her dress with trembling hands.

Jeff laughed and kissed the place he had so thoroughly plundered. "Next time, let me work," he said.

She sidestepped away from the desk and bent to pull up her drawers, which had been hobble-like around her ankles. "Have you no decency?"

He shrugged. "None."

Fancy blushed and straightened her skirts. When she hurried toward the locked door, he was unrolling the paper that had so sparked her curiosity. Despite a lingering wonder, she did not dare stay.

Miriam was just turning away from the front door when Fancy entered the main hallway, flushed with satisfaction and shame. The older woman smiled in a way that made her blush that much harder.

"There's a message for you," Miriam said, her blue eyes twinkling as she extended an envelope.

Somewhat tremulously, Fancy reached out for the missive. On its front, someone had penned, MR. AND MRS. J. CORBIN.

Fancy wouldn't have gone back into the study at that particular moment, for anything. Therefore, she opened the envelope and shook out the folded paper within. It was a telegraph message, sent from Port Hastings.

> WE COULDN'T BE HAPPIER AT THE NEWS OF YOUR MARRIAGE. WILL YOU BE IN WENATCHEE FOR KEITH'S WEDDING? PLEASE CONFIRM OR DENY.
>
> LOVE, MOTHER

Fancy blinked rapidly and then refolded the paper with care. Miriam had gone back to the kitchen and she was alone with some very contradictory thoughts. In all the excitement and uproar, she had entirely forgotten about Keith and Amelie and their upcoming wedding. It would be lovely to actually witness the ceremony.

On the other hand, despite Katherine Corbin's assurance that "we couldn't be happier," Fancy had grave doubts about facing the woman. How would such a person truly view a daughter-in-law who had made her living prying a stubborn rabbit out of a hat? Surely, Mrs. Corbin had had higher hopes for her son.

Fancy cast one look back at the closed doors of the study. Warm with passion only moments before, she now felt chilly and hollow. If only she could be sure of acceptance, the way Adam's Banner had probably been. After all, Banner was a real doctor, with an education. . . .

Drawing a deep breath, Fancy squared her shoulders and went back to the study, something she would have sworn, only seconds previously, that she would not do. "Jeff?"

He looked up from the huge paper spread out on his

desk, frowning with companionable distraction. "Already?" he teased, after a moment's recovery. "Frances, you are insatiable."

Fancy blushed, rooted to the spot, and held out the telegraph message. "This just came," she said.

Jeff's brow furrowed into worried lines and Fancy felt a pang as he came to snatch the paper from her hand. Behind him, the mysterious design rolled back into a cylinder with a rhythmic whisper. Again, Fancy's curiosity was piqued.

She was edging toward the desk when Jeff stopped her cold with a joyful exclamatory sound and a wondering, "Good God, I forgot all about the wedding. Do you want to go?"

Fancy twisted her hands, one within the other, and her smile was a bit shaky. The thought of meeting Jeff's family en masse suffused her with terror, but she could not ask her husband to miss such an event because of her own fears. "Don't you?" she hedged.

Jeff's eyes were distant, filled with pleasant speculation, and Fancy felt oddly shut out. "Yes," he said, after a long time. "Shall I wire back that we'll be there?"

Fancy's throat tightened and tears burned behind her eyes. Still, she smiled. "Yes," she said, with resolution.

Jeff turned away, calling for Walter, and there was a lilt in his voice and in his step. Fancy bit her lower lip, drew a deep breath, and then remembered the huge, rolled paper on the desk. She scurried over and spread it with her hands. When she did, her heart bulged into her throat, filling it so that she could barely breathe.

On the paper was a carefully drawn plan for a clippership. Tears blinded Fancy as she rolled the paper up again and turned away. Nothing mattered now—not the prospect of being presented to Jeff's family and being found wanting, not the ever-present threat of Temple Royce, not the guilt inherent in failing to tell her husband or the authorities who had been responsible for that tragic explosion on the ship.

Jeff was going back to sea. He'd designed a ship for that purpose, and he hadn't even bothered to confide the fact to his own wife!

Little wonder, she reflected, despairing. He probably expected a scene, complete with tears, recriminations, and foot-stomping. Fancy lifted her chin. He'd be surprised, then, because she meant to take the news with unfaltering dignity, even though the very prospect was devastating.

When Jeff returned, apparently having dispatched Walter with an answering telegraph for his mother, Fancy was kneeling on the windowseat, staring sightlessly out at the lush lavender and white lilacs in the garden.

She heard the desk chair squeak as he sat down and she squared her shoulders lest she fall apart.

"I've missed my family," he confided in faraway tones after a long silence. "Spokane is a nice place, but it's too far from the water. Fancy, what if we built a house in Port Hastings?"

What indeed? Port Hastings had a harbor; he could come and go easily from there, leaving Fancy and any children they might manage to have under the watchful eye of his family.

Fancy lifted aching shoulders in a shrug, never turning from the window. "All right," she agreed somewhat brokenly.

Jeff failed to notice her lack of enthusiasm and went on speculating. "Of course, Port Hastings is Temple's home ground—"

For one wild moment, Fancy dared to hope that he would dismiss the idea for that reason. But, of course, Jeff was not the kind of man to make decisions on the basis of fear, and she was not really surprised when he didn't.

"The hell with Temple," he muttered.

Fancy's throat ached with the effort not to cry. "W–What kind of house would we build?" she managed.

"Whatever kind you want," Jeff answered, and it was obvious from his tone that his thoughts were on something else, now—probably the design for his new ship.

"I want one with a widow's walk," she said, turning to look at her husband through blurred and stinging eyes.

He was, as she had expected, bent over the plans. She didn't need to see his face to know how absorbed he was in them. "Fine," he said, and Fancy knew that he had not really heard her.

She crept out of the study, bruised to the core of her spirit. Outside on the brick street fronting the house, a carriage was coming to a stop.

Unable to face a round with Meredith Whittaker or any of the other socialites who had been calling diligently all week, Fancy bunched her skirts in her hands and scrambled up the stairs. She could not take refuge in the master bedroom—Jeff might find her there and then there would be no hiding her devastation.

In desperation, she wrenched open a door at random and hurried inside. The room was shadowy and cool and it offered what Fancy needed most—privacy to assemble her thoughts and her dignity again.

She flung herself down on a neatly made bed, smaller than the one in the room she and Jeff shared, and cried until her supply of tears was exhausted. That took considerable time, given her state of total despondency, and when Fancy finally sat up again, her eyes were puffy and her throat was raw.

She could risk going into the room across the hall now, having recovered some composure. There, she splashed her throbbing face with cold water until she was almost herself again.

The door opened as she was drying her cheeks with a soft towel. "Fancy?"

The gentle concern in Jeff's voice almost undid her again; it was a long moment before she could turn and face him with a smile on her face. A questioning smile that took the place of words she could not quite trust herself to utter.

"Are you all right?" Jeff was frowning, tilting his head in order to look into her eyes.

"I–I just had a headache," Fancy lied. The smile on her face was an aching mockery now, almost impossible to sustain. "Do we have company?"

Jeff grinned, though some of the curiosity lingered in his eyes. "We sure do. Why don't you come and say hello?"

"If—if it's Meredith, I—"

Jeff chuckled. "It isn't Meredith," he assured her, extending one hand.

Because she so often did this man's bidding without thinking first, Fancy accepted the hand. Having done that, there was no going back, for Jeff pulled her good-naturedly out of the bedroom, into the hallway, and down the stairs.

Phineas Pryor was sitting in the study, looking wan but essentially himself. He rose from his chair facing Jeff's desk and executed a courtly half bow, his eyes twinkling. "Mrs. Corbin," he said in cordial greeting.

Fancy gave a cry of delight—there was a measure of relief there, too—and flung herself unceremoniously into her friend's arms. "You're better!" she exalted.

He hugged her and then shrugged. "My sister is an angel of mercy," he said. "These few days of her tender care have restored me."

Fancy recalled her abrupt departure in the runaway balloon and felt guilty. "We didn't mean to leave you that way—"

Phineas laughed and, after Fancy had taken a chair near his, sat down again. "Didn't appear you had all that much choice. When I heard what happened, I figured old Phineas would just have to look after himself and I got up and drove my wagon here." He paused, indicating a stack of items beside his chair. "Brought your things, too—your signboard, your props, all that."

Fancy thanked him; she had worried over her belongings, especially the gifts Jeff had given her.

Jeff was perched on the edge of his desk, his arms folded. "We had to leave the balloon with a friend of mine," he said.

Phineas chuckled. "Ran out of hydrogen, did you? I reckoned that would happen. I've been worrying that that Royce fellow and his men might have caught up to you."

Jeff's jawline tightened. "I'll deal with Temple," he said, more to himself than Phineas or Fancy.

Fancy felt a new dread, unrelated to Jeff's impending return to sea. "You don't mean you'd actually seek him out, do you? He hasn't bothered us—why not let sleeping dogs lie?"

"Sleeping rattlesnakes are another matter," replied Jeff, and that distance was in his eyes again.

Fancy was nearly frantic, though she held her emotions in careful check. Thunderation, it was agony to think of Jeff sailing away and not returning for weeks or even months, but the idea of his facing so vicious an enemy as Temple was infinitely worse. Why, Temple would kill him, and do it gladly! "Jeff, you can't!"

The same man who had loved her with such tender ferocity a short time before was now harsh and cold. "Enough," he said, silencing her with a look.

Phineas shifted uncomfortably in his chair and then thrust the conversation off in another direction with a cheerful, "You going back for the balloon, Jeff?"

Jeff replied in the affirmative and Fancy heard little of the ensuing conversation. Too many disturbing pictures were whirling through her mind.

At Jeff's invitation, Phineas stayed to dinner, and Fancy was hardly more attentive then. She listened when Jeff told Phineas that they were traveling to Wenatchee to attend a wedding at the end of the week, then settled back into her own uncomfortable reflections.

After Phineas had taken his leave, promising to return the day after with the spare tanks of hydrogen gas stored at his sister's house, Jeff turned, grinning, from the front door.

"Phineas is living, as he put it, 'high on the hog,'" he remarked.

Fancy was distracted. "Wh–What?"

"Didn't you see that carriage? He rented it just to come calling."

"Oh," Fancy said witlessly. How could she be expected to think of Phineas's hired carriage with so many other things on her mind?

The next morning, bright and early, the hired carriage appeared again. This time, however, the passenger was not Phineas but a slender young lady with copper-brown hair and great, chocolate-colored eyes. Her name, she informed Fancy, was Bethany Pryor and she was Phineas's sister.

Fancy was taken aback; she had expected an entirely different sort of woman—a fusty old maid, for instance. But Bethany was hardly that.

"I've brought the hydrogen," she said matter-of-factly as she stood on the porch, indicating the carriage with a gesture of one hand. "Phineas wasn't feeling very well today."

Fancy forced herself to stop staring and absorb what the young woman had said. "Is he very ill?" she asked.

Bethany stated emphatically that he was not. Then, as Fancy escorted her into the parlor, she burst out laughing. "You're perplexed, aren't you, Mrs. Corbin?"

Fancy gulped. "Well—"

"Phineas is old enough to be my father," chimed Bethany, "but he really is my brother. Honest."

"I believe you," Fancy said quickly.

Bethany laughed again. "Good," she said, sitting

down on the parlor settee with a heartfelt sigh. "I do hope you'll come and visit us, even though Phineas is not at death's door, Mrs. Corbin."

Fancy sat down in a chair nearby, liking Phineas's young sister and wishing that she would not have to go away so soon. After attending the wedding in Wenatchee, she and Jeff were going on to Port Hastings to see to the building of their house. Probably, they would not be back in Spokane for a very long time, if ever. "Please, call me Fancy," she said quickly, halting her wandering thoughts before they could progress to the two matters that bothered her most—Jeff's upcoming confrontation with Temple Royce and the construction of the clippership that would take him away.

"And you're to call me Beth," responded the buoyant visitor, fussing with her gloves. "I'm afraid I can't stay very long—as soon as the driver unloads those infernal hydrogen tanks, I've got to be off on my errands."

Fancy wished that she had errands—Jeff had been away from the house since breakfast and she was bored. Alas, Miriam's sister, Evelyn, was due at any moment to fit more of Fancy's new clothes. With the trip to Wenatchee and then the coast only days away, the sewing, measuring and pinning had increased to a frenetic pace.

"I've told Phineas that I could do his patent medicine route," Bethany went merrily on. "I know the business as well as he does and he does need to rest. I do get weary of teaching. Why, I could drive his wagon and sell the merchandise as well as any man, and I could fly that infernal balloon, too."

Fancy bit back a giggle. "I'm sure you could," she said.

"I could indeed," insisted Bethany. And then she stood up before Miriam could get near with the tray of cookies and the pot of tea she had probably hurried to prepare. "Well, I'll be going now. I hope we meet again sometime."

Fancy felt bereft at the thought of her going. "Couldn't you just stay for a cup of tea?"

"Oh, no," trilled Bethany pleasantly and then she was gone. The hydrogen tanks were stacked on the porch in neat array.

"Well!" huffed Miriam, looking put out. "This is the finest orange pekoe, too!"

Fancy chuckled, but somewhat sadly. It was going to be hard to leave Miriam, as it had been hard to leave Isabella and Keith's housekeeper, Alva Thompkins. "Don't be offended, Miriam," she said. "I don't think Bethany stays in any one place for very long."

"Reminds me of a mouse in a mitten," complained Miriam, trudging off toward the kitchen again.

Alone—Fancy was in a melancholy mood and it seemed to her then that she was always alone—she went back into the parlor to take a solitary cup of tea. When that was gone she consumed two large sugar cookies out of sheer self-pity.

"Many more of those," reprimanded Evelyn, staggering under a load of yard goods, "and I'll have to let out the seams in all these new dresses!"

Startled and properly chagrined, Fancy put her third cookie back on the plate. Evelyn had brought two assistants along and soon the mistress of the house was standing on a hassock while they all pulled at her skirts, tugged at her bodice, and stabbed her with pins. By the time it was over, which wasn't until midafternoon, Fancy was so undone that she fled upstairs, put on her old dress with the stars stitched to it, and went outside in search of Hershel.

She found him in a covered hutch in the back yard, fatter than ever and very content in his prosperity. It was obvious that Walter, Miriam's husband, had devoted much time to his comfort.

Needing the reassurance of something familiar, in much the way she had needed to wear the starred dress again, Fancy cautiously opened the hutch door and reached inside to pet Hershel. "We're getting spoiled, you and I," she said. "If we ever have to stand on our own two feet again—pardon me, I know you have *four* feet to stand on—we'll be in trouble."

Hershel's pink nose twitched and he looked largely unconcerned.

"Furthermore," Fancy went on, knowing that she was prattling but needing that, too, "you're entirely too fat for any top hat I've ever seen."

At that moment, another carriage came to a rattling halt on the brick street and Fancy turned her head to see who was calling now. She prayed that it wasn't Meredith Whittaker.

Hershel took advantage of her distraction and leaped out of the hutch, heading straight for Miriam's cherished vegetable garden. Fancy, after a second of recovery, gave immediate chase.

She caught Hershel in a row of new parsnips, but only after tripping on the hem of her dress and landing full out in the loamy dirt.

Looking upward in dread, she saw Jeff standing before her, with a stunningly handsome dark-haired man. "Frances," he said, his eyes dancing with mirth,

"I would like you to meet my brother Adam. Adam, my wife."

Flushing, Fancy clambered to her feet and offered a hand in greeting—a very muddy hand.

It was the measure of Dr. Adam Corbin that he accepted that hand without a moment's hesitation.

Chapter Fourteen

JEFF STOOD AT THE SIDEBOARD, POURING BRANDY INTO two snifters. It was clear to Adam that the barrier between his brother and himself remained, and yet there were changes in the man, too. Subtle variances that could probably be ascribed to that lovely little nymph in the star-spangled dress.

Jeff's broad shoulders stiffened beneath his shirt, and it was a long moment before he finally turned around, drinks in hand. "What are you doing here, Adam?" he asked evenly, quietly.

Adam did his best to look nonchalant. He shrugged and sat back in the chair facing Jeff's desk, lifting one booted foot to rest on the opposite knee. "Are things so bad between us that I need an excuse?" he countered.

Jeff handed Adam a glass and took the chair behind the desk, setting his own brandy aside. "I didn't think anything could get you away from Banner and that hospital of yours," he said.

Adam sighed. He'd been working harder than ever lately and the train trip had been a long one. "We're going to talk, Jeff, and reasonably. About Papa and why I didn't tell you he was alive until—"

"Until it was too late," Jeff broke in, his eyes dark with pain.

The elder brother ignored the interruption. "First, I want to tell you that I think your wife is beautiful."

A grin tugged at the corner of Jeff's mouth. "Mud and all?" he drawled.

"Mud, stars, and all," confirmed Adam, grinning. "I've always had confidence in your good taste, brother, but she exceeds all expectation."

"She does, doesn't she?" mused Jeff in tender tones that betrayed much. "The odd thing is that Fancy feels inferior to almost everybody. I think the prospect of meeting Mama and the rest of you has her terrified."

"We'll try not to be too overwhelming," Adam promised, with a quick grin. "Though I can't speak for O'Brien."

Jeff shook his head. "Still referring to your wife as 'O'Brien,' are you? My God, you're romantic."

Adam shrugged. "She answers to it," he said.

There was a softening in Jeff's face; he sat back in his chair and looked thoughtful. "How is Banner, Adam?"

"Bone mean and breathtakingly beautiful, as always." Adam paused; despite Jeff's obvious feelings for his own wife, he couldn't be sure how he would take the news. "She's expecting again," he said, finally.

To Adam's relief, Jeff grinned. "Congratulations. Do you think you'll get another set of twins?"

Adam rolled his eyes, though the thought of Danny

and Bridget, his children, filled him with pride and a need to go home. "God forbid," he said.

Jeff laughed and Adam felt the old closeness to his brother, just briefly. He prayed they could regain it again permanently.

Humiliated almost beyond bearing, Fancy thrust Hershel back into his hutch and firmly locked the door. Trust that miserable rabbit to get her into trouble and just when she would have liked to have made a good impression, too.

Of course, that had probably been a foolish hope in the first place—she had never done anything that could be expected to impress someone like Dr. Adam Corbin. No doubt he would go home to Port Hastings and tell the family that Jeff had married a mud-streaked hoyden.

Because she knew Miriam would be working in the kitchen, Fancy risked going in the front door. The low hum of masculine voices told her that Jeff and Adam were shut away in the study.

Not for a moment did she consider intruding. Determined not to cry, she marched up the stairs and into the master bedroom. What she saw in the bureau mirror nearly dissolved her, however—her hair was falling down, her cheeks were smudged with wet garden dirt, and there was a leaf clinging to the peak of her right breast.

With a sad sort of self-mockery, Fancy stood up very straight and said, "May I present, ladies and gentlemen of the upper classes, Mrs. Jeffrey Corbin?"

A soblike laugh caught in her throat and she turned away before her face could crumble. Resolutely, she prepared for a much-needed bath.

The combination of hot water and scented bath salts was a soothing one, and by the time Fancy had soaked awhile, and then scrubbed, she felt better. She even began to see the humor in chasing a rabbit through the vegetable garden and falling flat on her face in the process.

She got out of the bathtub, opened the drain, and dried herself quickly. Then, dressed only in satiny drawers and a matching lace-trimmed camisole of soft ivory, she chose a fresh dress with great care. Perhaps, if she looked especially nice and behaved with some degree of propriety, she might be able to redeem herself.

An hour later, when Fancy went downstairs again, it appeared that she had done just that. Adam and Jeff were out of the study now, and they both took in her carefully coiffed hair and whispering lavender silk dress with admiring eyes.

"Hello, again," Adam greeted her, with a brotherly smile that eased a great many of Fancy's apprehensions. Then, before Jeff could make a move, he offered a gentlemanly arm. "I believe dinner is about to be served. May I?"

Fancy did not even look at Jeff—she returned Adam's smile and took his arm. "Thank you," she said.

Miriam had set the table and, after everyone had been seated, she began serving. She was obviously pleased that Adam was there, and she worked with a lilt in her step and a twinkle in her eyes.

Jeff watched her with wounded amusement and then commented, "I do believe Miriam likes you better than me, Adam."

"Doesn't everybody?" grinned Adam, lifting his wineglass.

There was an uncomfortable moment in which, Fancy was sure, everyone at the table was thinking of one Banner O'Brien, who had indeed cared more for Adam than Jeff.

"I understand that your mother is active in the Woman Suffrage movement," Fancy put in quickly, hoping to change the subject.

A flicker in Adam's deep blue eyes, eyes just the color of Jeff's, thanked her for the diversion. "Active is not the word. Mama will probably recruit you to the cause."

"The hell," growled Jeff with surprising feeling. "No wife of mine is going to go traipsing around making speeches and passing out fliers—"

Adam laughed. "Your innocence is heart-wrenching," he told his brother.

Fancy was nettled. "If I wanted to make speeches and pass out fliers, Jeff Corbin, I would."

Adam gave his brother another affectionately mocking glance and again lifted his wineglass. "Don't try to fight it, Jeff," he said. "Hell hath no fury like a woman oriented toward politics."

Jeff gave Fancy one bone-slicing look and turned his full attention to his brother. From then on, the conversation concerned the upcoming wedding in Wenatchee, their sister Melissa's escapades at college, and whether or not Grover Cleveland belonged in the White House.

Temple Royce settled back in the bathtub, a cheroot clamped between his teeth, an outdated newspaper in his hands. Christ, he was tired, and every muscle in his body ached, and if he didn't have lice he'd be lucky.

Beyond the hotel window, which was open to the breezy June night, he could hear the clang of trolley car bells, the nickering of horses, and the voices of street urchins, prostitutes, and drunks. Shutting Spokane out of his mind, he settled down to read.

The territorial legislature was harassing the federal government about statehood and Mrs. Katherine Corbin was harassing them, in turn. Wall Street was predicting another panic and three days ago a man had gone crazy up at Colville and murdered his whole family. Temple was about to close the newspaper and fling it aside when the name *Corbin* caught his eye again. He was used to seeing Katherine's name, but this was different.

It seemed, according to the brief item on the society page, that the Reverend Keith Corbin meant to marry one Miss Amelie Rogers on the forthcoming Saturday at the First Methodist Church, Wenatchee. Temple grinned and relit his cheroot, which had gone out.

Saturday. Wenatchee. And, like as not, the whole troublesome Corbin family would gather in one handy place. Temple suddenly felt buoyant; the grinding fatigue of tracking Jeff from hell to breakfast was gone.

There was a solid rap at the hotel door. "Boss? You in there, Mr. Royce?"

"Come in," said Temple, drawing deeply on his cheroot and smiling up at the cracked plaster ceiling.

The rest of Temple's men had long since gone back to Port Hastings, grousing that they were tired of sleeping on the ground and chasing a man who seemed to have all the substance of a ghost, but Rothstein had always been loyal. He'd have gone into the devil's privy if Temple ordered it.

"I been watching Corbin's house," the massive man said with gruff discouragement.

Temple was still relaxed, though there was a quickening within him. "And?" he prodded idly.

"That crazy doctor is there. Now we ain't just got Jeff to deal with, we got his brother, too."

Temple reached for a nearby towel with a wrenching, angry motion of his left hand. There were reasons, and sound ones, why he couldn't risk a confrontation with Adam Corbin. "Damn it all to hell," he muttered.

But then, as he stood up and dried himself and reached for his clothes, Temple remembered the convenient wedding and calmed down again. There was no need to fret about the Corbins, and no need to stay in Spokane.

"We'll get some dinner and maybe some women," he told a surprised Rothstein. "And then we'll catch a westbound train."

"You givin' up?" Rothstein muttered, slack-jawed and yet a little hopeful, too.

Temple put on his last clean shirt and reached for a string tie. "You know better than that," he said, smiling into the mirror.

It was too warm for a fire that night and the windows were open, curtains wafting in the lilac-scented breeze. Fancy cuddled closer to Jeff in their bed, taking comfort from the warm strength of him.

Their lovemaking had been especially intense and, in the glowing aftermath, most of Fancy's doubts and fears were at bay.

"Your brother is very handsome," she said, her head resting on Jeff's bare shoulder.

"Yeah," came the somewhat grudging response.

Surprised, Fancy lifted her head to look into Jeff's

face. "You're still angry with him, aren't you?" she asked, saddened.

Jeff sighed heavily. "No," he said, at length. "I tried to be, but I couldn't. Adam did what he had to do—I understand that."

Fancy knew that he was not talking about the conflict over Banner O'Brien, but the matter he had mentioned once and then refused to discuss further. Something about their father. Resigned to the fact that she would probably never know anything more about that particular secret, she again rested her head on that sturdy shoulder.

Jeff's fingers tangled themselves gently in her hair. "Adam does have something that I want," he remarked presently.

Fancy was achingly alert. In the past few days, she had allowed herself to hope that Jeff's feelings for Banner had settled into brotherly admiration. Was he about to shatter that fragile confidence? "What?" she dared to ask.

"Children," replied Jeff.

Fancy's beleaguered spirit soared. Her time of the month was overdue by several days and she cherished a tender hope that Jeff's child might already be growing within her. It was her one security, knowing that, if Jeff did go away to sea or even die at the hands of Temple Royce, she would yet have a living part of him. For always.

But the time for telling had not come; she couldn't mention her suspicions until she was certain. "You—you want children?"

Jeff laughed a low, rumbling, cozy laugh. "Dozens."

"Dozens!" blustered Fancy.

"Well, five or six, at least."

Now it was Fancy who laughed. "That's better."

Jeff rolled over so that he was looking down into Fancy's face. The expression in his indigo eyes was tender, questioning. "Do you like babies, Mrs. Corbin? I just realized that I've never asked you—"

"There are a great many things you have never asked me, Mr. Corbin. But yes, I do like babies. I love babies."

He traced the outline of her jaw with an index finger, pushed a gossamer tendril of hair away from her face. "Let's start one, then," he said in a gruff whisper.

"It isn't as though we haven't tried," Fancy reminded him gently.

He kissed her, his lips searching and warm. "One can't be too diligent about these things," he breathed. And then his head was moving downward and his mouth was claiming the peak of Fancy's left breast.

"One certainly can't," gasped Fancy in fevered agreement, arching her back, glorying in the moist, heated demand of his mouth.

Whereas their earlier lovemaking had been languorous, building gradually to an almost intolerable pitch, this joining was quick and fierce. Their two bodies buckled in magnificent unison, met violently in the force of a simultaneous release.

Jeff gave a growling cry, while Fancy sobbed her husband's name and clutched at him with frantic hands, all the while silently cursing clipperships, the sea, and the man who would separate them forever if he could.

As the time to leave Spokane drew nearer, Fancy found Meredith less of a trial. She had been foolish to be jealous of this woman because it was clear that, if Jeff had ever wanted Meredith Whittaker, he could have easily taken her.

But he hadn't.

Meredith frowned at the billows of pretty gowns and hand-embroidered underthings spilling from this trunk and that. "That Evelyn must work like a demon," she said without admiration.

Fancy smiled, folding a pale green shirtwaist and laying it carefully in the largest of the trunks. The parlor looked, she thought with amusement, like the inside of a pillaged baggage car. "Evelyn has several helpers," she explained.

Meredith fingered a soft gray skirt trimmed with jet beads and now her frown was thoughtful. "Lovely work," she said, grudgingly.

"Isn't it?" chimed Fancy, going on with her folding and arranging. She didn't have to do it—Miriam would have—but it was a joy to touch such lovely garments and imagine herself wearing them. "You might want to have Evelyn make some things for you."

"Not likely," bristled Meredith, but then she summoned up a rather shaky smile. "Miriam told me that Adam is here. Is he?"

Fancy shrugged. "Yes. Why would Miriam lie?"

Meredith didn't bother to answer, though her smile faltered. "It's a shame, the way the Corbin men are marrying off all at once."

"Must be an epidemic," quipped Fancy, struggling against a spate of unmatronly giggles.

Meredith was scowling, clearly at the end of her patience. "I can't understand what Jeff sees in you!" she blurted out. "Or what Adam sees in that Banner person, for that matter!"

Fancy was stunned by the outburst and, before she could think of anything fitting to say, Adam appeared.

"Did I hear my wife's name fall from your lovely lips, Meredith?" he asked, and though he was smiling, there was a glittering chill in his eyes.

Meredith stiffened. Color surged up over her snow-white bosom to pulse in her face. "Adam—hello—"

"Hello," he returned, with a sort of exaggerated, biting patience.

Without another word, Meredith grabbed for her beaded handbag and her stylish parasol and fled.

Adam folded his arms and grinned again. "What did I say?" he asked.

Fancy smiled and shook her head. "I'm not sure. Whatever it was, our Meredith understood."

"I hope so." Adam replied, perching on the arm of an overstuffed chair and folding his arms. He was wearing a dark suit despite the warmth of the day, and somehow he managed to look perfectly cool. For a time, there was a companionable silence during which Fancy went on with her packing and repacking, her fussing and smoothing.

Adam broke the peace with a directness Fancy had already guessed was typical of him. "Meredith said she didn't know what Jeff sees in you. Do you know, Fancy?"

Suddenly, Fancy's throat was twisted and tight and her heart was beating too fast. "I don't think I do," she answered honestly when she could get the words out.

"He isn't good enough for you, you know. Just the way I'm not good enough for Banner."

Even if she'd had a week to think Fancy wouldn't have known how to respond to that remark. So naturally she remained silent.

Adam smiled. "I knew you were right for my brother the minute you dived into the parsnips to catch that rabbit," he said.

Fancy flushed at the reminder. "Right for him?" she whispered, truly confused but hopeful, too.

"My brothers and I are hard to live with, Fancy. We're given to towering rages and grand passions and we tend to be attracted to women who are—well—unconventional."

Fancy was even more confused than she had been before. In her mind, Amelie Rogers, Keith's intended, represented the perfect Corbin wife. And she certainly couldn't be described as "unconventional." "Isn't Banner—"

Adam chuckled. "Conventional?"

"Well—yes. I was sure that she would be."

"Were you? Well, you've got a surprise coming, then. O'Brien is a spitfire."

Fancy put one hand to her forehead and sat down. "Now that I think about it, a woman doctor would have to be spirited," she reflected. And then she looked up into Adam's face with wide and vulnerable eyes. "I'm not very spirited, you know," she confessed as an afterthought.

Adam arched one raven black eyebrow. "Aren't you?" he countered with gentle disbelief. "Jeff tells me that you've been on your own for several years, that you've traveled all over the territory performing. Do you really think that's what ordinary women do, Fancy?"

Fancy felt an intangible light warming her mind, reaching into the shadowy parts of her spirit. "I suppose not," she said.

Adam shrugged as though to say that his point was made and quietly left the room.

Fancy sat for a long time, alone in that sunny, spacious parlor, smiling to herself.

The train chortled into Colterville and came to a noisy stop, whistle shrilling, smokestack puffing. Fancy was reflecting on the changes in her life since she'd been here last and jumped in surprise when Jeff elbowed her gently in the ribs.

"I'll get the balloon and put it on the next train," he said. "I want you to go on to Wenatchee with Adam—I'll meet you there tomorrow."

Adam cleared his throat and looked out the grimy train window, pretending an interest in quiet, uninspiring Colterville.

"I'm staying with you!" flared Fancy.

"You'll be safer with Adam," replied Jeff, standing up in the aisle now. "Will you just do what I tell you, for once?"

"No!" Out of the corner of her eye, Fancy could see Adam's broad shoulders moving in silent laughter.

With patronizing patience, Jeff bent to kiss her briefly on the mouth. "Frances, Frances, you do try my forbearance," he said. And then he turned and walked away.

Fancy looked at Adam in silent question and he gestured for her to follow Jeff. "I'll make sure your rabbit gets off the train," he promised, his eyes dancing.

Impulsively, Fancy stretched to kiss his forehead. "My trunks? You'll get those, too?"

He nodded. "Hurry, Fancy."

Soaring on a swell of happiness and rebellion, Fancy leaped out of her seat and rushed down the aisle. Jeff was already a good distance up the road, so long were his strides, and he had almost reached the livery stable by the time Fancy caught up with him.

He whirled and glared at her, amazed at her audacity. "What the—you little—"

Fancy laughed and the train whistle shrieked, drowning out whatever else her husband had meant to say. Just as Jeff caught her elbow in a furious grip and started propelling her back, the train pulled out, Adam waving expansively from one window.

Swearing—he clearly hated to be defied so flagrantly—Jeff wrenched Fancy off in the other direction again. Reaching the livery stable, he literally flung her down onto a bale of souring hay out front.

"Sit there!" he ordered. "Right there, God damn it! And so help me, Frances, if you move—"

"I won't," promised Fancy, in sunny, docile tones. But already the spiky hay was poking through her skirts in a very uncomfortable fashion.

Jeff waggled one index finger in her face. "If you do, I swear I'll beat you."

It was an empty threat and they both knew it, but Fancy wasn't about to push. She had managed to stay here, with him, and that was all she cared about for the moment. "I promise I'll behave," she said sweetly.

"It's a sin to lie," snapped Jeff, and then he turned and marched angrily into the livery stable.

When he came out again, having rented a sizable wagon and a team of two sorrel horses, Fancy was still sitting obediently on that bale of hay, the picture of wifely submission. Except, maybe, for the violet sparkle in her eyes.

"Could I stand up now?" she asked, batting her thick lashes.

The proprietor of the livery stable looked at her in stark admiration. "Now there's the kind of wife a man needs."

Jeff reached out, his mouth losing an obvious battle with a smile, and wrenched Fancy to her feet. "Like he needs the black plague and high taxes," he muttered.

Fancy was enjoying the game. "Have I displeased you somehow, darling?" she simpered, trying to look remorseful. "Oh, if I've been naughty—why, I just couldn't live with that!"

The stable manager took out his handkerchief and wiped his eyes, moved to deep emotion by such a display of old-fashioned womanhood. "Glory be," he said in wonder.

Jeff fairly flung Fancy up into the wagon seat. "Bullshit," he muttered.

The drive to Eustis Ponder's farm was a long one, and it was late afternoon when they arrived. Isabella scurried outside to greet them, her face alight, drying her work-roughened hands on her apron. Fancy leaped down and hugged the woman with unrestrained joy.

"Land, I've missed you, Fancy!" Isabella cried, returning the hug with equal exuberance. "Can you stay long?"

"Overnight," said Jeff, busy with the horses. And when Eustis hurried in from the fields only moments later, the men greeted each other with almost as much enthusiasm as the women had.

Isabella had obviously hoped for a longer visit, but she was a woman conditioned to making do with what was offered and she ushered Fancy into the house for pie, coffee, and gossip.

"You look a mite happier than when last I saw you," Isabella remarked when they were settled at the table.

Fancy was trying to enjoy each moment and not let her mind stray ahead to days when she might be alone again. "I am."

"The way you love that man shines out all over you," Isabella chirped. "Won't be long till there's a baby to bind you even closer."

"I hope you're right," she said softly.

Isabella glowed, having caught some nuance from Fancy's words and come to a conclusion of her own. "Mercy me, you're late for the monthly, aren't you?"

Fancy nodded. "I haven't said anything to Jeff, though," she confided. "I want to be absolutely sure first, and it's too soon for that."

Isabella's strong, calloused hand came across the table to squeeze Fancy's. "You make sure to send me a letter the day you find out," she ordered.

Fancy promised that she would.

Jeff's hand was cupped around Fancy's breast, warm and insistent. The spare room was so dark that she could only make out the wheat-gold glint of his hair, the shadowy slope of his bare shoulder.

"Stop that!" she hissed.

"Why?" came the reasonably put response.

"Because I don't want Eustis and Isabella to hear, that's why!"

A long, chortling, and all-too-convenient snore came through the thin wall.

Jeff laughed. "Eustis," he said, "is a true friend."

Fancy was blushing so hard that it hurt. "Men!" she spat out.

The hand was stroking her breast, tracing the nipple,

making it ache. "Now where is that sweet, obedient, cloyingly compliant little chit that made a fool out of me at the livery stable today?"

Fancy squeezed her eyes shut, determined to ignore the sweet havoc he was wreaking upon her breast, to sleep. "I wouldn't know," she said.

Jeff rolled easily out of bed with a long-suffering sigh, pulling Fancy after him. Just as easily, he pulled her nightgown up over her head, flung it aside, and then kissed her, his tongue plundering her mouth until she was weak. To repay him, she knelt, and in kneeling, she came into power.

Jeff trembled, uttered a muffled groan and surrendered to the ruthless pagan who gave him no other choice.

Chapter Fifteen

FANCY LEFT THE PRIVATE COMPARTMENT WITH AS MUCH dignity as possible, her head high. The train seemed to be careening down the tracks toward certain destruction and she had to grip the occasional seat back to keep from falling as she made her way along the aisle to her place.

Jeff, already resettled in his own seat, looked up at her with a salacious grin and then pretended to concentrate on the newspaper he had bought in Colterville.

Fancy glared at her husband in silent defiance and sat down opposite him. Beneath her stylish new traveling dress and her hand-embroidered camisole, the thoroughly tongued and suckled peaks of her breasts chafed.

"I warned you," Jeff said in an amused whisper, crackling his newspaper once for emphasis.

Fancy stiffened, folded her arms across her breasts, and looked out the train window. They were traveling along the broad and angry Columbia River now, drawing nearer to Wenatchee with every passing second. "I didn't think you were serious!" she hissed.

"You liked it," said Jeff.

Fancy suppressed an untoward urge to plunge the sole of one shoe through that cursed newspaper of his. There was no denying that she'd enjoyed their brief and scandalous encounter in the compartment, but her pride was nettled, all the same.

She colored, remembering what had gone on in that tiny room. Jeff had all but dragged her back there and, once the door was closed, he'd calmly unbuttoned her dress, lowered her camisole, and taken his pleasure at her bare breasts. This with passengers and the occasional conductor walking by in the narrow passageway outside!

When he had satisfied himself at her nipples, Jeff had had the gall to divest her of her drawers and lift her onto the upper berth, so that she sat facing him, without hope of escape. He had then nuzzled his way into the moistness and warmth of her and brought her to a savage, gasping release with a calm greed that infuriated her even now.

Lowering his newspaper, Jeff smiled at her. It was as though he had been looking into her mind, marking the passage of her thoughts and the direction they took. "That was revenge for last night, among other things," he said.

"Beast," muttered Fancy, albeit half-heartedly. The train was thundering its way over an impossibly high trestle that seemed most unsteady to her. One look down into the swirling currents and eddies of that dangerous river sent her bounding across to sit beside Jeff.

There was a look of tender tolerance in the ink-blue eyes that swung to her pinkened face. "The train isn't going to fall into the river, Frances," he said moderately.

"Fancy," she corrected doggedly, clasping her hands together in her lap. Her skirts, freshly pressed that morning at Isabella's, were now crumpled and somewhat dusty. Would anyone be able to guess, from her appearance, that she had just been ravished in a train compartment?

"Your thoughts might as well be written on your forehead," Jeff observed, in a low tone that stirred that strange, wanton part of her to life again.

"Oh?" she said, trying to look nonchalant.

He laughed and shook his head and went back to his newspaper.

It was a relief to Fancy when the train jolted and shrilled to a stop at Wenatchee, for more reasons than one. The nearness of Jeff, the intangible power of his body over hers, had caused her a delicious sort of misery. More than once she'd considered taking his hand and leading him back to that compartment.

There were angry clouds in the summer sky, but the Corbin family was waiting at the ramshackle train station anyway, and Fancy's first sight of them was alarming. There seemed to be so many of them.

"Courage," teased Jeff, ushering her toward the group, his grasp firm but unhurting on her elbow.

A beautiful, fair-haired woman with delicate features and eyes as blue as Jeff's hurried forward immediately.

"Is this our Fancy?" she demanded gleefully, casting only one glance at her towering son.

Jeff chuckled. "Yes, Mama, this is Fancy."

Katherine Corbin flung her arms around her daughter-in-law and hugged her fiercely. "Welcome, welcome!" she cried. And then, still holding Fancy by the shoulders, she turned her head to look back at the others. "Look—isn't she wonderful?"

Fancy swallowed, disconcerted. She had not expected such a warm greeting from a woman who had every reason to think her unsuited.

At that moment, the most beautiful woman Fancy had ever seen stepped forward, green eyes sparkling, cinnamon hair done up in a loose and appealing knot at the top of her head. "Wonderful is hardly the word, Mama," she smiled.

"Fancy, this is Banner," Jeff said quietly, and with a gentle sort of pride that stung his wife.

"H–Hello, Dr. Corbin," Fancy managed to say.

"Dr. Corbin!" scolded the vision. "We're sisters now, Frances. Won't you call me Banner?"

Fancy felt rumpled and road-weary. Her hair was coming down from its pins, thanks to Jeff Corbin's lust, and her pretty dress was probably a mass of wrinkles. Her throat worked, but no response was forthcoming.

"Back off and let her breathe, O'Brien," ordered a familiar masculine voice from somewhere in the blur.

The emerald-green eyes snapped with annoyance, but Banner subsided enough to present a young girl with dark hair and eyes of the clearest crystal blue. "This is Melissa," she said.

Melissa's smile was eager and bright with mischievous delight. "Hello," she said without the slightest shyness. And then her gaze swung to Jeff's face, impish. "I don't know how a great lumbering sea dog like you ever managed to win such a bride," she informed her brother.

Jeff laughed, locked his arms about Melissa's waist, and swung her unceremoniously around in a circle that forced everyone else, including Fancy, to step out of range. "I've missed you, brat," he said.

Melissa hugged his neck and, when he set her down again, there were happy tears in her eyes.

The whole scene was a colorful mist to Fancy, and she was grateful when Keith suddenly appeared before her, smiling his gentle smile. "Aren't you glad you already know Amelie and me?" he teased, kissing her forehead. "Welcome to the family, Fancy."

Fancy hugged him, her heart in her throat, and then smiled at Amelie, who looked slightly overwhelmed herself.

"I'm afraid your rabbit got away," announced Melissa, facing Fancy squarely. Her serious expression melted into a delighted grin. "Don't worry, though—he's in the house somewhere. Poor Alva is hysterical!"

"Are we going to stand around here in a mob or what?" Adam demanded with gruff impatience.

Everyone laughed, including Fancy, and then they were off toward a line of three buckboards.

"We have our own wagon train," said Banner, falling into step beside Fancy.

Fancy felt more secure now; she had half expected to be met with horrified disbelief, but now that she had been greeted with warmth instead she was almost dizzy with relief. "Did you bring your babies?" she asked Adam's wife.

Banner shook her head. "They're at home with

Maggie, our housekeeper," she said, and there was a brief sadness in the depths of her clover-green eyes.

A few clamorous and confused minutes later, they were all seated in the seats of the wagons, Katherine, Keith, and Amelie riding in the first, Adam and Banner in the second, Jeff, Fancy, and Melissa in the third. The balloon was being sent on to Port Hastings aboard the train.

Melissa talked incessantly all through the short trip back to Keith's big stone house. Fancy listened with half an ear, already feeling deep affection for Jeff's young sister. Mostly, though, she was remembering the day she had come to this place with Mr. Shibble's troupe. She'd thought of that experience as a cruel ending at the time; instead it had turned out to be a beginning.

There were pink tea roses growing up the sides of the gazebo where she and Hershel had performed; she marveled that she hadn't noticed that before.

"I hope you aren't angry about the rabbit," Melissa said, penetrating Fancy's thoughts at last. "I only wanted to hold him."

Fancy smiled and patted her sister-in-law's small hand. Hershel was a symbol of another time and she didn't need him quite so much as she had before. "We'll find him," she said.

The wagons came to noisy, simultaneous stops, and before Jeff could so much as secure the brake lever and let go of the reins, Melissa had caught Fancy's hand in her own and was tugging at it insistently.

A shriek from inside the huge stone house indicated that Hershel had been found or at least sighted. Laughing, Katherine reclaimed her daughter-in-law firmly, linking her small, strong arm with Fancy's. "Do try to be patient with us, darling," she enjoined in an amused whisper. "We become easier to accept with time."

Accept? Fancy had never worried about accepting them; quite the reverse had been true. She couldn't speak for the lump in her throat.

Banner and Melissa joined the entourage, followed somewhat hesitantly by Amelie, while the men remained behind to see to the horses.

"Get back here, you pink-eyed critter!" screamed Alva as they drew nearer the house. Katherine laughed and encircled an uncertain Amelie with her free arm. Fancy found herself liking her mother-in-law even more.

The inside of the house was cool and spacious and again Fancy remembered her first day there. She'd had no hope then of being a Corbin—the thought hadn't even occurred to her—but now she was a part of the family.

An inviting luncheon had been set out on the dining room table. Harried and driven by an annoyed Alva Thompkins, the Corbins finally gathered there, all of them talking at once.

Fancy, having washed her face and hands and repinned her hair in the upstairs room where she had first encountered Jeff Corbin, was just beginning to feel like a lady. Her worries about being accepted by the family were gone for the most part, for they had not only accepted her, they had welcomed her. She smiled across the table at Amelie and lifted her fork to eat.

At that very moment, Hershel struck. He came leaping across from a sideboard and landed, hind feet slipping in a wild bid for traction, in the middle of a platter of glazed ham. Gaining his footing, he calmed instantly and approached the green salad, where he nibbled at an overhanging lettuce leaf.

There was a stunned silence, during which Fancy wished that she could quietly die, and then Melissa and Banner gave simultaneous shrieks of laughter.

"I was hoping for roast chicken," said Adam without inflection of any kind.

Eyes dancing, Keith turned to shout toward the kitchen. "Alva, we found the rabbit!"

Fancy saw the whole scene through a shimmering blur of mortification. When Jeff calmly stood up and grasped the furry intruder in both hands, she pushed back her chair and fled.

In Jeff's room, she flung herself down on the bed and sobbed.

A gentle hand came to rest on one of her shoulders and the mattress gave way a little as a skirted figure sat down on its edge. "Oh, Fancy, don't cry," Banner pleaded gently. "It's all right, really it is."

Fancy wailed. Her good impression was ruined. Ruined! How had she ever hoped to fit in with these people? Why had she deluded herself that she could? "I never should have married Jeff!" she cried. "I knew I would be a shame to him—"

Banner's voice was instantly firm. Gone was the gentleness. "Frances Corbin," she ordered, "you sit up this minute and look at me!"

Fancy obeyed, sniffling inelegantly. The command had been put in such a way that she would not have thought of ignoring it.

Banner's green eyes were snapping. "Jeff loves you," she said forcefully, "and he needs you. You could never be a shame to him in any way, and I don't want to hear that sort of nonsensical drivel from you ever again!"

Fancy was aghast. "But—"

Now Banner was waggling an angry index finger in her face. "We all thought Jeff was lost!" she went on. "But you saved him, Fancy. You and your rabbit and your dress with stars on it!"

"H–How did—I mean—"

Banner lowered her finger and smiled. "Keith told us all about it, Fancy—how you came here and blasted Jeff out of his black moods and his self-pity—"

"I have been spoken of in kinder terms," observed Jeff wryly from the doorway.

"But not truer ones," retorted Banner crisply, at the same time taking both Fancy's hands in hers and squeezing them in reassurance.

Fancy lowered her eyes, a blush aching in her cheeks, unable to look at Jeff. Banner stood up and quietly left the room.

There was a short, pulsing silence. Now, Jeff would reprimand Fancy for owning a rabbit that would step in his august family's dinner. She braced herself, hands knotted together, head down.

"Frances," Jeff ordered sternly, "look at me."

She couldn't.

He came and sat down beside her on the bed. "Frances," he repeated.

"I'm sorry," she whispered.

And, to her complete surprise, his arm came around her shoulders, strong and warm. "Banner was right, you know. If you hadn't come prancing in here and thrown my supper all over me that night, I don't know what would have happened."

Fancy gaped at him, wide-eyed. "But I—Hershel—"

He laughed and the sound was low and gruff and profoundly comforting. "Hershel is part of your charm," he said. "Fancy, I love you."

She sniffled and a smile formed itself on her mouth. "Last time you said that, I kicked you out of bed," she said.

He kissed her briefly once, and then again in a more lingering fashion. "I remember," he breathed.

O'Brien was grinning as she took her chair at the table. "I don't think they'll be down for a while," she said, to the family at large.

Watching his wife, Adam was reminded of the way her satiny belly was rounding to accommodate his child and of their reunion the night before. He sat with his legs just a little farther apart.

Fork in hand, O'Brien met his smoldering gaze with impish understanding. All the same, a slight blush crept up her flawless face and lost itself in the cinnamon tendrils curling along her forehead. If he signaled her, in the secret way, would she obey him?

Adam decided to find out. Setting his wineglass down, he cleared his throat and tugged thoughtfully at one ear.

O'Brien blushed even harder, but she laid aside her fork and stood up again, her eyes lowered but hardly submissive. "I–I don't think I'm very hungry," she said, and then she turned and left the dining room.

Adam waited until he heard her footsteps on the stairs before excusing himself from the table and following.

"Please pass the rabbit," said Keith with humorous resignation.

"Bag balm?!" hissed Fancy, lying naked and warm on the bed.

Jeff laughed and knelt astraddle of her, taking a great dollop of the soothing potion onto his fingers. She whimpered softly as he rubbed balm into her right nipple.

"You'll taste terrible," he said gravely, but then he proceeded to attend the opposite nipple with more balm and slow, tantalizing motions of his hand.

Fancy had expected something quite different when Jeff had undressed her, but this was very pleasing. A feeling of heated luxury surged through her. "Aren't you—aren't you going to t–take me?"

"Oh, yes," he said, moving downward, kneeling between her legs. The cooling cream was now being applied to the secret, tender place—around and around his fingers went, in gentle mastery, up and down, around and around.

"Oooh," crooned Fancy, closing her eyes and arching her back.

"Do you like that?" Jeff asked in deep, idle tones.

Fancy bit her lower lip, not wanting to admit that she did.

He caught the very core of her passion between gentle fingers and plied it, smoothed it, roused it to aching obedience. "Fancy," he insisted.

"Yes!" she gasped. "Yes, yes—"

"How much?"

A great tremor went through Fancy, followed by a frantic, molten need. "V–Very much."

"Shall I take you?"

Fancy blushed at the scandal, the sweet wickedness. The breeze from the open window floated over her, somehow fanning the inferno within. She stretched in sweet, eager comfort. "Yes," she whispered.

"When?"

Fancy reached out with shaking hands to undo his belt and the buttons of his trousers. She learned instantly that he was not so calm as she'd thought. "Now," she conceded raggedly. "Oh, now—"

Groaning, Jeff got up from the bed just long enough to take off his clothes. Then he lay down again on his back and turned Fancy to sit astride him. His shaft glided easily inside her, thanks to the balm, but it was as imposing as ever.

Grasping Fancy's hips in his hands, Jeff began to raise and lower her upon his mastery, slowly at first, and then with fury. She reached a blinding release that made her fling her head back and bare her teeth over a hoarse growl of satisfaction and then was free to watch Jeff.

He was so beautiful, so very beautiful, even with the angry scar reaching the length of one powerful arm. Finally, with a gravel-rough cry of her name and an upward thrust of his muscular hips, he gave up what her velvety passage had drawn from him.

Fancy fell to him, stricken and exalted, and they slept, legs and arms entangled, until sunset.

Katherine watched her youngest son with carefully veiled concern. Of all her children, Keith was the least like Daniel. Like herself, he was a crusader.

He sat on the gazebo steps, unaware of his mother's presence, holding Amelie's hand and talking to her in words Katherine couldn't have heard, would not have even tried to hear. The wind, coming in over the river, ruffled his toasted gold hair.

Katherine felt a pang. Tomorrow, he would be married. She liked Amelie and should have been happy to have her join the family, but a strange feeling of foreboding was wriggling in the very core of her intuition.

Turning away, lest she be noticed, Katherine tried to quell the sense of impending tragedy but could not. She had met it too many times before to discount it as a mother's fancy.

Melissa met her in the middle of the screened porch, looking petulant. "I wish I had a husband!" she complained.

Despite the uneasiness that still plagued her, Katherine smiled. "What on earth prompted that remark?" she demanded good-naturedly.

In the kitchen, Melissa flung her arms out in a gesture of impatience, nearly overturning the dirty dishes Alva had stacked beside the sink. "It's boring around here if you're not paired off with somebody. Keith and Amelie can't see anything but each other and the rest of them are taking naps!"

Katherine bit down on her lower lip. Naps? Not if she knew her sons, and she did. "You know how it is when you get old and doddering," she teased.

"Any minute now they'll be fusty in the bargain!" Melissa cried with vehemence.

Katherine smiled and thunder crashed in the dark skies overhead. Instantly, her merry mood was gone again. Daniel, she thought, for it was her habit to speak silently to her husband when she felt afraid, Daniel, something terrible is going to happen.

A downpour hammered and dashed at the roof and Katherine shuddered. Amelie and Keith came bounding into the kitchen, sopping wet and laughing.

Katherine drummed up a smile, which immediately faltered. Why was she so frightened? Why?

"I suppose you're going to go upstairs and take naps, just like everybody else!" cried Melissa, glaring at her brother and his dripping bride-to-be.

With a wet hand, Keith ruffled his sister's carefully coiffed hair, a gesture he knew she hated. "Naps, is it? Brat, you're younger than I thought."

"Keith," Katherine reprimanded softly, but she wanted to gather him in her arms, hold him, protect him. From what, though? From the sweet, innocent-eyed Amelie, who so obviously loved him?

By then, Melissa was squealing with glee and Keith was stomping around after her, making monster sounds. Amelie hung back, watching with wide, shy eyes.

Katherine watched a tenuous daring building within her future daughter-in-law. "You'll wake the others!" the child nearly strangled to say.

At this, Keith threw back his head and roared with laughter. Poor Amelie looked so confused that Katherine ached for her.

"Let's get you something dry to wear," she said kindly, extending a hand to Amelie.

They were halfway up the back stairs when Amelie burst out, "Why did he laugh that way, Mrs. Corbin? I didn't say anything funny!"

As if on cue, a lusty masculine groan came from behind one of the doors on the second floor. Katherine cleared her throat in a belated effort to cover it.

Perhaps she should have come up alone for the dress she meant to loan Amelie, rather than dragging the poor child along. "I wouldn't worry about it," she said soothingly. "Men do laugh at the strangest things."

Amelie's bright green eyes widened as though she might be brewing a fever. "They're not s–sleeping at all!" she cried in revelation.

Katherine wanted to drag both her elder sons from their beds and beat them. She refrained from comment and staunchly led the way to her own room.

Looking almost haunted, Amelie went behind a folding damask screen to strip off her wet clothes. "Is—is the whole family so—well, so ardent?" she wanted to know.

Katherine rolled her eyes heavenward and fetched a blue cambric gown from her trunk for Amelie to put on. If this dear little innocent thought Keith was any different from his brothers, just because he was a minister, she had a dreadful shock coming. "Ardent?" she echoed, feigning confusion.

The blue cambric, draped over the top of the screen, slithered to the other side. "I did see Adam swat Banner right on the—right on the bottom!"

Katherine bit down hard on her lower lip. Living in the same house with Adam and Banner, she had seen, quite inadvertently of course, much worse. "My husband and I," she began gently, diplomatically, "were always very affectionate with each other. It's natural that our children are that way, too."

A snow-white face peered around one end of the screen. "All of your children? Keith, too?"

Katherine willed herself to evaporate and, of course, failed. "I think you should ask him that, Amelie. After all, it is a rather personal matter."

Amelie looked terrified and Katherine remembered that she didn't have a mother. "I couldn't do that!"

"But he will be your husband."

Amelie groped her way to the bed and sat down. The moment she did, she bounded up again, and the significance of that was not lost on a sympathetic Katherine. "Does it hurt?" the woman-child whispered.

Katherine sat down on the edge of the bed, prompting Amelie to sit beside her. "It does hurt a little the first time," she said quietly. "Then, if you truly love your husband and he loves you, making love can be very pleasurable indeed."

"I do love Keith," said the bride-to-be.

Katherine took Amelie's hand and squeezed it. "Then you needn't worry because he certainly loves you in return."

"I'm scared!" confessed Amelie in a feverish rush. "B–But when Keith kisses me—"

Katherine smiled and at this silent urging, Amelie went on.

"When he kisses me, I feel all these strange things! Even if I'm wearing a summer dress I get terribly warm, and my heart beats faster and faster until I think it will explode!"

"Those things are normal, Amelie." It was time to brave the hallway again and Katherine hoped that her sons and their wives were resting now. Quietly. "Let's go downstairs and have some tea with lemon and honey."

The sky beyond Katherine's window was now dark and furious and split with faraway lightning. Again, she felt that creeping, helpless dread.

And Amelie seemed to feel it, too. She stood up and

went to the window like a sleepwalker, her gaze fixed on the rain. "We wanted to be married outside," she said, "in the churchyard."

A chill, inexplicable and fierce, went through Katherine. Then she took herself firmly in hand. Why, if Daniel were here he'd say that she was being fanciful and silly. "Perhaps the sun will shine after all," she said brightly. "Come now, dear—let's go and have that tea."

Amelie turned and nodded, but there was a worried look in her eyes. Katherine wondered sadly if this lovely child was not too timid for all that lay ahead. Was it wrong to wish that she could have been more like Banner or like Jeff's Fancy?

Downstairs, in the big, cozy kitchen, Melissa and Keith were lighting lamps and stoking up the fire in the cookstove. Alva, overwhelmed by the episode with Fancy's rabbit, had retired to her room to nurse a headache.

Keith looked up and his blue eyes caressed Amelie with a tenderness Katherine had never seen the likes of, even in him. She knew then that she would not have to warn him to be gentle when the time came.

By the time the tea had been brewed and a rousing, rainy day game of whist had been struck up, Katherine had almost forgotten that she was afraid.

Chapter Sixteen

THE PREVIOUS NIGHT'S RAINSTORM HAD PASSED, THOUGH the sky was still dark and cloudy. Feeling oddly oppressed, Fancy turned away from the bedroom window and began searching for something suitable to wear to a wedding from the one trunk Adam had taken off the train for her. Her other new clothes had remained in the baggage car, to be shipped on to Port Hastings.

Jeff, sprawled across the big bed in such a fashion that Fancy wondered how there had been room for both of them on that one mattress, stirred in his sleep. "No—" he said gruffly. "No—"

Fearing that he was dreaming of the explosion aboard the *Sea Mistress,* as he often did, Fancy hurried to the bedside. Guilt mingled with the sweeping tenderness she felt as she gently smoothed tarnished-gold hair back from his forehead and whispered, "It's all right, Jeff. It's all right."

He settled down again, without waking, and Fancy bent to kiss his forehead softly. At this he muttered some nonsensical endearment and rolled over onto his stomach.

Fancy was confronted with the dreadful scar slashing across his back. In some places, it was as wide as her hand. A lump rose in her throat. What if she awakened him and told him that he had Temple Royce to thank for that scar, that she could swear to it in a court of law?

But Jeff probably knew, or at least suspected that Temple was responsible for that disaster. And if that were true, why risk incurring his wrath by bringing the subject up again?

Fancy stepped back from the bed and turned away resolutely. This was to be a happy day, complete with a wedding. She would not spoil it with thoughts of Temple Royce.

She washed and dressed in a black sateen skirt and a white shirtwaist. Later, when it was time, she would change into something less prim. Maybe Banner, Melissa, or Mrs. Corbin could help her select just the right gown.

The house was very quiet as Fancy made her way down the stairs leading to the kitchen. There, Alva was busy building a fire in the cookstove. She glanced at Fancy and then looked away again without a word of greeting.

"I'm sorry about what happened yesterday with Hershel," Fancy ventured, stung. As briefly as they had known each other, she thought of Alva as a friend.

"No matter," replied Alva, slamming down a stove lid, then reaching up to adjust the damper.

Fancy sat down at the kitchen table, feeling weary

despite a good night's sleep. Distant thunder grumbled in the sky. "What is it, Alva? Why are you so angry with me?"

Alva whirled. "You left here without sayin' so much as a fare-thee-well, that's why!"

Fancy was startled out of her doldrums and she sat up very straight in her chair. "At the time I felt I had to get away," she said evenly. "You would have tried to make me stay."

Alva was busy again, pumping water into a coffeepot, measuring grounds into its basket. "I would have at that," she said with grudging agreement. "It was lonesome here after you went."

"I'm sorry," Fancy said sincerely.

"You going on to Port Hastings, you and your husband?"

Fancy dreaded the prospect. In Port Hastings, Jeff would order his ship built. How long did it take to construct such a vessel, anyway? How long did she have before he sailed away and left her? "Yes," she said, trying to shift her thoughts to more pleasant matters. "But you won't be lonely anymore, Alva—not after today. Amelie will be here."

"Amelie!" hooted the housekeeper, rattling stove lids again.

"Don't you like her?"

Alva sighed and began taking mixing bowls from shelves, whisks and spatulas from drawers. "It isn't that," she said quietly. "Miss Amelie is a nice enough lady, but—well—I don't know that she's strong. Any woman married to a Corbin has got to be that and more."

Fancy was circumspectly amused. No doubt, Alva regarded Keith as her chick and felt protective toward him. "Do you have those same reservations about me, Alva?"

"No," said Alva firmly. "You're like Dr. Banner—you can look after yourself if need be, and it would be my guess that you can handle your man. These Corbin men need wives who are just as ornery as they are."

When it came to Adam and Jeff, Fancy could believe that Alva's assessment was correct. They both tended to be tyrants and dealing with them was a job, however rewarding. But Keith seemed a different sort; gentler, more pliable. "Keith is hardly the 'ornery' sort, Alva," she observed.

The coffee was brewed and Alva took it off the stove and filled two cups from its spout. Then she sat down at the table, facing Fancy. "You think he isn't a man, just because he preaches the gospel?"

"Of course not, but—"

"But nothing. That poor little Amelie child won't make him happy."

Fancy took a cautious sip of her steaming coffee. "He loves her!"

"Maybe," said Alva, and then the conversation was over because Melissa came bouncing into the kitchen, chattering about the organdy dress she was going to wear to the wedding.

Even after the wedding party and the many guests had arrived at the church, the sky was still dark and threatening and the wind was high. Everyone, it seemed to Fancy, was a bit uneasy.

She smoothed the skirts of her lavender lawn dress and hoped that they could all be settled in their pews before another storm came.

The other members of the party seemed to be in no

hurry to go inside, however—Mrs. Corbin was chatting with some of the local women, old friends of hers, perhaps, and her sons were conferring near one of the wagons. Banner and Melissa had disappeared into the tiny parsonage nearby, probably to help Amelie with her wedding dress and veil.

With a sigh, Fancy looked toward the river. It seemed to churn, that green-gray water, railing at the angry sky and the wind. A chill danced up and down Fancy's spine and she shivered.

Guests were arriving steadily and the bell in the church belfry sang a soft, sad song in the wind. But then, in an instant, the sun broke through the dark clouds and warmed the small gathering, drawing pleased exclamations from the women.

Fancy smiled. It appeared that Amelie would get her wish; Keith had mentioned that she wanted to be married in the churchyard. It was all so romantic, unlike her own wedding. . . .

Amelie came out of the parsonage, wearing a beautiful, billowing gown and a flowing veil. Fancy knew a moment of uncharitable envy, remembering that she herself had been married in her star-spangled dress with a snake trainer to say the holy words.

"I'll make it up to you," whispered a knowing and amused masculine voice from her side.

Fancy looked up into Jeff's face and marveled; it was disconcerting the way he so often seemed to know what she was thinking. Did he also know that she had seen the plans for his new clippership? "If you don't go away to sea," she said, and before Jeff could reply to that everyone was being ushered into place for the ceremony.

As Amelie had hoped, it would be performed outside, under a towering oak tree. A retired pastor, who lived in the parsonage because Keith didn't use it, would officiate.

The sun grew brighter and brighter as the rites progressed, and the wind settled. Still, Fancy felt uneasy. She gave herself a mental shake and put the feeling down to petty jealousy.

Keith had just slipped a wide gold band onto Amelie's finger when the unthinkable happened. There was a thunderous roar, a bright flash, and Fancy was flung to the ground with hurricane force. There were screams and a frightening, ringing sort of thud. Pinned beneath Jeff's rigid frame, sheltered by it, Fancy grappled to be free.

Jeff lifted his head; she saw his features tighten. "Jesus God," he muttered.

Fancy was writhing wildly, trying to see what had happened. "Let me up—what are you—"

"Are you all right?" Jeff demanded sharply, staring down into her face.

There was a wailing sound somewhere, and people were sobbing. Horses shrieked in terror and pain. Fancy nodded and Jeff lifted himself off her and helped her up.

The church was gone—completely gone. Nothing remained except a pile of smoky rubble. Women and men were getting to their feet, the women crying, the men looking stunned and pale. Some of the guests lay still on the ground.

Clinging to Jeff's arm because she would have fallen without its support, Fancy tried to absorb what she was seeing. It was then that she noticed the billow of white silk and tulle lying prone beneath the oak tree. Banner and Adam knelt on either side of Amelie, while Keith stood at her feet, staring down at her in shock.

Adam looked up into his brother's face and solemnly shook his head.

A keening howl of grief and protest rose over all the other sounds, rendering them meaningless. Tears of disbelief and horror stung Fancy's eyes and she stumbled toward the scene under her own power, for Jeff had let go of her to go to Keith.

His eyes wild, his clothes mussed, Keith flung Jeff's arm away. "No," he said, in a hoarse, choked voice, "by all that's holy, *no—*"

Fancy could not bear to look at Keith or at Amelie. Instead, she watched Banner, who still knelt on the ground, her coppery hair mussed, her face smudged with dirt, her skirts full of splinters.

"W–What happened?" Fancy pleaded to no one in particular. The sun is shining, she thought. It is the day of the wedding. And yet people are weeping, people are hurt. . . .

Fancy forced herself to look at Amelie and then had to turn away, swaying. *People are dead.*

"Get the bags, O'Brien," Adam's voice said crisply, brusquely, from somewhere in the pounding void. "They're in the buggy."

Banner scrambled past, dashing at her face with the back of one hand.

"What happened?" Fancy asked again, and again no one heard her.

Keith bellowed once in outraged protest and disbelief like a man gone mad. There was a dense, acrid smell in the air—dynamite, like they used in the coal mines sometimes at Newcastle. Fancy staggered around the side of a wagon and threw up again and again and again.

Dozens of men were arriving now on horseback. They wore pistols, carried rifles, moved in a twisting haze before Fancy's eyes.

"Move aside, miss," one of them ordered kindly, taking Fancy's arm.

"What the hell happened here?" rasped another.

Fancy couldn't answer. There were horses down, as well as people. Some of the animals were still screaming and one had a great, jagged piece of wood piercing its neck. She flinched as shots were fired, putting the injured beasts into a permanent and merciful sleep.

The world seemed to spin around and around, then buckle up and down. Fancy's knees gave way and she sank into a sleep of her own.

When she awoke, Jeff was crouching on one side of her, Katherine Corbin on the other. "What—" she croaked.

Katherine's Corbin-blue eyes were bright with tears. "There was an explosion, Fancy. Amelie is dead."

Fancy remembered the heap of white fabric on the ground and began to shake her head. No, it was too horrible, it couldn't happen, no. No!

Smelling salts were passed under her nose, assaulting her senses, jolting her back to reality. Sick, Fancy tried to sit up, and would not have succeeded without help from Jeff.

"Is anyone else—was anyone—"

"Three people are dead, as far as we can tell," Jeff broke in grimly. "A lot more are hurt. It's a good thing Adam and Banner are here."

Fancy wavered, covering her face with both hands. She had to be strong like the others. She had to. No one had time to pamper her and, besides, she might be needed.

She lowered her hands, drew a deep breath, and rose shakily to her feet. Amelie's tiny, inert form was being lifted into a wagonbed. Keith scrambled in beside her, his face filthy and wet with tears.

There was debris everywhere—even the church bell lay in the grass beneath the oak tree, silent now. Fancy forgot Jeff and stumbled toward Banner, who was removing a spear-sized splinter from a man's shoulder.

"H–How can I help?" she whispered.

The man moaned and Banner did not look up from her work. "We need blankets," she answered. "Tell these people that we need blankets and wagons."

Fancy found a man wearing a badge and a look of sick horror and relayed Banner's message. The wagons came, in due course, and so did the blankets, and the wounded and dead were taken away.

"I'll take Fancy and Melissa home," Katherine said, looking up into Jeff's face, which was as stunned and ravaged as her own. "You go to Keith. He'll need you."

Jeff nodded distractedly, kissed Fancy's forehead, and went off to find a horse.

Melissa was weeping softly and, as the three women walked toward a waiting wagon, Fancy slipped one arm around her sister-in-law's waist in mute support.

Eustis Ponder sat in the wagon seat, his wrinkled face wan. "Lord, Kate, I'm so sorry," he said to Katherine, leaping down to offer her his hand.

"You—you came to the wedding," said Katherine, in a dazed voice. And despite her strength, she swayed a little.

"We was late," said Eustis, lifting Katherine up into the wagon seat. "Heard the blast, though."

Fancy and Melissa got into the bed of the wagon, which was littered with bits of straw and hay. "Where's Isabella?" Fancy asked worriedly.

"She went to Doc Haverson's place, with Adam and his missus," Eustis answered, taking the reins in his strong hands. "Isabella's done some nursing in her time and they're going to need help."

Fancy sat back against the side of the wagon and closed her eyes. All the same, she knew that the sun had passed behind a cloud and it would be a very long time before its warming light would shine on the Corbin family again.

Jeff was crying. It was a soft, hoarse sound, but it drew Fancy up out of her laudanum-induced sleep. She stretched out her hand to touch him in the darkness.

"I'm so sorry," she whispered.

The bed seemed to shake with the force of his grief, though he was clearly trying to suppress it.

Fancy's brain was fogged, but her heart was fully alert, feeling her husband's pain, making it a part of her own. She drew Jeff into her arms and held him.

"I love you," she said.

"Temple," he cursed, as though she had not spoken, sobbing the word.

Fancy shivered. "What?"

"Temple," Jeff spat. "Temple killed my brother's wife—those other people—"

Sick horror washed over Fancy. She remembered the blast, the screams, the horses bleeding and keening on the ground. "Temple is far away," she managed to utter. But she knew that she was wrong. She also knew that she had to tell Jeff the truth about that other explosion or die under the weight of the knowledge.

She ran the fingers of one hand through Jeff's rumpled hair in a tender motion, though she knew that there was no preparing him. "Temple was responsible for what happened on the *Sea Mistress,*" she said in a whispering rush. And then she stiffened, waiting for the inevitable storm.

Jeff drew out of her arms slowly. "What?"

"I heard him—heard him boasting about it that night. That's when I ran away and that was why Temple was looking for me."

The silence was chilling.

"I–I was afraid to tell you, Jeff—afraid you would blame me—"

The covers on the bed were flung back and the briskness with which Jeff tore himself from her was sharply painful, like tearing away a bandage from a new wound. "Jesus—" he whispered, in the thick darkness.

Fancy ached. She squeezed her eyes shut and tears trickled out anyway. "It wasn't my fault, what Temple did."

He was far away from her. Only a few feet from the bed where she lay and yet beyond reaching or touching. "Thirteen men died that night, Fancy, and four more were crippled. I knew Temple was behind it, but there was no way I could prove it."

Fancy swallowed, unable to respond.

"But your testimony would have been proof. He would have gone to prison—"

She bolted upright, furious and full of pain. "I was a saloon singer!" she cried. "A magician! Who would have believed me?"

"I would have. The marshal might have, too. It would have been a place to start, something to work with."

"I'm sorry."

"Sorry," he drawled, in cruel, marveling tones. *"Sorry?"*

"Jeff, please—"

Suddenly, he was grappling for his clothes, struggling into them. Everything was over, every dream was dashed, he was never going to forgive her for keeping silent. And could she ever forgive herself? If she had spoken up, Temple might not have had a chance to strike again. Amelie and the others might not be dead.

The next three days were the fiber of which nightmares are woven. Amelie's funeral was held beneath the oak tree where she had been married, conducted by the same aging pastor. Keith watched in heart-wrenching silence as Adam, Jeff, Amelie's father, and Eustis carried her coffin through the deep grass to the graveyard, where she would rest forever.

More words were said over her then, hollow words, ancient words that held no comfort. And then the casket was lowered into the ground, and Keith whirled and strode away toward the river.

A tendril of hair danced around Fancy's face and she brushed it aside, watching him. She knew, as did the others, that it would not be a kindness to approach Keith now.

But she could not help but see the way he lowered his head, the way his broad shoulders moved in meter with his grief. With a quick motion of his right hand, he unfastened the clerical collar at his throat and flung it into the river.

Fancy bit her lower lip and turned away in despair. At another time, she might have sought Jeff out, drawn comfort from him, given comfort. But Jeff had not spoken to her or touched her since the day of the wedding, nor had he slept in their bed.

"Fancy?" The small, anguished voice made her turn. Melissa was standing there, her face ravaged. "Oh, Fancy, it's too terrible!" she sobbed out.

Fancy held out her arms and Melissa flung herself into them, trembling. She wept as Melissa wept.

"There, now," Fancy said presently, sniffling. "Everything will be all right."

It was at that moment that she looked up and saw Jeff watching her with cold, skeptical eyes that seemed to say, *"Will it?"*

Fancy met his gaze squarely; though he had wounded her, she would never let him know. When he walked away, she rested her cheek against the side of Melissa's head and said again, "Everything will be all right."

She didn't believe it for a minute.

Fancy stood in front of Hershel's hutch, the one she and Jeff had built together the day they first made love. It was dark inside the barn, but she hadn't bothered to light a lamp.

With a trembling hand, she opened the hutch's small, hinged door and reached inside. Hershel's fur was soft and soothing to the touch. "Maybe we'll go back into the magic business, you and I," she said.

The voice behind her made her start. *"That's* where I saw you," said Adam in tones of gruff revelation. "You were singing in Port Hastings aboard the *Silver Shadow."*

Fancy waited for her heart to flutter back down to its proper place in her chest before answering ruefully, "Fancy Jordan. She sings. She dances. She does magic."

Adam struck a match and a lantern flared to flickering brilliance. "Does she also plan to leave her husband?" he asked forthrightly.

Fancy lowered her head. "It might be better—Jeff is so angry."

"Jeff needs you," said Adam, coming closer, closing and latching Hershel's cage.

"Y–You don't understand. I told him something that—"

"I know what you told him," Adam broke in, not unkindly. "You overheard Temple Royce boasting about blowing the *Sea Mistress* to hell and gone."

"Yes."

"Jeff knew that Temple was behind that—we all did. He has another reason for being angry with you, Fancy."

Fancy could only stare up into her brother-in-law's rugged, tension-ravaged face.

Adam sighed and took her arm in a gentle hand. "Let's sit down and talk," he said.

Fancy let him lead her to the very bale of hay where Jeff had done such lovely, wicked things to her on that day over a month before. She blushed at the memory but sat down, and Adam sat on another bale across from her.

"Fancy, Jeff is using what happened in Port Hastings as an excuse to hold you at bay. If you'll be patient with him, he'll come around."

"Why would he want to do that?" whispered Fancy, truly mystified and just a bit hopeful, too.

"What happened to Amelie was a shock to him, of course—it stunned all of us. But I think Jeff in particular was reminded that we're all mortal. Any of us could die at any time. In short, I believe his reasoning is that if he convinces himself he doesn't care about you, you won't be taken away from him."

"But if that's true, he's wasting so much—"

"Exactly. But he'll realize that, Fancy. Right now, he's looking at Keith and he's thinking, 'There, but for the grace of God, go I.' "

"Don't you feel that way, too, Adam? Aren't you afraid for Banner?"

He sighed. "I don't think I could bear to lose her. But O'Brien and I are both doctors, Fancy, and in our business you're never allowed to forget that life is all too fragile."

One tear rolled down Fancy's cheek and dropped off into her skirts. "I love Jeff so much," she said brokenly. "I really don't know what to do, though—"

Adam caught one of her hands in his own and squeezed it. "Wait, Fancy. Be patient. Most of all, go on loving him." He paused. "Do all the magic you know, for both your sakes."

Fancy could only nod.

A stall door rattled as they were standing up, ready to go back into the house and join the rest of the family. Stepping into the center of the barn, they saw Keith leading a spirited black gelding out into the summer night.

"Keith," Adam called. "Wait."

Keith was slipping a bridle over the gelding's head, and if he'd heard his brother, he ignored him.

"Where are you going?" the eldest brother persisted.

The youngest flung a saddle blanket over the beast's back, and then a saddle. "Away," he said hoarsely, wrenching the cinch into place.

"Away where?"

Keith's broad shoulders moved in a shrug. His

features were partially visible in the light of the lantern Adam carried and it hurt Fancy to look at him, to see the depths of his grief.

"Right now, I don't really care."

"What about your parish? What about all these cussed apple trees of yours?" demanded Adam, harsh in his desperation.

Keith shrugged again and buckled the cinch. His jaw was set and it was clear that he didn't plan to answer.

"Keith."

Tormented azure eyes glittered in the lantern light. Fancy wanted to walk away, wanted not to hear, but she couldn't move. She remembered the way he had wrenched off his clerical collar that morning and flung it into the roiling Columbia.

"What about God?" she asked softly, and then could have bitten off her tongue because she hadn't meant to speak. She had no right to.

"God," scoffed Keith, on a long, raspy breath. "There is no God."

Adam reached out a hand to his brother, drew it back at the menacing look of warning the gesture inspired. "Keith, listen to me—the pain will stop. You'll be able to think clearly again—"

Keith swung up into the saddle and the gelding danced beneath him like an evil beast, part of the night, a pet of the devil. "Said the man whose wife waits for him with a baby in her belly," he broke in bitterly.

"You can't run from this, Keith. It will follow you."

A sudden and ragged sob, terrible to hear, tore itself from the depths of Keith's chest. "Don't stand there and preach to me, God damn you! Your wife isn't dead—you have Danny and Bridget—"

"Get down from the horse," Adam went on smoothly, reasonably. Fancy wondered if Keith heard the tears in his older brother's voice the way she did. "We'll talk. We'll get drunk. Anything. We'll get through this, Keith."

"I couldn't get drunk enough to forget that damned bell!" roared Keith. "It—it crushed her—the bell from my own damned church—"

"I know," said Adam, and he was holding out his hand now. "Please. Stay."

But Keith shook his head. "I can't, Adam," he breathed. "I can't."

And then he was gone, perhaps forever. Though he was shaken, Adam took Fancy's arm in a firm grasp and escorted her back to the house.

Chapter Seventeen

THOUGH THE HOUSE WAS FINISHED, IT STILL SMELLED OF sawdust and fresh paint. Every window was taller than Fancy herself, and she stood before one that faced toward the harbor, her mother's letter in one hand. An early-winter snow slanted past the glass.

Even from that distance, the new ship was clearly visible, its bare timbers and towering masts a constant reminder that Fancy was losing her husband. She sighed. Surely, she had already lost Jeff.

Oh, he shared her bed. But for all its ferocity, Jeff's lovemaking was somehow distant, not born of love but of the undeniable needs of a healthy male body. She had the feeling that any woman would have done.

The child, due in late February by Banner's calculations, moved within her. Despite the tears blurring in her eyes, Fancy smiled. She had this baby, she would always have this baby.

"Mrs. Corbin?" sang a bright, nasal voice from the vicinity of the front door. "Mrs. Corbin, you here, mum?"

"In here, Mary," she called, turning back to the window as the new housekeeper entered the spacious but still only partially furnished parlor.

"Saints be praised, it's a chill day!" Mary babbled, and Fancy smiled again. Mary was young, redheaded, and frankly Irish, and she had a talent for lifting her new and inexperienced mistress out of a dark mood. "Would you like some tea, then? I could make it that fast."

"That would be nice, Mary," replied Fancy. Her vision was clearer now, but she still didn't dare to turn around and show her tear-streaked face. "Thank you."

The snow was coming down faster now; by nightfall it would be deep indeed. What fun it would be to play in it, to roll up a snowman or to make angels in the pristine whiteness.

Fancy sighed again and looked down at the letter, twice-read already. It was a comfort to know how happy her parents were, living at the Wenatchee house, overseeing the orchards. Fancy's father thrived on the fresh air and her mother had pretty clothes to wear and Alva Thompkins to look after her. The two women were great friends, sewing together, planning gardens, reading aloud to each other from the many books in Keith's fine library.

Fancy folded the letter, and now she did not see the clippership that haunted her days and nights like a specter. She did not see the snow or the bustling spectacle of Port Hastings. No, she saw Keith riding away that night after Amelie's funeral, his soul broken in his eyes. No one had heard from him since, though

Jeff, in a rare moment of communication, had said that the banker had told him that Keith had drawn twice on his private funds. One draft had been sent to Sacramento, one to a place called Los Alamos, in the New Mexico Territory.

Now, living in a beautiful new house, a child growing inside her, and with all the money and security she could ever have hoped for, Fancy felt as much a lost wanderer as Keith. Jeff was so rarely home; his every waking moment was consumed either by that blasted clipper or consultations with the Pinkerton agents he and Adam had hired to search for Temple Royce.

So far, not a trace had been found. Fancy half hoped that Temple would never be located—if he was, Jeff would kill him and no doubt hang for it.

"Mrs. Corbin? Mrs. Corbin, the tea's ready."

Fancy started and turned from the window to smile at Mary. The thin winter light danced in the girl's short, springy curls. "Thank you."

"Was a fair walk," hinted the housekeeper brightly, "up that steep hill. That snooty Maggie McQuire from the big house went right by me in a *carriage,* if you please—didn't even offer a lift!"

Fancy bit her lower lip, amused. For some reason, Katherine's Maggie had taken an instant dislike to poor Mary, and the two of them were always at odds. Maggie had not approved of Jeff's building a house of his own—it had been her opinion that both he and his new wife belonged with the rest of the family in the enormous brick mansion farther up the hill.

"I would go mad," had been Jeff's only comment on that suggestion, and Fancy hadn't cared where they lived as long as they were together.

"She thinks I'm an upstart!" Mary prattled on indignantly, her shrill voice penetrating Fancy's reflections. "And me doin' the best I know how!"

"Hush now," Fancy said softly, "and have some tea."

Mary's mouth rounded for a moment, even though she had been hinting for just such an invitation. "And the captain would kill me right and proper if he caught me sitting with the mistress!"

Sad again, Fancy tucked the letter from her mother into the pocket of her blue sateen skirt. There wasn't much danger of Jeff catching his housekeeper having tea with his wife—it was only midday and he wouldn't be home until long after dark. "We'll stand, then," Fancy said to mollify Mary.

"You stand? And in your condition? No, no, mum, you sit right here by the fire and I'll have my tea in the kitchen."

Fancy's throat was thick with a lonely sort of despair. "Oh, Mary," she said, "don't go. Please."

Mary poured tea for them both and sat, though she looked poised to leap up should there be a knock at the front door or a sound from the kitchen. She was an enigma to Fancy, always wanting to do daring things and then having doubts about them when the time came.

"Honestly, mum," Mary blurted out, in her startling and sudden way, "it breaks my heart to see you look so down in the mouth, that it does. What's the captain thinkin' of, to leave you here alone so much?"

Fancy closed her eyes and tried to take comfort from the crackling warmth of the fire on the hearth. Actually, the house was heated by a modern, if cantankerous, wood-burning furnace in the cellar, but Fancy loved the cheery fireplaces that graced this room, the dining room, the kitchen, and the master bedroom. "You're being too familiar again, Mary," she said, not unkindly.

"I'm always that, ain't I? And sorry I am for it, too. I–I didn't mean anything by it, mum."

"Finish your tea, Mary."

A slurping sound indicated Mary's eagerness to be obedient. She nearly choked when there was a knock at the front door.

"Saints in heaven, I'll wager it's that nosy Maggie McQuire, lookin' to see if I'm keepin' proper care of you!" Mary cried, bolting out of her chair and anxiously smoothing her hair and her skirts as she hurried into the entryway.

Fancy didn't bother to point out that Maggie never used the front door but the one leading into the kitchen, and that without knocking.

At the lilting sound of Banner's voice, Fancy was cheered. She was rising out of her chair to offer a proper greeting when her sister-in-law swept into the room in a swirl of snow-dusted green woolen and gleeful complaints about the weather. Due to bear her own child in less than two months, Banner created constant scandal by refusing to stay at home and hide her obvious condition.

"Sit back down in that chair, Frances Corbin," she ordered, doffing her bonnet in front of the fireplace and setting it down on the hearth. "You look pale."

"Don't she now?" fretted Mary.

Banner gave the housekeeper an arch look and Mary fled to the kitchen for another cup and saucer. "She's a scamp, your Mary," she observed without rancor. "I don't imagine things ever get dull around here, with her to—"

Fancy struggled with the hurt expression that had risen instantly to her face, but the falling off of Banner's comment proved she'd been too late. For all the luxuries, for all Mary's constant chatter and mischief, things were indeed dull in that house. And lonely.

"That waster!" Banner sputtered, lowering herself cautiously into a chair. "Who does Jeff think he is, treating you like this?"

Fancy loved her husband and even now she felt compelled to defend him. "It was a shock to him that I knew Temple had blown up his ship and still kept it from him."

"Gull globs," scoffed Banner. "He's just throwing one of his famous six-month tantrums!"

"He does have a temper."

Banner's hands were resting on her enormous round stomach. "Don't say that so adoringly. If he wasn't so big, I'd take a switch to him."

Fancy was even more defensive. "Adam has a bad temper, too," she pointed out.

"Yes," admitted Banner readily, "but he just flies mad and yells awhile and then it's all over."

It seemed time for a change of subject, if the peace was to be kept. And since Fancy loved her sister-in-law with all her heart, she cherished that peace. "How are things at the main house?"

Banner laughed. "Pure insanity. Mama is organizing another suffrage campaign—we're all to stand on street corners and pass out fliers. Adam is stomping around raving about women keeping their places and the printer's helper is trembling in his shoes."

"What about the twins?" pressed Fancy, grinning. Danny and Bridget, Jeff's niece and nephew, were the delight of the entire family.

"When I left, they were trying to find Hershel. He's loose again and Maggie's threatening to make him into a stew."

Fancy chuckled at the pictures flashing through her mind. But she felt a certain nostalgia, too, for the days before Jeff Corbin, when she and Hershel had made their way together in a frighteningly big world. There had been lots of hardships then, but not this aching sense of loneliness. That was new.

"In any case, that's why I'm here. Mama sent me over to beg you to help," announced Banner.

"To catch Hershel?"

"To pass out fliers. Fancy, suffrage is important! Why, the most stupid, lice-ridden lumberjack can vote, but you and I can't!" Banner's beautiful cheekbones flushed with the heat of her conviction. "Are we going to stand for that?"

"I suppose not," mused Fancy.

And so it was that, not half an hour later, she found herself standing, bundled up and scarfed to her eyes, in front of Wung Lo's Laundry, a stack of fliers in her mittened hands. RISE UP, YOU WHO LOVE JUSTICE AND RIGHT! the papers read. EVERY GOOD CONSCIENCE WILL DECREE THAT WOMEN MUST VOTE!

Fancy managed to press a few into the hands of passing women, but the men went so far as to cross the street to avoid her. The snow was falling faster and harder and her feet throbbed with cold. After an hour of almost constant rejection, her political convictions were wavering dangerously. Men were too hard-hearted and selfish to ever let women have the vote anyway, so why was she standing out here under a streetlamp, freezing to death?

Across the street, the door of the newly built Port

Hastings Hotel and Restaurant swung open, and a familiar laugh caught Fancy's attention. Jeff. That was Jeff. And she hadn't heard him laugh like that since before her confession about Temple Royce.

She stepped forward, peering through the snow, and was nearly run down by a passing lumber wagon. Clinging to Jeff's arm, smiling up at him, was a beautiful woman with red hair and stylish clothes. . . .

Meredith! Meredith Whittaker! What the devil was *she* doing in Port Hastings?

But the answer was all too obvious. Pain scraped the inside of Fancy's heart until it was hollow, was displaced by a bracing rage. After looking both ways, she stomped across the snowy street and confronted her husband by hurling two hundred suffrage fliers in his face.

Jeff gaped at her, pale with either shock or rage—she couldn't tell which and she damned well didn't care. "What the hell—" he rasped.

Although Meredith pouted as he peeled her fingers from his arm and stepped toward Fancy, there was a wounding look of triumph in her green eyes, too.

Fancy was too hurt, too furious to speak. She knew that she must be a sight, with her protruding stomach and her mufflers and the babushka scarf that covered her hair and kept her ears warm, but there was no helping that.

Slowly, Jeff bent and took one of the fliers into his hand. As he read it, a scowl formed in his features. "Have you been bedeviling passersby with this nonsense?" he demanded coldly.

Fancy felt as though her rage lifted her, made her taller, so fierce was its upward sweeping within her. How dare he stand there and reprimand her for having honest political convictions and doing something about them, and he with his mistress on his arm, just coming from a tryst!

Fancy drew back one foot and kicked him soundly in the right shin. A humiliating, sobbing sound was coming from her throat all the while, and her chest was heaving up and down.

Jeff grimaced, swore as he grasped his shin. "Fancy, for God's sake—"

Fancy kicked him in the other shin and whirled, stomping through the scattered orange fliers. That she collided directly into Adam Corbin was the kind of luck she would have expected.

He grasped her shoulders, scanned her face with startled indigo eyes, and then glared over her head at Jeff. "Well," he said. That was all, just "well." But it conveyed his anger and his disapproval, none of which seemed to be directed at Fancy herself.

"I guess I'd better go and meet Mother before she gets worried," announced Meredith in a simpering voice.

"Do that," Adam bit out, still supporting Fancy with his hands, still preventing the flight she was desperate to make. And those blasted sobs that she couldn't control were still shaking through her and rasping past her throat.

"Adam—" Jeff began lamely.

Two grim-faced women walked by, staring. "Aren't we a lovely family?" Adam asked, smiling acidly.

They scurried on, muttering, and Adam calmly lifted Fancy into his arms and planted her in the seat of his buggy, which was waiting in the road.

"God damn it, Adam," Jeff hissed, "wait a minute! Where do you think you're taking my wife?!"

"Oh." Adam looked surprised as he draped a robe over Fancy's lap and turned to face his brother. "Is this your wife? I wouldn't have known it by the way you treat her."

Jeff's eyes, dark with an emotion she couldn't have named, sliced to Fancy's face. "Frances," he said, "get out of that buggy."

Fancy lifted her chin. Her dignity was gone, so she clung to the pretense of it. "Go to hell, Jeff Corbin," she replied.

Adam shrugged and grinned at his brother, though the expression in his eyes was crisply lethal. "There you have it," he said, climbing into the seat beside Fancy and taking up the reins.

Jeff looked murderous. As the buggy rattled away, he drew back one booted foot and kicked a cloud of suffrage fliers into the snowy air.

As they drove up the steep and slippery hill to the main house, with its attached hospital and clinging, snow-laced ivy vines, Fancy had second thoughts. Suppose, in his anger, Jeff sought Meredith out again?

Fresh grief swept through her, stinging, too powerful to contain. What difference did it make if he did? There was no doubt in Fancy's mind that he had already betrayed her. What did one more time, or a thousand more, matter?

It mattered. It all mattered terribly. Fancy covered her face and wept with noisy abandon.

"For what it's worth," Adam said in brotherly reassurance, "I really don't think Jeff would betray you."

That was too much to hope. It was wishful thinking, and Fancy had done enough of that. "He didn't even give me a wedding ring!" she wailed.

Adam draped one arm around her shoulders and

gave her a comforting half hug, but he said nothing more until they reached the main house. There, he lifted her down and escorted her through the front door.

"O'Brien!" he yelled.

Fancy had recovered enough to remind him that Banner was still passing out suffrage fliers near the sawmill and thus couldn't be expected to answer his call. Maggie came instead.

Throughout the rest of that afternoon, Fancy was fussed over and pampered and commiserated with and, for all that, she felt worse with every passing minute. Jeff was not going to come and claim her, she was convinced of that. He was probably with Meredith again.

Fancy closed her eyes, lying there on the bed and in the room that had been Jeff's. She felt as discarded as the books that he no longer read, the model of a clippership on the mantel that he no longer valued, the clothes that he no longer wore.

She was like the things in that room—a *wife* that had been Jeff's.

Fancy's throat drew tight with tears and she curled up into a little ball, desperate to shut out reality. Had it not been for the baby living inside her, she would have gladly died.

Jeff reeled a little as he stormed into Adam's cluttered office. "Where is she?" he demanded.

Adam sat back, removed his spectacles, and slipped them into the pocket of his shirt. Calmly, he swung his feet up onto the surface of the desk. "Who?" he baited innocently.

Jeff felt sick. He'd had too much blue-ruin whiskey on the *Silver Shadow*. Clasping the doorjamb in both hands, he willed himself not to throw up. "Where is Fancy?" he asked in a softer voice, one that betrayed his desperation.

"Upstairs, sleeping. And just in case you're thinking of storming up there, cavalier-style, let me say that if you try it I'll turn you inside out."

"She's my wife!"

"Oh? And what does that make Meredith?"

Jeff was wavering dangerously. He stumbled to a chair and fell into it with a groan. He wasn't due for a hangover until tomorrow, but the damned thing was starting early. "Meredith?" he echoed stupidly.

"The lady you were sporting on your arm today," Adam prompted without sympathy.

"Christ," Jeff bit out, rubbing his eyes with one hand. "You know who Meredith is—"

"Do I? Fancy believes she's your mistress."

Jeff's hand fell from his face. "What?!"

Adam shrugged. "After all, you have been neglecting her for months. And today she saw you coming out of a hotel—"

"Good God, is that why she kicked me? She thought that Meredith and I—" Jeff shot to his feet and immediately regretted it. "She thinks I would do that?!"

"Sit down before you pass out," ordered Adam.

Jeff sat, gratefully. And then, perhaps because of the raw whiskey he had been consuming for the past several hours, he began to cry. His sobs were dry and they hurt, but he was not ashamed of them. Not before Adam.

"Talk to me, Jeff," his brother commanded moderately when the first spate of unbridled misery had passed.

"I love her—doesn't she know I love her?"

"I don't think mind-reading was a part of Fancy's act, Jeff."

"I built her a house—she has carte blanche at every store in the territory—every store in the goddamned west! I—"

"Do you know what she said to me today?" Adam broke in. "She said you didn't even give her a wedding ring."

"For God's sake, if she wanted a ring, why didn't she buy one?"

"And you call me insensitive! At least I gave O'Brien a wedding band!"

"I'm going to be sick!" Jeff yelled, jumping unceremoniously to his feet and running for the door.

"I'll be in the kitchen brewing coffee," Adam answered with resignation, blowing out the lamp on his desk.

The sight of Fancy, curled up in his childhood bed as though to shield herself from some shattering injury, wounded Jeff. He fell into a chair where as a boy he had often sat dreaming of the sea, and stared toward the harbor.

It didn't draw at him the way it once had, that great ocean beyond the Strait of Juan de Fuca, with its mysteries and its terrors.

Behind him, Fancy stirred and whimpered softly in her sleep. Jeff wondered what she was dreaming about. Meredith and her husband's imagined infidelity? The explosion in the harbor last Christmas Eve? The horror of Amelie's death?

He sighed and tilted his head back. "Temple," he whispered, "wherever you are, whatever you're doing, I'll find you. If it takes the rest of my life, I'll find you."

"Jeff?"

Jeff turned his head and saw that Fancy was sitting up in bed. The room was dark and he couldn't make out her expression.

"D–Do you love Meredith Whittaker?"

He laughed, but it was a broken, mirthless sound and it hurt his throat. "No, and I don't sleep with her, either. She's in town to visit her sister or something."

Her need to believe him was almost tangible and it shamed Jeff. God, why had he been so hard on her when she was the reason for everything he did, every breath he drew?

"I would forgive you," she said.

Jeff ached. "I've never been unfaithful to you, Fancy. Not with Meredith or anyone else."

She began to cry, softly. Brokenly. Jeff went to her without thinking and gathered her into his arms.

"Fancy," he breathed, anguished at the depth of her pain. "Oh, Fancy, I'm sorry."

Fancy stiffened. "For what?" she demanded, pushing back from him a little.

"For treating you the way I have. Will you forgive me?"

"That depends on whether or not you were lying about Meredith!"

Jeff laughed and this time it felt good, so good. "What a contradictory creature you are, Frances Corbin! You just told me that you would forgive me."

"Did you or did you not make love to that redheaded hussy?"

"I did not."

"Then I forgive you."

"What if I'd said I had?"

She shuddered in his arms with tearful laughter. "Then I would still have forgiven you. It just would have taken longer, that's all!"

Jeff held her close and buried his face in the rose-water- and tear-drop-scented softness of her hair. "I love you, you little rabbit rustler," he said.

"You smell terrible! Have you been drinking?"

"Copiously," replied Jeff. "And it was romantic of you to point it out."

Fancy wrinkled her nose. "Yeesh!" she exclaimed.

Jeff shrugged with suitable humility. "There's nothing for it—I'll have to take a bath."

He watched with love and satisfaction and a sense of homecoming as her eyes widened. "A bath? Why, you couldn't heat water at this hour! Everyone is asleep—"

Jeff caught her hand and pulled her gently off the bed with him, chuckling. "You haven't seen the famous Corbin bathtub, I see."

"Is it like the one in Spokane?"

He wanted to kiss her but refrained out of delicacy. After all, he had been drinking blue-ruin all evening and then he'd thrown up in the side yard. "Not exactly," he answered, lowering his voice to a whisper as they ventured into the hallway. "The pipes show and there isn't any fancy tile or anything like that, but it serves the purpose."

They sneaked down the shadowy passageway to a door roughly midway between one end of the house and the other. "I was hoping we could have a tub like that in our house," Fancy confided in a whisper.

"We will. If that's what you want, that's what you'll have," Jeff promised, touching the tip of her nose.

Inside the dark room where the bathtub waited, Jeff took a match from his shirt pocket and struck it with his thumbnail. Light, flickering and soft, danced with the shadows. But he did not light the waiting lamp, but instead chose a single candle, which was kept on a shelf underneath the washstand.

The pipes thundered and roared when he turned the proper spigots, but water poured into the bathtub, hot and inviting.

Since Fancy was wearing only a thin, lace-trimmed chemise, she was undressed and in the water, sighing with delight, before Jeff had even shed his boots. He looked at her with mock annoyance.

"About those fliers you threw at me today," he began in a husbandly way.

She tossed her head and looked back at him, impish and infinitely appealing in the poor light of that one candle, flickering now on the tub's broad edge. "It was a matter of conscience," she said. "I agree with your mother—if women don't fight for what's rightfully theirs, they'll never have it."

Jeff shed his shirt, his trousers, his socks. "Does this mean you're going to be a crusader like Mama?"

Reclining luxuriously in the tub, she smiled and rested both hands on her rounded, protruding stomach. "Later. I don't expect I'll have much time after your daughter arrives."

"Suppose my daughter . . ." He stepped into the bathtub and sat down, facing her. The water was still running and the pipes were making a clatter that would raise the dead, but he didn't care. ". . . turns out to be a son?"

Her eyes were very wide and vulnerable. "Wouldn't you love a girl as much as a boy?"

It hurt, loving a woman this much. Even at its best, it was a keenly piercing thing. Far more hazardous than sailing the seas. "Of course I would, Fancy. What makes you ask a question like that?"

She lowered her head and her slender alabaster shoulders moved in a touching shrug. "My papa wanted me to be a boy—that's why he named me Frances."

Jeff sat up a little straighter. "He said that? Straight out?"

"Yes."

He reached back, turned off the water. The boilers clanked and there was a whooshing sound inside the walls. "Let me touch this place where you shelter my child, Fancy," he said.

She rose to her knees and he closed his big hands around her stomach, marveling at the shifting and kicking, the blatant life, within. He was so moved that he would have wept again as he had downstairs had she not cupped his face in both her hands and whispered, "I would be properly attended, Jeffrey. Now."

Chapter Eighteen

"WITH THAT BUMBLING MARY TAKIN' CARE OF HER," boomed Maggie McQuire, in housekeeperly reprimand, "it's no wonder our Fancy's so frazzled!"

Before Maggie could start making dire predictions, Jeff took Fancy's arm and escorted her outside to the buggy that awaited them. There, after lifting Fancy into the narrow seat, he squinted up at her and the Chinook wind ruffled his wheat-gold hair. "Do you want to stay here, Fancy? With Maggie?"

Fancy shook her head. She wanted to go to her own house, for all its vast emptiness. It was on the tip of her tongue to ask Jeff if he would spend the day there with her, but she didn't quite have the courage for that. The weather, snowy and cold only the day before, was glorious today, caught up in a false spring that the Indians and old-timers called a Chinook.

"I guess you'll go down to the shipyard today," she ventured softly, avoiding his eyes so he would not see the pain and worry in her own.

"I do have some things to do, yes," he said cryptically, taking up the reins in his strong hands. "I'll be home for dinner, though."

Fancy felt a little start; it was rather pathetic to be so delighted over sharing a simple midday meal, when it was the norm in other marriages. "I'd like that," she said shyly.

They drove home through patches of melting snow and stubborn grass and over rutted roads. The wind was indeed warm, and the sun was bright in the sky, and though it was November, one would have almost believed that it was April instead.

At the door, Jeff got out of the buggy, then helped Fancy down. As Mary appeared on the porch, he bent and whispered, "Get rid of her for the day."

A rush of pleasure warmed Fancy and pulsed in her cheeks. A thousand errands for Mary leaped into her mind. "What shall I serve for dinner?" she asked in a dignified manner, trying to hide the way he had disconcerted her.

"Yourself," Jeff replied, and then he was back in the buggy again and driving away. For once, the knowledge that he was probably on his way to that half-finished clippership in Port Hastings harbor did not devastate her.

"I was worried about you, mum—gone all night like that!"

Fancy entered the large foyer, tugging off her gloves as she went. "I'm sorry, Mary—my husband and I spent the night at the other house. I should have sent a message."

Always quickly mollified, Mary beamed. "Ain't it a lovely day, Mum? All sunny and warm—"

Fancy thought of the scandalous aside Jeff had muttered when she had asked him about dinner and flushed slightly as she reached to hang her cloak on the brass coat tree. "I've a whole list of things for you to do," she began. "You won't mind walking down to town, will you?"

Mary was delighted. "Oh, mum, a day like this is just perfect for walking! And I thought I'd be stuck indoors the whole time!"

Sometimes Mary's exuberance was tiring, but Fancy smiled. "Once you've finished your errands, you can spend the afternoon as you like. Visiting friends or something."

Mary laughed. "So the master's coming home today, is he?"

Fancy blushed again. "That is no business of yours, Mary," she said firmly. "Come along, now, and I'll write out the things I want you to do."

Half an hour later, Mary left the house with a spring in her step and mischief in her eyes. Try though she might, Fancy couldn't be angry with the woman for her presumptuous and familiar manner. All that mattered on this beautiful Chinook day was that she'd won out over that dratted clippership for once. That wouldn't last, of course, but perhaps the new closeness between Jeff and herself would.

Fancy meant to see that it did.

During the coming hour, she rushed about, hair falling from its pins, face flushed, baking the flaky dried apple scones that Jeff loved, fluffing sofa cushions, going over her wardrobe again and again in search of just the right dress.

She could not decide between a sedate mulberry broadcloth and her favorite lavender cambric, which became her but was worn perhaps too often. Fancy was still standing beside the bed, caught in this quandary, when her senses leaped in one startling chorus—Jeff was home.

She turned and there he was, standing indolently in the bedroom doorway, grinning at her, taking in her flour-splotched skirts, her falling hair, her flushed and startled face. In his hands he held, of all things, the old black top hat from Fancy's performing days.

"Here," he said, extending it. "See what you can pull out of this, Mrs. Corbin."

Fancy's throat was tight and she was filled with mortification that he should see her like this when she had so wanted to be beautiful for him, perfumed and elegant. Perhaps appealing enough to keep him home from the seas. "What—"

A peculiar mewling sound came from inside the hat he was extending. "See for yourself," he said.

Fancy drew a deep breath, puzzled and quite shaken, though she couldn't have explained why. She approached and reached cautiously into the hat and warm, soft fur met her touch. "Not a rabbit!" she whispered, closing her hand around the small body and lifting.

"No, not a rabbit," Jeff laughed, his indigo eyes shining.

"A kitten!" Fancy cried, delighted, holding the ball of white fluff in both hands. It purred and looked up at her with trusting ice-blue eyes.

"It seems to me that any good magician could pull more than a kitten out of a hat this big," Jeff remarked. "Try again."

Fancy set the kitten on the floor, where it brushed itself against her skirts and swatted at her petticoats. Wide-eyed, she reached into the hat again and came out with a little box of dark blue velvet.

Lifting the hinged lid, she gasped, for inside the box was a ring, a golden band set with alternating diamonds and amethysts. "Oh, my—" she breathed, overcome. "Is it—"

"Yes," Jeff said firmly and with mock sternness. "It's a wedding band. I wouldn't want other men thinking you're fair game."

Fancy held out a trembling left hand and he slipped the ring onto the appropriate finger. When she looked up, Jeff's face was distorted by a shimmering blur of tears. "W-While you're at sea, you mean?" she whispered.

"While I'm where?" he asked, looking honestly surprised.

Fancy turned the ring on her finger; it fit perfectly and the brilliant stones danced. "While you're sailing that ship," she said.

"Sailing that—" He caught her shoulders in his hands. "Is that what you thought, Fancy? That I was going to leave you to sail again?"

She could only nod.

He cupped her chin in one hand and lifted. His face was very close to hers. "I love ships, Fancy," he said softly, forthrightly. "But I love you far, far more. And I won't be making any voyages unless they're short ones."

Hope leaped within her, a searing, brutal, and yet fragile hope. "Exactly what do you mean by short?" she demanded, the kitten still catching at her petticoats.

"You know, brief," explained Jeff. "Two days, three. The kind of trips that you and the baby could take with me."

Fancy gave a shout of glee and flung her arms around Jeff's neck and her feet were completely off the floor. The kitten dangled from her hem for a moment and then fell, with a soft thump, mewing in disgruntled protest. "I thought—oh, Jeff, I was sure—"

He held her tightly to him. "I'm sorry, Fancy," he breathed into her neck. "I didn't know you thought I planned to go back to the sea. If I hadn't been so damned stubborn—"

"Don't," she whispered, and she silenced his self-recrimination with a kiss.

Passion howled around them like a fierce wind, and then through them. Between consuming kisses, they stripped each other of every garment, wanting nothing to impede their joining.

When Fancy stood before Jeff in a pool of skirts and petticoats and satiny drawers, he bent to take slow, sweet suckle at her breast. She moaned and flung her head back as he plundered her, his strong hands stroking her rounded stomach.

But there was an urgency in them both that forestalled their usual inclination to linger long over their loving. Jeff swept Fancy up into his arms, carried her to the bed, and fell to her there, strong and hard upon her.

His domination was complete, but Fancy welcomed it. She cried out in triumph as he entered her in a swift but gentle thrust.

He paused, looking worried. "Did I hurt you?"

"Oh, no—no—oh, Jeff, love me! Make me yours—"

And he did. Their bodies moved in splendor, rising

and falling as one, arching in the final, quivering exaltation that wrung a hoarse shout from Jeff and a keening, animal whine from Fancy.

Fancy was setting out cream near the cookstove in the kitchen for the kitten. The dried apple scones had burned, the acrid scent heavy in the air, but neither she nor her husband cared.

"The balloon?" she puzzled, standing up straight again.

Jeff was politely eating one of the scones, having broken away the charred edges she had crimped so carefully. "It's a perfect day for it, Fancy," he argued in quiet tones. "Tomorrow it will probably snow again."

Fancy despised that balloon and had hoped never to have to deal with it again in any fashion except to kick at it surreptitiously when she happened to pass it in the barn, but there was little that could trouble her on this fine day. After all, she had her wedding ring, at last—she had a child growing within her and, best of all, she knew that Jeff would not be leaving her for the sea. They were in perfect accord.

"Well—"

He grinned and flung what remained of his scone into the fireplace. "I promise we won't fly away this time, Fancy," he assured her. "I'll make sure the cable is fastened and we won't go any higher than, oh, a hundred feet."

Fancy felt a little thrill of adventurous fright. It would be fun to look down on Port Hastings and on that clippership that would never carry her man away from her. "If you promise," she said.

"On my honor," he replied.

The balloon danced and shifted against the blue sky,

straining at the ropes that held it to the grassy clearing behind the main house. Clearly, except for buying the kitten and the ring, Jeff had devoted all of the morning to bringing it there and inflating it.

Sensing that she was about to have second thoughts, Jeff laughed and lifted her carefully into the wicker gondola. She gripped the side with white knuckles as he went from one stake to another, releasing the ropes until there was only one that held them.

Temple Royce appeared so suddenly that Fancy didn't have time to scream out a warning. He struck Jeff from behind and the one rope that held the balloon to the ground began to unfurl with alarming quickness.

Fancy felt the balloon surging higher, but her own peril was the last thing on her mind at that moment. Jeff was scrambling to his feet, stumbling toward the rope. Its looped end dragged along the ground.

"Thank God," she whispered. For Jeff was not dead as she had first feared, but only dazed.

He lunged for the rope and Temple, looking like the mad and hunted creature he was, lunged for him. They rolled in the wet grass, over and over. The balloon drifted higher.

"Jeff!" Fancy screamed, and her cry was lost on the wind.

Both Temple and Jeff got to their feet, neither of them aware, it seemed, that Fancy was about to fly off in a craft she had no idea how to navigate or land. There were trees, tall and ready to pierce the orange and white balloon, and beyond them, the endless Pacific Ocean. . . .

Fancy cried out again and Temple looked up at her and laughed, waving one hand in farewell. He stepped backward and, in that moment, the looped rope caught around his right ankle. There was no more slack now and nothing to hold the balloon to the ground.

Temple shrieked in startled horror, hanging upside down now by one booted foot, and the balloon went higher still. Jeff grabbed for him with both arms and missed, landing on his stomach.

"God help us," Fancy muttered, sick with fear. "Help us all."

Temple was flailing and struggling at the end of the rope now, his head coursing a dozen feet above the ground. They were wafting seaward and Jeff was shouting something but Fancy couldn't hear him for the wind and the pounding of her own blood in her ears.

Suddenly, as they neared the tall Douglas firs that rimmed the clearing, there came a strangled scream from below and the balloon stopped, with a sickening lurch. Tree branches brushed the sides of the gondola and clawed at Fancy's face, filling her lungs with the paradoxically festive scent of Christmas.

Trembling, certain that she would topple to the ground at any second, Fancy gathered all her courage and peered over the side. What she saw made her forget her own plight.

Temple still hung from the balloon rope, arms and legs outspread, face caught forever in an expression of staring horror. A tree limb had gone through his chest and now protruded from his back.

Fancy slithered to the floor of the gondola, shaking, her eyes clenched shut. Never, ever, as long as she lived, would she forget what she'd just seen or the desperate fear she still felt.

"Jeff," she whispered, "Jeff, Jeff."

And she heard his shout from below. "Fancy! Fancy, are you all right?"

"Yes," she managed to cry out. Above her, the balloon was making a frightening, hissing sound and she could feel the gondola shifting in the thick branches, like an endangered bird's nest.

She was going to die now, right there. In a tree! Her baby would never be born. . . .

"Don't move!" Jeff called hoarsely. "Sit perfectly still and I'll get you down, Fancy! I promise I'll get you down."

Fancy began to cry. The wind was buffeting the balloon from the other side now; she could feel it coming loose from the branches, leaning precariously toward the clearing. The hissing sound told her that it was slowly deflating.

With a jarring motion that made Fancy utter a choked scream, it broke free of the tree. The gondola rocked as if to spill her out and then steadied, fixed to the tree by Temple's body.

Fancy got to her knees and risked looking down. Jeff was there—oh, God, to have him hold her, to be safe again—his head tilted back. It must have been thirty feet to the ground.

"Stand up, Fancy," Jeff ordered calmly, and she saw that there were other people running into the clearing—Adam, Banner, Melissa, even Katherine.

"I can't!" wailed Fancy.

Jeff ignored her words. "Remember how I made the balloon land that other time, Fancy?" he asked reasonably. "Pull the white cord—slowly. Very slowly."

Fancy's knees were made of jelly, but she stood up, reaching for the cord in question, her eyes closed tight.

"No!" Jeff roared. "That's the gas valve! Pull the white cord!"

Fancy forced herself to open her eyes. Her stomach was leaping within her and her throat burned with bile. But she looked up and the white cord was there. Her hand trembled so that she could hardly grasp it, but she did, after long, torturous moments of struggle, manage to catch hold.

"Pull it very slowly," Jeff ordered. How could he be so calm?

Resisting a frantic need to wrench at the cord, Fancy pulled it gradually downward. There was a splintering sound as the balloon descended, and she knew without looking that Temple had fallen.

And then the gondola was within two feet of the ground, and Adam and Jeff were both grasping its edges in strong hands, hauling it the rest of the way down. Jeff caught Fancy by her shoulders and wrenched her out, holding her close, muttering senseless words into her hair.

She wailed with terror and relief, clutching at his shirt with her hands. Jeff lifted her into his arms and, with his wan mother scrambling along at his side, carried her out of the clearing.

Fancy lost consciousness before they reached the main house, and awoke to find herself on an examining table in the hospital wing, with Banner peering down at her. "Jeff, Adam—she's awake!"

There was a scuffling sound and the little room seemed to undulate. Only Jeff's face, Jeff's glorious, snow-white face, could be trusted not to writhe and shift.

"Fancy," he whispered hoarsely, and there were tears on his cheeks. "Oh, Fancy."

She reached up and drew his head down, holding

onto him, tangling her fingers in his hair. It was so good, so gloriously good, to touch him. "D–Did I lose the baby?" she managed, voicing her worst fear.

"No," answered Banner in a tearful voice before anyone else could reply. "No, the baby is fine."

"Thank God," sobbed Fancy. "Oh, thank God—"

"Let her rest now, Jeff," came Adam's voice, from the void.

Obediently Jeff drew away, out of her arms. She was drifting, drifting—but comfortably. Arms lifted her and she was placed on a soft bed. Rails clanked into place and a blanket was tucked around her.

It was good to sleep.

Temple Royce's grisly death was the talk of Port Hastings for months. Most of the populace, for reasons of their own, were glad that he was gone.

There were some, of course, who claimed that Jeff and Adam Corbin had murdered him to avenge real or imagined wrongs, but those in authority looked upon this theory with disdain. Had Royce died in a more ordinary fashion—at the point of a gun or a knife, for example—the idea would have had some credence. But impaled on a tree limb, fifty-some feet above the ground? No. The judge and the mayor and the marshal shook their heads in unanimous disbelief. Temple Royce had been a smuggler, a thief, perhaps even a murderer, if what the Corbins said about the sinking of the *Sea Mistress* and the tragedy at that Wenatchee wedding was the truth. Like as not, the fates had dealt with him in their singular and irrevocable manner.

Except for gossip over teapots and poker tables, the ubject was closed.

Banner's manner was brisk and professional. "Get ut of this room this instant, Jeff Corbin," she said, olling up the sleeves of her dress and washing her ands in the basin that steamed near the window, nelting the pretty curlicues of frost that had gathered here during the night.

"Don't you want me to find Adam?" Jeff asked lesperately. He had driven all the way to the main ouse and back in the cold chill of that February dawn, nd was only now realizing that his shirt was untucked rom his trousers and misbuttoned in the bargain.

Banner looked at Fancy and winked. "That's a grand dea, Jeff," she said. "You go and find your brother. I hink he's in the Klallum Camp."

Jeff bent over the bed and kissed Fancy's wan but appy face. "You'll be all right, won't you?"

A pain caught Fancy just then; it seemed that her ipbones were being pried apart. Having a baby was roving to be arduous business. "Yes," she managed to ay, still smiling.

Jeff raced out of the bedroom and when he was gone, Banner, trim again after the birth of her healthy aughter some weeks before, laughed. "We're well rid f him, I think," she said.

Fancy moaned and arched with another pain. W–Will it take a long time?"

Banner was drawing down the blankets to examine er and Fancy was very glad that she could be attended y a woman. It would be embarrassing to have Adam oing all these things, brusque and businesslike though e was. "Sometimes first babies take awhile," came the thoughtful answer. "With any luck, though, we'll be all done before Jeff gets back."

The door opened and Mary came in, her eyes wide, clutching her wrapper around her. "Does it hurt much, mum?" she asked in quiet awe.

Banner darted the housekeeper a look that said she would brook no hysterics. "It's a worthwhile pain," she observed, finishing her examination and covering Fancy again with the sheets and blankets. "You get something for it."

Mary glowed. "Aye! A wee baby—no better gift than that, now is there?"

Banner smiled. "No," she agreed, more gently. And then she sent the housekeeper bustling off to heat water and gather fresh linens. "I was saving those jobs for Jeff," she confided wryly, "but now that he's out of the way, they'll serve the same purpose with Mary."

Fancy felt another pain building within her and tried to divert her thoughts from it. She and Jeff would have a child soon, a child of their very own. Their house would be wonderfully noisy, the way the main house always was.

It seemed that Banner washed her hands a thousand times during the next hour. When the pain was bad, she talked of her own children, the twins Danny and Bridget, and the baby Elisabeth.

Fancy was perspiring and every part of her seemed to strain with the effort of birthing that child. She breathed deeply when Banner told her to and gripped her sister-in-law's strong, sure hands when the suffering grew to intolerable proportions.

"Scream if you want to," Banner enjoined. "Sometimes it takes your mind off the pain."

Obediently, Fancy screamed. She was glad, then,

that Jeff had been sent on a wild goose chase and could not hear her.

"Is Adam r–really at the Klallum Camp?" she asked, between bouts with that consuming, clenching agony.

Banner shrugged. "Who knows?" she asked, flipping back the covers to examine Fancy again. "All right, this is it," she said coolly. "I can see the baby's head. I want you to push as hard as you can, Fancy."

Fancy pushed, gasping. This final, greatest pain seemed to clasp her like some wild and furious beast.

The door burst open just as the baby burst into the world. Banner's hands were busy with it for a moment, and then it squalled in outrage.

"A boy," Jeff breathed, and Fancy turned her head on the damp pillow and saw that he was standing just inside the room, his magnificent face suffused with joy and wonder.

"Let me see him!" Fancy cried, craning her neck.

Banner smiled and laid the squirming, furious child on his mother's stomach. "Don't mind the cord now," she cautioned gently. "We'll take care of that in a minute."

Fancy touched her baby boy with a trembling hand. He had a thatch of untamed, wheat-gold hair and the dark blue eyes that all infants have. His red face was squenched with fury and his tiny hands and feet flailed in protest.

"Being born is something of an affront, isn't it?" Banner asked soothingly, collecting the child from Fancy's stomach.

"He looks like you," Fancy said, looking into her husband's face. "What will we name him?"

Jeff kissed the tip of her nose. "Anything but Hershel," he answered.

Fancy laughed, exhausted and aching and full of heady triumph. "We could name him for Phineas," she teased.

"That isn't a bad idea," mused Jeff ponderously.

"Never!" cried Fancy. "I was only teasing!"

Jeff feigned disappointment. "Eustis?" he suggested.

And Fancy knew then that he was teasing as well. Her heart was full of love and pride at the wonder they'd wrought together. "We could name him for your brothers," she said. "Adam Keith Corbin. Or Keith Adam—"

Jeff laughed. "I love my brothers, Fancy, but there is such a thing as confusion, you know—especially in this family."

Fancy yawned, craving sleep with a sudden and all-consuming lust. When she awoke hours later, Jeff was stretched out on the bed beside her, fully clothed, holding her close.

"I'm about to suggest a compromise," he announced, as though there had been no pause in their conversation about the baby's name. "Your father's name is Patrick, isn't it?"

Fancy nodded. The room was shadowy and quiet and all that mattered in her world was right there, either touching her or within easy reach.

"Then why don't we name our son Patrick Keith," Jeff mused. "I like that."

"They'll call him Pat," Fancy protested, "or even Paddy!"

Jeff shook his head. "No. He'll always be Patrick."

And he was.

There had been a party to celebrate spring and the launching of the new ship, and Fancy was flushed with laughter and the music that lingered in her head and heart. What a joy it had been, singing and dancing on the decks of a ship shamelessly named for her!

"*Corbin's Fancy,* he calls it," she told the greedy infant at her breast. "Can you imagine that? Everyone danced and sang—"

The door of the bedroom creaked open, letting in a golden spill of light from the hallway. Jeff was there, holding something large and square under one arm. Presently, he lit a lamp at the bedside and sat watching Fancy as she finished tending their child and then laid him in his cradle to sleep.

Then, grinning, he stood up and placed the square object on the wall, where a picture of a rose arbor had been. It was Fancy's signboard from the days when she had performed with Hershel, now framed and behind glass. FANCY JORDAN. SHE SINGS. SHE DANCES. SHE DOES MAGIC.

"We've taken care of the singing and dancing," Jeff said, turning back to rake the length of her with smoldering indigo eyes. "That leaves the magic."

Fancy smiled and went to him, and the lamp Jeff had lit flickered out.

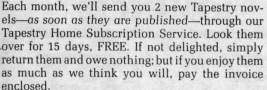